A Love Story for Bewildered Girls

A Love Story for Bewildered Girls

EMMA MORGAN

PENGUIN BOOKS

PENGUIN BOOKS

UK | USA | Canada | Ireland | Australia
India | New Zealand | South Africa

Penguin Books is part of the Penguin Random House group of companies
whose addresses can be found at global.penguinrandomhouse.com.

First published by Viking 2019
Published in Penguin Books 2020

001

Copyright © Emma Morgan, 2019

The moral right of the author has been asserted

Typeset by Jouve (UK), Milton Keynes
Printed and bound in Great Britain by Clays Ltd, Elcograf S.p.A.

A CIP catalogue record for this book is available from the British Library

ISBN: 978-0-241-98468-0

'Regret is like a carpet stain – scrubbing at it is not going to help.'

– Great Aunt Beatrice

This is Grace Marshall Eppington

Grace liked her earrings. That was the first thing she noticed about the woman: the long silver earrings that grazed her neck as she turned her head. Grace was attracted to earrings like magpies are attracted to shiny things, which could be blamed on the few nice memories that she had of her mother, a ballet dancer who always wore pairs that swayed from side to side as she walked, as though she was a Bedouin woman wearing her dowry in her ears as she rode atop a camel across the desert.

'I like your earrings,' Grace said, and would have put her hand up to touch one except that she was holding her nearly empty wineglass between both hands as a shield against the man next to her, who was trying to discuss drains.

'Thanks,' the woman said as she flicked her eyes over Grace and turned away. Her long neck. Her sixties blond pixie cut like Mia Farrow. Her earrings swaying. The woman presented her back to Grace and Grace wanted to lean forward and kiss the mole on the nape of her neck. But she didn't believe that would be appropriate with someone whom you had just set eyes on for the first time. Grace believed that would be classed as really quite strange.

Was Grace really quite strange? Was she the sort of person who normally kissed strangers on the backs of their necks? No, she considered herself quite ordinary, with the oval face and dark eyes of an early photo of a sensible Edwardian lady, a bluestocking given to bicycling, plain wholesome food, and improving lectures. Her short mousy hair had been badly cut and then buzzed at the back by her sister Eustacia with blunted clippers and she had a permanent stoop from years of being over-conscious of her five-foot-ten lankiness, but she was not bothered about being Jane Eyre plain at all, although it seemed that the woman with the earrings obviously was. Grace stood looking at the woman's back in a black top tight enough to show that she was not wearing a bra, and tears came into Grace's eyes as though she had stubbed her toe.

Grace had, up to that point, been enjoying herself; she was slightly drunk, in the early phase when you felt voluble and cheery, the phase before you started either crying, fighting, or snogging unsuitable people in the cupboard under the stairs, and she had been talking to a group of friends before the drain man had trapped her in a corner. She could see one of them, Andy, whom she had been having a good discussion with about whether Juliet Binoche or Nicole Kidman was the more talented, signalling across the room now to ask her if she needed another drink. She liked parties, although, as a child, she hadn't gone to a lot of them; her family was a hermetic world that never invited outsiders in apart from the bin men and the postman at Christmas for sherry. And, of course, the hunt sometimes met at the bottom of the drive but that didn't count, surely. Beforehand she had combed her hair and tried not to spit toothpaste down the T-shirt she had put on that if seen in a bad enough light would appear to have been ironed. She was wearing clean jeans. What more could she do? She straightened her eyebrows carefully with the tips of her fingers and spit. That was the reactive effect on personal grooming that growing up with three sisters had had on her.

'Yes,' said the drain man, whose name she had forgotten, 'it's the pigeons that keep dying on the roof that block the drainpipe,' and Grace tried to reabsorb her tears by sniffing and then, when this didn't work, wiped her eyes quickly on the back of her sleeve. She turned so that the woman disappeared from her sightline completely. Her friend Dolores, the party's hostess, tapped her on the shoulder. Dolores was under five foot, her bosom upholstered to sofa-like proportions with 'patting'. She wore American tan tights all year round and her navy handbags always matched her shoes. 'Classical, my style is classical, like Margaret Thatcher.' She'd ended up in England because she'd married a Yorkshireman she'd met when she worked as a blackjack dealer at a casino in Alicante. 'Nicky, he was so handsome, but he was bad, bad, bad. Like the devil. He went with the girl from the Four Crowns. The barmaid. She had big tits and who knows about her vagina,' and she had mimed this on their very first meeting, when Grace had moved in down the street four years ago. Dolores liked to regale her with intimate details about her sex life that Grace didn't want to know, and had, on more than one occasion, shown Grace her appendix scar. She also enjoyed forcing large quantities of Spanish foodstuffs on Grace to take home with her, as a result of which Grace had a chorizo habit.

'I've got to go,' said Grace.

'No! No! Don't go! It's so early. There is a very nice girl over there in the corner. You need sex, I know you do, or you will dry up like an old sponge.'

'Thanks a lot,' said Grace.

'I will fetch her,' said Dolores.

'Please don't,' said Grace, but Dolores had already gone.

As the drain man reached past her to get a bottle off the nearby table, Grace slipped out of the hot room while her other friends' backs were turned, avoiding Dolores, who was trying to drag a woman across the room towards her. In the street she gulped for fresh air and went six doors down to her own house.

She ran upstairs to the bathroom and, bending over the sink, turned on the cold tap hard enough so that when she bent towards it water sprayed on to the floor. As she doused herself she realized that she didn't even know the woman with the long earrings' name. She stood up straight and looked in the mirror, water dripping down her face and on to her T-shirt. Oh, she thought, and watched her mouth form the sound, oh.

Her sister Eustacia was right when she said that one day it would hit Grace like a tonne of bricks.

'You'll just know,' she told her.

'How?' asked Grace.

'When you know you know,' said Eustacia, putting her arm around her, and Grace thought that her sister must be having a funny turn.

'How long did it take you?' Grace asked her sister Tess.

'About ten minutes. Give or take.'

'And you, Bella?' she said to her other sister Arabella.

'What?'

'To fall in love with Ray. Did you know immediately?'

'Oh God no! When I had sex with him for the first time I found he was covered with a layer of hair like a gorilla.'

'But you married him!'

'I gave him an ultimatum. Monthly waxing or no more shagging.'

'And he agreed?'

'Why wouldn't he?'

'But I still don't get it, how will I know?' said Grace with frustration.

'You won't have a choice,' said Tess.

'That's an addiction,' Grace said. 'Or a compulsion. Neither of which are good.'

'One day it will just happen,' said Eustacia. 'It'll be so quick you won't have time to think about it.'

4

'Not unlike losing your virginity,' said Bella.

'Thanks,' said Grace, with a degree of sarcasm that was not lost on her sisters.

Tess put her arm around Grace from the other side to Eustacia and Grace felt squished.

'Don't worry about it, sweetheart,' she said, 'it won't be painful, it'll be easy.'

'Quite unlike . . .' said Bella.

'How would I know?' said Grace.

'Fair point,' said Bella.

Grace was thirty-two and so had been waiting for love for a long time while pretending not to wait at all. At convent school she had been used to unrequited crushes on girls called Rebecca and Camilla, the snooty ones she had mooched around after, girls who at best ignored her and at worst ridiculed her and called her 'a creepy lezzer'. In adulthood, she had recovered from this bad start but none of her relationships had worked out as she had hoped. The truck driver she had liked a lot but who had turned out to have poor personal hygiene and Grace had had to make her excuses. The nurse she had met at a lesbian walking group called Pack of Dykes with whom she had enjoyed several months of sex and hiking, until the nurse decided to emigrate to Australia and had not even enquired if Grace wanted to go too. The personnel officer who said, 'My girlfriend's in Bridlington this weekend,' and, although abashed, Grace went home with her anyway. The postgraduate psychology student who wore braces and chewed on marshmallows, her mouth a mass of metal tasting of sugar, who had said she had thought about it and decided she would prefer a man. The economics lecturer whom Grace wanted to get up and leave in the middle of the night because the woman had made noises not unlike a seagull's.

At least, unlike the straight friends of her age who were

being looked at pityingly for being left on the shelf, Grace's single life seemed to be envied. She had lost count of the number of women who had called her 'lucky' because she was supposed to have no biological imperative. Grace was not running out of time, it was presumed, her eggs were not mouldering, there was no internal clock ticking away. The statistics that she knew from her friends about post-thirty downhill rates of conception. She could draw herself a graph. At least she was free from the competitive stereotypes of 'cupcake-baking earth-mother' versus 'cold, venal and childless career woman' that seemed to be foisted on her friends. Straight people are ridiculous, she thought when they complained about this but didn't say it. It had often occurred to her that she wasn't forced to fit into the narrow strictures that they were, didn't have the external pressures to present a perfect image to the outside world at all times, and this made her grateful.

Grace owned a redbrick house on a back street in an area of Leeds that had become far too fashionable for her liking, a house with wooden floors she had stripped herself and whose radiators she knew how to bleed. That was another thing that straight people seemed to assume about her – that she was good with tools, and it annoyed her that this was true. She had a meaningful and stimulating job as a psychotherapist, a job which she had worked hard to gain, and which she was, she liked to think, adept at. She had plenty of friends with whom to do the social activities of an engaging sort that were planned into her week. She had, of course, her large family spread across Yorkshire and she saw her favourite sisters often. As lives went it seemed to be flowing along nicely. But, as it turned out, all the time she had been waiting in secret for something or someone to hit her so hard that she would run out of breath, like the way a wave in a rough sea bowls you over, slams you into the sand, and nearly drowns you.

Grace didn't sleep with the woman that night, although she wanted to. She wanted to more than she had wanted anything else in her life before. So it seemed that some of her sisters were right all along. They were absolutely bloody right.

This is Violet Amelia Mayweather

This morning Violet had woken up with 'the fear' and had remained in its vice-like grip all day. As a result, she was not only in her pyjamas at 6 p.m., but also still in bed, and was by now extremely hungry, having not yet been able to put her feet on the floor, let alone get as far as the kitchen. If only Annie had been home, she could have texted her from under the covers, 'Please could you possibly bring me some Marmite toast?' and Annie would probably have brought her some, even if it did come accompanied, at the bare minimum, by the sternest of expressions. Unfortunately though, she hadn't woken up until Annie had left the flat to go to work that morning and so she hadn't eaten and all she had had to drink was the stale water in the glass on her bedside table. This was probably just as well, because the bathroom also seemed too far a journey to make. It was pathetic, this inability to move, she kept telling herself. She was a healthy twenty-eight-year-old woman and it was as if she had lost the use of her legs. She hadn't even phoned Starchild to say she couldn't come to work. She hadn't done anything at all, except sleep and wake dry-mouthed to spend several hours staring at the ceiling trying to repress all thoughts and then giving up and burrowing back down into her bed to find the relief of sleep again. Her bed had become her entire world, it was a flimsy boat in the black sea of 'the fear' that surrounded it. There might as well have been monsters under her bed with long suckered tentacles which would reach out and grab her if she so much as put a toe from under the duvet. These are the imaginings of a child, she thought, in the hope that castigating herself might work as a motivational force. It didn't. 'Pusillanimous', she thought, that's the word for me, and wished that she could remember what book that was from.

It was one of the many things that Violet envied about her best friend Annie – her lack of 'the fear'. In the past Annie had questioned her about it but it was like trying to explain the feel of a snowball in your hand to someone who had been brought up in the tropics. The complete absence of fear of anything or anyone was part of Annie's make-up. 'But what exactly are you afraid of?' Annie had asked her soon after they first met. 'I think,' Violet had said, 'the question is – what am I not afraid of? And the answer to that is dachshunds, coffee cake, and little old ladies with lipstick on their teeth. That's about it.' Annie had looked at her with that 'what on earth are you rabbiting on about you daft cow' expression that Violet now knew often preceded one of the stock phrases that Annie had, unconsciously, got off her mother. 'You've just got to get on with it.' That was one of the most common. 'Pull your socks up, they're not going to pull themselves,' was another. But Violet's favourite was, 'Other people have it much worse than you, you know,' followed by an example of someone who did have it much worse than her. From anyone else Violet might have found these phrases abrasive and completely lacking in empathy, but from Annie she found them comforting in their familiarity and sometimes repeated them to herself, not as maxims to live by, but as tiny talismans against the darkness. They didn't sound the same in her accent though.

Hopefully Annie would be home soon, and Violet was pleased about that because she was increasingly hungry and thirsty. Annie, the moment she stepped into the room, would cause the creatures with the tentacles to shrivel back into their gloomy holes and therefore Violet might finally be able to get up. There was no one else apart from Annie who could come to her aid. Her mother was in Cheshire with her stepdad, which might as well be a million miles away from Leeds. She had grown up a shy and socially incompetent only child whose fantasy world involved an imaginary friend called Zazou, and it wasn't until she met Annie that she learnt what a real friend was. And as for the men in her life, well, they came and went with the speed of motorboats. What her mother described as 'flings' and Annie as 'borderline promiscuity'. But she didn't care about that because Annie was her anchor in an unstable world. There was no way, though, that she was going to that party they had been invited to this evening, given by some woman that Annie knew who worked in HR. She feared an argument about this. Annie liked arguments even more than parties but Violet was an argument incompetent and found parties awkward at the best of times. The word 'party' still conjured up an afternoon when she, aged six, had been forced to eat red jelly in the shape of a rabbit by a bossy mother and had thrown up something that looked like bits of bloody lung on to the woman's shoes. She had been sent home in disgrace. It wasn't that she didn't find other people interesting, but that they always asked you questions like, 'And what do you do for a living?' and the banal answers she had to give dispirited her and made her ashamed of herself. And how could she go to a party when she couldn't even brush her teeth or get dressed? What was she supposed to do? Wear her pyjamas?

Not only having failed with Annie, she had never managed to explain to anyone else either what it felt like if she went outside when she had 'the fear'. Everything was amplified – all the sounds came at her through loudspeakers, it all seemed horribly strip-lit, the texture of the softest surfaces was sandpaper rough, and the prospect of having to talk to anyone or obey any demand made upon her was terrifying. She could hardly cross a road or go into a shop, the potential for imminent disaster was so great. It felt as if ordinary people had knives in their pockets which they might produce at any moment. She feared for her life. It sounded bonkers, she knew that. 'I am probably bonkers,' she said to herself. From the kitchen the phone rang and her heartbeat increased. It might be Annie, telling her she had to work late, and Violet tried to weigh up whether this was a good thing or not. It would mean that she didn't have to go through the argument about the party but on the other hand it would also mean that she remained without food. Annie would have deliberately left the phone on the kitchen island to make sure that Violet had to leave her bed to get it, and Violet's mobile was in her coat pocket in the hall and therefore also unreachable. Her stomach growled. What she would really like was some chocolate raisins. She thought about going and looking out of the window on to the street and whether that would make her feel better. It might, or it might make her feel like a princess trapped up here in a castle with no hope whatsoever of escape. The phone stopped and then started again. That was likely to mean that it wasn't Annie at all but Annie's mother, a woman she found in equal parts comical and ogreish. There was no way she was talking to her. She pulled the covers back up over her face.

This is Annie Barnes

'Get up,' said Annie, an hour later, trying to pull the duvet off Violet.

'I can't,' said Violet, holding on to it with both hands as hard as she could.

'You can,' Annie said and yanked again so that Violet was pulled towards the edge of the bed. It looked likely that she would soon end up on the floor.

'Why must I?' asked Violet through teeth gritted with effort.

It was becoming a tug of war with an inevitable conclusion because the difference in size between them made them a comedy pairing. Violet like a miniature Snow White, with swinging black hair that she hid behind to avoid direct contact with the world, as pale and small and delicate as a doll, Annie with the proportions and the colouring of Sophia Loren, all curves and attitude, 'stacked', as she liked to describe herself. Before meeting Violet, Annie had always felt towards small women what she felt towards chihuahuas, that she would quite like to kick them, and it was a testament to their friendship that Annie never had. She had made allowances for Violet because, on their first ever outing to a Manchester student bar that smelt of marijuana and slops, Violet had confided in her that she hated being small.

'Men pick me up given the smallest opportunity. And women say to me, "You're so tiny. What size do you take?" Like it's a compliment.'

'But come on, there must be some advantages. You're teeny tiny, you're pretty, men love that. I'm sure you've got plenty to pick and choose from,' said Annie.

'You are really beautiful, Annie,' said Violet, who was nibbling on an ill-advised sausage roll to try to sober up.

'I know, but I have far fewer to pick from,' said Annie. 'I'm more of a specialist taste. But you, you're a pocket Venus. Everybody loves you, I'll bet you.'

'Men who want to protect me, yeah. Men who want to look after me and have me sit on their knee and be their little girl.'

'That's disgusting. No one ever asks me to do that.'

'I mean, why would you want to sit on their knee? Unless you were a ventriloquist's dummy.'

More of a problem for Annie was that Violet's fashion sense was non-existent to the point of being embarrassing, as she would only wear clothes from charity shops; she found it comforting to wear things that someone else had already worn. Annie disapproved of this because it resulted in Violet wearing scout's jumpers and Hello Kitty T-shirts and dungarees, as she could still fit into a twelve-year-old's garments. Annie disapproved of trousers on women, apart from for exercise purposes, let alone of anything that covered your cleavage. If God had given you it, why the hell not show it, was her rationale, but all attempts to persuade Violet into something more suitable or even new had failed.

Annie managed to get the duvet off at last and threw it on to the floor. It had hardly been a fair contest; she had at least a four-stone advantage. Violet curled up into a ball and wrapped her little hands around her little knees.

'Come on, shift your arse,' said Annie, remaining by the side of the bed. 'If you get up I'll tell you my favourite word.'

'I should think it's probably "litigious",' said Violet.

'If you don't get up now I'm going to carry you into the shower and turn on the water! And then you'll be bloody sorry!'

'Are you threatening me?' asked Violet, who had hooked one hand around the bedpost.

'That was not a threat. That was a statement of intent. Don't slander.'

'That's libel.'

'You know it's not libel.'

'I just wanted to make a point,' said Violet.

Annie knew that she was wishing the duvet wasn't so far away so that she could crawl to get it. Annie took the opportunity to kick it behind her.

'And what,' Annie asked, with the increasing exasperation and the hands-on-hips gesture that might normally have roused Violet into action, 'is your point?'

'That I really don't want to get up and I really don't want to go to the party either,' said Violet.

'Why I put up with you I do not know,' said Annie. 'By the way, this room is a complete tip,' and Annie threw something at Violet which turned out to be a dress she had been looking for. She clutched it to her chest.

'Are you by any chance my mother?' asked Violet.

'Your mother's got no tits to speak of. So no,' said Annie. 'Get up. Going to the party might do you good.'

'I'm not coming,' Violet said and turned her back.

Annie didn't do inertia or depression or anxiety or whatever the hell this was herself. She had no truck with it, just like she had no truck with knickers that cost under twenty quid, dirty bathrooms, integral spotlights, cars made by Ford, washing up without Marigolds on, shower gel or speed bumps. She should have known that this assertive approach was not going to help. Violet, normally so pliable, became intransigent in this state. Why did what Violet called 'the fear' suddenly come upon her, seemingly out of nowhere? Dunno. What about going to the doctor? No. Why not? Dunno. She'd been having these episodes ever since Annie had met her and it was best, Annie had found with years of experience and irritation, to leave her be until she came back out of her snail shell. The leaving of things to come to fruition on their own did not come naturally to her but she had learnt to bite her lip. More or less.

'I'm not coming,' said Violet again.

'You could have said that before!' Annie said, and she picked up the duvet and threw it back at Violet, who slid under it with a sigh.

Annie stood as the party milled around her, looking at the therapist's card that Dolores had given her when she had apologized for Violet not coming, yet again, to one of these parties.

Dolores had told her that this was the obvious solution to Violet's 'sad shyness' as she called it and that the therapist was a friend of hers who was very good. Perhaps it was the solution? She considered the likelihood of Violet going to therapy. Her heels were hurting her, her shoes were always too tight, and she tried to alleviate this by wiggling her toes but that didn't work. 'You have to suffer to be beautiful,' her mother always said, and in Annie's experience she had found this to be true. Annie liked a bet but on her own skill set rather than racing. Drinking men under the table. Arm wrestling. She wouldn't have taken the bet on Violet going to see someone because the odds were non-existent. Not a long shot but a dead horse. She had tried to tell Dolores that it was pointless giving her the card but she had failed. Annie admired Dolores's tenacity, it was almost as strong as her own. She looked up to see a man entering the room who looked as if he could easily bump his head on the door lintel. Six two, thought Annie, but no rugby player, too thin, and with shoulders not meant for the scrum. There were a lot of props in her family. He wouldn't have lasted a minute. The man had a blond short back and sides and looked freshly laundered. He was dressed in a way Annie always went for, Levis and a well-ironed expensive shirt. Not designer, proper clothes. She reckoned that he was older than her by about ten years. He approached her. Across a crowded room, she was aware of the cliché. He had good posture and beautiful oxblood brogues.

'Penny for them,' he said. 'Can I get you a drink? There's not much choice I'm afraid. Warm white or warm red or a bowl of red liquid that looks suspiciously like sangria.'

'My gran always used to say, "Spend a penny," when she went to the loo and I used to look down it to see if she'd dropped one,' said Annie. 'Do you iron your own shirts?'

She reached forwards to stroke his sleeve. He seemed to like that.

'No, I have a man who does it for me.'

'Your boyfriend?' she asked.

'No,' he said, coughing, 'I have a man who comes in and does that kind of thing for me. I pay him.'

'A cleaner,' she said.

'I don't think that Pike would like to be called a cleaner. I think he would be mortally offended.'

'Well, a housekeeper then? Will that do? What is his job title?'

'Factotum perhaps.'

'Facwhat? That sounds like a disease of the rectum,' she said to see if it would make him laugh, not because she didn't know the word. It did make him laugh and his laugh was charming because he crinkled his long nose before he tipped his chin up, not a weak chin Annie was pleased to note, but later she realized that the whole outcome of their relationship hinged on that moment. He laughed at what he believed to be her ignorance. He had taken her as someone different from the person she was, right from the beginning.

People always judged her by her voice. When she went to London for meetings they mimicked her behind her back, she knew they did. They talked about *Coronation Street* and flat caps. When pissed the arseholes doing their articles asked her if she had had a privy out t'back. When she was younger she had once asked a man to step outside with her when he had said that, and he had had the sense to look scared. Now she only smiled in a way that didn't go as far as her eyes and didn't bother about it, knowing that she was better than all of them. And yes, she had grown up in a tiny terraced house in a Lancashire mill town but so what? Her dad had made enough money in the building trade to buy them a brand-new house in a suburb, complete with five bedrooms, a conservatory, and a utility room. Both of her brothers were engineers like their mother had planned. Her highest aim in life was to make sure that her children would never have to get their hands dirty at work. They'd all done well. But was that ever good enough? Her dad would always be a builder at heart, even if her mother did say 'property developer'. They'd always be money that had been made. She could tell instantly that if he didn't have a trust fund now, his parents would do anything to avoid inheritance tax. They probably had money offshore and perhaps even a town house and a country house. She bet his dad never had to scrub his hands with Swarfega after a day at work. Should any of it matter? Wasn't that outdated now, positively Victorian, that distinction? But it was underneath everything like soil under tarmac. You fancy me, she thought, but you think my voice is amusing. You think I'm common. Sod you. When he came back to her and gave her a glass full of a liquid that was supposed to be wine she downed it in one.

'Got to be going,' she said.

'School night? What do you do?'

'I'm a lawyer.'

'That's interesting. I'm in advertising myself.'

'How fascinating,' she said.

'Are you being sarcastic?'

'It's only I think that's daft for a man. Poncing around with adverts about cars and that. Washing powder. Cat food. Or whatever you do. You don't look like the hipster type. Where's your beard?'

'Would you like to go somewhere nicer?' he said.

'No,' she said.

'Why not? Am I so terrible?'

She could tell that he thought himself charming; she expected that he always got what he wanted, or rather who.

'You've got a voice that sounds right up yourself, to be honest.'

And he laughed again, and she still liked the way he did it.

'Would you at least give me your number? Then I can take you out and impress you massively at a later date. I'm Laurence, by the way.'

'Larry? Like in Olivier?'

'Just Laurence.'

'Like I said. Up yourself.'

'What's your name?'

'078461114789. And if you can remember that off the top of your head I might even take your call, just Laurence.'

She knew as she walked away that she made an impressive back view, that her arse was like soft cushions you wanted to lay your head on and that she swivelled her wide hips like Marilyn in *Some Like It Hot*.

She knew he would phone.

This is Grace's profession

It was five to four. Grace had one eye on the clock and the other on the woman in front of her. Clock, woman, clock, woman, clock. It was rhythmical and more a matter of habit than need. It was soothing. She had good time management skills. This was an acknowledged fact in her office. She had been complimented on it and asked for her secret in the same way that people ask how you stop your meringues from collapsing. It was hardly a talent to boast of but it made life easier. She managed not to tap her foot. Clock, woman.

At school, the nuns hadn't given them much career advice. There was a nun called Sister Maria Concepción who was Spanish and had a lovely soft accent and she called Grace into her office and asked her about her future vocation. Grace sat looking at the bad quality reproduction of *The Light of the World* on the wall opposite and tried to think about it. She knew that

Sister Maria Concepción wanted her to say nun or missionary but she couldn't bring herself to do it. To broaden their spiritual horizons her grandfather Cyril had given her and her sisters the outlines of all the world's major religions that the nuns had ignored, and Grace had decided that atheism was the way to go; it seemed simpler and she didn't fancy any of the others, despite the temptation to be able to say, 'I'm a Zoroastrian.' She gave up religion immediately and easily, completely unlike the efforts it took to avoid chocolate at Lent, and never went back. She sat in the office looking at Jesus and it suddenly came to her like a vision of the divine. Psychology, she could study that. Why not? True, she couldn't spell the word very well but no matter.

'Psychology,' she said, 'I want to be a psychothingymagig.'

Sister Maria Concepción sighed deeply and held out her small hand and brushed one of Grace's with it.

'And you such an intelligent girl,' she said.

This Grace considered to be the best decision of her life so far but it wasn't until she started having therapy herself that she realized why it all appealed to her so much. Her upbringing had been what might be labelled 'eccentric', if not 'downright odd' or possibly 'dysfunctional'. No wonder she had wanted to try and figure things out. She had lived with her sisters and Cyril, a Classics professor, and their Great Aunt Beatrice, who still rode to hounds, although she was unsteady and had to be tied on to the saddle with red baling twine. They inhabited a rotting manor house with twelve bedrooms and no central heating on the edge of the North Yorkshire moors which was falling down around their ears day by day. Every so often their mother would come home, have a baby, and abandon it to Cyril's hands which were stained yellow by pipe tobacco. It seemed that her diaphragm was only useful for short periods.

She stayed a month or two, hardly eating anything and doing her ballet exercises for eight hours a day, until she got back into her lithe shape and then she was off again on tour. It was Cyril who dealt with the croup and the cradle cap, Cyril who stirred the Mr Matey bubbles in their baths and frightened them with bloodthirsty stories about the battle of Marathon and, when they were not much older, taught them to drive the Land Rover so that they could come and get him after the lock-ins in the local pub. Cyril named them after the heroines of Thomas Hardy novels: Arabella, Grace, Eustacia, and Tess. They were just grateful that he hadn't gone for 'Bathsheba'.

'Arabella, darling, or one of you,' was how their mother referred to them when they were children. 'Arabella, darling, or one of you,' was the story of her approach to rearing her daughters. As a result they didn't think of her as a parent but as a reluctant Father Christmas who appeared sporadically during their childhoods clutching black market cigarettes and vodka for Cyril and Beatrice and snow globes and dolls for them. And of course, there was the father/fathers issue. There were no photos, no evidence, and when, as teenagers, they decided to ask her, en masse, she waved her fingers airily at them all.

'Oh, you know darlings, men,' she said, and they could get nothing more out of her.

When picked apart Grace's early life provided years of material to work on. She, although it seemed somehow wrong to admit it, loved all the attention that the therapist focused on you. After all, although Cyril and Beatrice had coddled their foibles, there were always so many of them that they became a single entity – 'the girls'. To have one person sit and listen to you for hours and months and years was such a luxury and she knew that her clients enjoyed this too. After all, what is more interesting to us, when it comes down to it, Grace often thought, than our own weird stories; that didn't stop her however from sometimes still being surprised by the things her clients were happy to divulge to her.

She had been seeing this morning's client for three months. There were extensive notes about her in the folder on her desk. Denise. Dentist. Aged fifty-six. Married to Arthur for thirty years. Three grown-up children. Could probably be described as 'still an attractive woman for her age', which Grace presumed translated as 'slim'. Grace frequently wondered why straight women were so obsessed with their looks in comparison to the lesbians she knew. Not that they were without standards – they washed for example, they had their hair cut, they wore deodorant – just that their standards didn't seem to be so very stringent. She had looked in *Vogue* once and found it bizarre, the worshipping of things as ephemeral as stupidly expensive dresses and bags and shoes. And the strange adolescent models with their sticking-out bones. It must be such a burden to have to keep up with that sort of rubbish, such a waste of money and effort. She wondered if this was all to do with the male gaze and having to submit yourself to it, of having to morph during adolescence from tomboy to sexy. She had always looked upon men as equals but perhaps that was because she didn't have to conform to their idea of pleasing and attractive. It was interesting, she should read up about it. She looked down at her plain grey shirt and plain black trousers and was relieved that at least they had no toothpaste or mud on them. She looked at Denise's make-up and wondered how she got it to stay on her face and how long it took her to put it on in the mornings.

'We've been pretending we're horses again,' said Denise, pressing her thin lips together but speaking in a very matter-of-fact voice.

Grace nodded. At the beginning of her training she might have wanted to say, 'Excuse me, you're what?' but she had long ago accustomed herself to these sorts of confessions.

'Not just in bed any more,' said Denise, 'it's kind of spilled over. We have horse names now. And when we go for a walk we like to pretend we're trotting and when we're going faster we call it cantering. That might be going too far, don't you think?'

'What do you think?' asked Grace. She was so used to answering a question with a question that she no longer noticed she did it.

'I mean, we wouldn't want anyone else to know, especially not the children. No one else but you does, he's Monty, an Arabian stallion, and I'm Minty, a pure-bred American palomino. I asked Monty, Arthur that is, if it would be OK to talk to you about this and he said he didn't mind at all. He knows you wouldn't tell anyone. You won't tell anyone, will you?'

'No,' said Grace, and this was true of course but the fact was that she often wanted to tell her sisters and her friends all sorts of things that her clients told her about. Dolores for example would have been completely delighted to hear some of it. Her sister Bella would have had a field day. It was one of the worst things about being a therapist – the client confidentiality clause. Because sometimes the things people said were just so interesting it seemed a shame not to share them.

'We've bought a salt lick but I can't say I like it, and we're considering getting a water trough. We could put it on the patio we thought, next to the gazebo, and no one will ever be any the wiser. We thought we could tell the children it was for the birds to wash in. What do you think?'

She looked excited and Grace was glad for her and thought about saying, 'I think it's a bloody excellent idea. Why the hell not?'

'What do you think?' said Grace, mirroring Denise's cross-legged posture. 'Are you happy with these horse role-plays?'

'I love them! They make life ever so much more fun.'

She liked Denise. It was easier of course to enjoy your work when you liked your clients but she was a professional after all, she could listen to anyone, but not just anyone came because she was in private practice and she charged £80 an hour. Sometimes she felt bad about that, guilty even; maybe she could take on some of the less well-off or institute a sliding scale. If she was a truly good person she wouldn't have gone private at all, but she had long ago admitted to herself, after a traumatic stint in an underfunded alcoholic outreach pro-gramme, that severe pain was too much for her to bear. Was that a terrible admission on her part? Yes. But she liked her house which her clients paid for and after all, she justified to herself, wasn't she still being of service? Didn't everyone deserve to be helped? She did believe that and yet it still ran-kled her as she listened to banalities and repetitive complaints and obsessions and some mildly odd scenarios. Those were her daily bread and she could coast through them with ease. It made it that much easier to wake up in the morning. It made her day interesting, sometimes fascinating, but not over-stimulating or stressful. It made it, she admitted to herself now, possible to sleep at night.

'I'm afraid our session's nearly over for today,' she said to Denise, and leant back in her chair. 'Is there anything else you would like to go over before we finish?'

'I just wanted to tell you about the saddle,' said Denise.

The reality of it was that Grace loved her job.

After work that day Grace went to Manfred's on the way home. His shop as usual smelt of burnt coffee and anti-bacterial spray, the heating cranked way up in all weathers. She went there far too much, out of a combination of guilt that Manfred worked about fifty hours a week more than her and laziness. As a result, she seemed to spend a lot on items discounted because of their sell-by date.

'Ah Grace,' he said to her now. He was a very good-looking man Grace could appreciate if not be attracted to, taller than her, with one of those triangular swimmer's bodies and a long face framed by thick black eyebrows that nearly met in the middle. Grace liked to think of Manfred as a twenty-something romantic hero trapped in a corner shop but that was patronizing, as he never expressed any discontent at being there.

'Good to see you,' said Manfred, and Grace liked the fact that he always seemed to mean it. 'What can I do you for? I've got lovely frozen peas that came in two minutes ago. Sweet. Succulent. You'll love them.'

'I don't like peas very much.'

'You can't live your life on biscuits! I worry about your dietary requirements. Here, have a baklava.'

'How is baklava better than biscuits?' asked Grace.

'Freshly made by my mate. He's into his cooking. All home-cooked ingredients. None of your E55 rubbish. Have one.'

And he passed her a small sticky slice. She put it into her mouth.

'And how's the love life?' asked Manfred.

'What love life?' asked Grace, trying not to spray crumbs over the counter.

'Young woman like you. Lots of beautiful girls out there.'

'Then why aren't you married yourself?' asked Grace.

'I'm picky,' he said, and grinned. 'Can I interest you in these eggs? You could make yourself a nutritious omelette. Bang in some of my frozen spinach and you'll be sorted. I'll give you them twenty-five per cent off seeing as there are only five. It's a bargain.'

This is Annie's solution to Violet's unstable mental state

As soon as she started to make money as a lawyer, Annie stopped dyeing her hair over the bathroom sink and went to the most expensive salon in town to have it done. Cheap hairdressers were one of the other things she didn't believe in; if a mess was to be made it was better to make it yourself. But oh, the relief of no longer having to rub at the stains on her hairline with the cigarette ash left over from her three-times-a-day cigarette. She liked to wear her hair swept to one side like a brunette Veronica Lake, and if you don't know how much it cost to get it to look like that then surely you wouldn't be able to afford it. Soon she also began to have a blow-dry twice a week. God forbid that she should wash her hair at home. It would take time for things to escalate but they did. One day there would be a personal shopper at Harvey Nicks, an underfed girl called Catrina whom Annie didn't like much, but who had perfect taste in form-fitting garments. Then there was the tortuous regime of waxing and the obsession with La Perla underwear. Moisturizer that shouldn't have been that expensive but was. What was it made of – diamonds? The sweet chemical smell of the dry cleaners that she loved to sniff when her clothes came back. Facials that tore every piece of dirt from her pores. There were deep tissue massages every two weeks and her trainer Nigel, who was the only person she would accept being shouted at by. Mani-pedis obviously and bags so expensive they could have fed a family of six for months. And shoes, too many shoes. Extensive eyebrow maintenance and a MAC habit. And that's what it felt like, like maintenance, like car upkeep. She did it all at high speed to fit it in with her workload. She viewed it as part of her workload. She was always immaculate, just like her mother, who had never had an off-duty day in her life. Her mother had never, not once, let her father see her without her make-up on. 'Even if you have to get up half an hour earlier, Annie, no man wants to see what he really married before he's even had his breakfast.'

As a child, she had despised the amount of effort her mother seemed to have to put in: all that time wasted in ladies' boutiques that smelt of Nina Ricci and hair salons that smelt of Elnett. But against Annie's better wishes her mother's standards had all stuck. The day-to-day of it was so tedious that her daydreams involved hems that were coming down and stocking ladders and going out bare-faced and with chipped nails. Violet had her hair cut in the local hairdresser's, where for twenty quid you could get a trim, a cup of tea, and a copy of OK, together with a range of conversations about cellulite and bad boyfriends. Annie half wished she could adopt this casual approach but she couldn't even get past the front door.

'It's like you're a celebrity and I'm a civilian,' said Violet. 'Come on. I dare you. Wear your slippers to Manfred's. They're nice slippers. Go on. You can do it. There aren't any paparazzi outside.'

'I can't.'

'But Manfred wouldn't care! He loves you.'

'I can't and that's that,' said Annie. 'Are you going to work?'

'Should do,' said Violet.

'Violet.'

'You're "Violeting" me.'

'Are you going to work or not?'

'Maybe.'

'Then I suggest you put some clothes on.'

Violet was not so much dirty as chaotic, a tendency which had led Annie to impose draconic restrictions on her natural strewing tendencies. 'And I'll thank you to keep this to your room' was, Violet would swear, Annie's most common utterance to her in the first months of them living together as she threw a forgotten object at her. Now Annie's newest theory was that the fewer choices Violet had to make, the more she would be able to do things other than lie on her bed looking at the ceiling or sleep a sleep so deep that it took an old-fashioned alarm clock placed in a saucepan to wake her up.

'You can't not go when you don't feel like it,' said Annie.

'You and your Protestant work ethic,' said Violet. 'Anyway, you think both of my jobs are stupid.'

'That's because they are stupid. You sell angel candles and crystals and other crap to new age idiots. And occasionally you take people's coats off them in a club that smells of spilt pints and men who are wearing too much Lynx. Neither of these jobs can be classed as meaningful or profitable vocations. You have a degree. Why the heck aren't you using it?'

'It's only an English degree, which you have been telling me is good for nothing since the day I met you. And some of the people I speak to of a day are very spiritually advanced, I'll have you know. And some of the men are OK.'

'They're leching bastards who would screw anything that moved.'

'That's no way to speak of people who talk to angels!'

'You need a proper job. Then you'd be more . . . motivated.'

'Do we really have to do this now?' asked Violet.

'I've bought you a laundry basket but there's no way I'm picking up your dirty knickers, so get up and sort out all this washing. I presume it's washing, since it's on the floor.'

Violet ignored her and rolled over.

Annie's latest solution to 'the fear' was de-cluttering. Violet could sometimes manage to brush her teeth and wash her hair now that Annie had removed all of her bathroom excess, leaving behind only Colgate, Radox and Herbal Essences. Bit by bit Annie had applied the idea of reduction to the rest of the flat she owned.

'It makes you realize,' said Annie on the phone to her mother one night, 'how much rubbish you accumulate. All those CDs you never listen to. All those bank statements.'

'I've been telling you that for ages,' said her mother. 'Just what the lady on *House Doctor* used to say. She dressed ever so nicely. It changed my opinion of them.'

'Decorators?' asked Annie.

'Americans. After all it's such a big country, there must be some decent people. I've decided to give them the benefit of the doubt. I'm going with your Auntie Dorothy to New York for a shopping trip,' said her mother.

'Pardon?' said Annie.

'Before Christmas. We've got a very good deal. Apparently, that Bloomingdales is as good as John Lewis.'

'You're leaving the country? You never even leave Lancashire.'

'Annie, you know that's not true,' said her mother with a sigh. She would be sitting in the hall on a loveseat she'd had Annie's dad make especially, talking on an actual real telephone because she believed neither in cordless nor in mobiles. 'I've been to Leeds to see you lots of times. And that time I went to London with the Women's Institute.'

'Cosmopolitan,' said Annie.

'Pardon? I have no idea what you're talking about, Annie. Everything used to be much simpler, you know. You bought two packets of sausages, one of frozen peas, and a bag of potatoes and that was dinner for all of you set. There's too much choice now, I think. That's why all of you young ones are so confused.'

'It's the yoghurt that does for me. Organic, flavoured, goat's milk, full fat, soya, Greek, with bobbly chocolate bits in. I want yoghurt. God, if I took Violet to Morrison's now she'd freak.'

'I do wish you wouldn't go there. I prefer Sainsbury's.'

'Well, I don't, all right?'

'I wish you wouldn't end your sentences in that slovenly way.'

'I know, mother. And you also wish I was married, had two children called Julie and John, and lived in a five-bedroom house down the road from you with a spa and spent the rest of my life doing my nails.'

'I do not. By the way, the Chiltons' house is for sale.'

'I'm not interested. I like my flat. I love my job. I like my life here.'

'I know. I don't mean to interfere.'

'Well, you are.'

Annie always tried not to let her mother wind her up but she knew it was a losing battle. She looked at her hair to see if she had any split ends but of course she hadn't.

'I want you to be happy.'

'I am happy. You want me to be what you think of as "settled".'

'And what's so terrible about that? I want what's best for you. What mother doesn't? I know your flat is very nice and everything but I wish you were nearer home.'

'It's near enough.'

'You know what I mean. Your father would like to see more of you.'

'Well, tell him to get in the car. What you mean is what mother would want her daughter living in the inner city with a deranged woman for a flatmate.'

'All I'm saying is that Violet is a very sweet girl and I like her but you shouldn't be sharing a flat with her any more.'

'At my age? Or because Violet is odd?'

'Well, what's wrong with me saying that? It's true.'

'Which one?'

'Don't try to get me in a muddle. It was fun for you when you were younger but, well, I don't like to say this but I've always been one for speaking my mind so I'll say it, she's a sponge on you.'

'A bathroom one? A trifle one?'

'Well, I was trying to have a sensible conversation with you, Annie, but if you refuse to see my point of view about Violet then I'll . . .'

'Force me at gunpoint into Sainsbury's?'

'You do too much for that girl and you know it. You shouldn't be wasting your time on her, not at your age. You're not getting any younger.'

By now Annie was halfway between exasperated and bored.

'Ah, I knew it was coming. The biological cut-off panic. The marital advice.'

'Well, why should I lie to you? It's true. You should have stuck with that nice Michael Wrigley.'

'You couldn't stand Michael Wrigley! You said, and I'll quote you here, "His father's got no money and his mother's no better than she should be." For God's sake, Mum! How many times do we have to have this bloody conversation? You're the one who thinks that no one is good enough for me! You're the bloody one who tells me not to let my standards down, not to give it away, not to bloody . . .'

'I will not be talked to in this manner, Annie. I will not be sworn at and spoken to in that tone of voice when all I am thinking of is your welfare, your fertility, and the future of my grandchildren. Annie? Annie?'

It was the first time Annie had ever put the phone down on her mother in her life. She felt a great sense of satisfaction followed immediately by an equally weighty sense of guilt. If she put them on a set of scales which would win? Gradually the guilt started to tip it, so that an ache appeared at the base of her brain, an ache she could feel would soon overtake her whole body with the urge to ring back. Should she ring her back and apologize? No, she bloody well wouldn't; she would occupy herself until the urge passed. Her mother was ridiculous – she was only twenty-nine for God's sake, she had plenty of time for the whole settling down thing. She shook her head and feeling clearer walked into her bedroom. What needed doing in here? Should she hoover? No, it didn't need it, she hoovered every other day with her Dyson in parallel lines. Dust? There was no dust. She had got all of this off her mother, it was the way she had been brainwashed to think that house-work was an atheist's version of the divine. She could get down on her hands and knees and scrub at the floor tiles in the bath-room with a toothbrush like her mother did, seemingly for fun but looking alarmingly like somebody praying. Oh god of cleanliness, here I am with my humble bleach, please have mercy on me. Why am I like this? She was suddenly furious with herself. Why am I just like her? I don't want to be like her. Her phone rang.

'For God's sake, Mum! What do you want now?'

'Interesting greeting. I am not, however, your mother.'

'Who is this? Why have you got this number?'

'It's Larry Olivier.'

'Why are you calling me?'

'For conventional reasons. Would you like to come out to dinner with me?'

'When?'

'How about Saturday?'

'I can do it in about half an hour.'

'Really?'

'That's what I said. Take it or leave it.'

'Then I will most definitely take it. Give me your address and I'll pick you up.'

'I'm not giving a strange bloke I don't know my address! Do you think I'm stupid? I'll meet you at Sukothai. Eight. I'll book.'

And she cancelled the call.

I'm not doing my bloody eyebrows, she said mentally to her mother. So there.

This is how Grace met the woman (II)

Grace was on her way back from Eustacia's house on the Yorkshire coast where she had spent the weekend with Eustacia and Tess and Tess's precocious twin boys. She had enjoyed seeing her sisters but the twins were annoying. If I could ever have a child it wouldn't be made to eat brown rice and miso soup and be banned from TV, Grace thought. I would feed it entirely on strawberry milkshakes and Pringles and expose it to many hours of rubbish kids' programmes in the hope that it would turn out easier to be with than Rowan and Linden. Their names irritated her. She couldn't help thinking that even if her children had grown up hyperactive and obsessed with Disney, she could have done a better job. Maybe it was different when they were your own, maybe all your good intentions went out of the window under the stress of sleep deprivation and screaming. Maybe she would have ended up being the type of mother who smacked their children in supermarkets and swore at them for dropping their sweets on the pavement. She would never have the opportunity to know.

When she saw the woman sitting on a low wall by the bus stop near the park reading, Grace had been thinking about her so much that she almost didn't recognize her. Grace felt slightly disappointed – she was still beautiful but she looked like the 'making of' documentary rather than the film itself. But maybe, thought Grace, this might be a good thing, and it allowed her to stop her car a hundred metres down the road and park. Before she could think about it too much she took a deep breath and walked back to the woman, although the temptation to pretend she hadn't seen her and hurry past turning her collar up like an undercover detective was strong.

'Hello,' Grace said, which seemed a normal sort of opener. What should she do with her hands? She put them in her pockets like a guilty schoolboy. There was sweat starting on her lower back under her jeans and more on her upper lip and her pulse was accelerating. This was strange. She was used to getting to know strangers and finding out their darkest secrets. Why should talking to this person on an ordinary street on an ordinary day make her anxious? And yet, if this was so very ordinary, why hadn't she told her sisters about this woman as she always did about anyone who was interesting.

'Hi,' the woman said, barely glancing up.

'I met you at Dolores's party the other day,' Grace said.

The woman had long earrings on again, this time with tiny silver beads at the ends. Grace wanted a gust of wind to make them swing.

'I don't remember,' the woman said. She was chewing gum. Grace hated gum.

'The party or me?'

There was no smile from the woman.

'You. I remember the party,' she said and kept on reading.

Grace was perturbed by her bluntness. She couldn't think of anything else to say for a while, so she stood there waiting for the woman to say something herself; but this tactic failed because she didn't seem bothered by the silence, she never even looked up. Grace, after some mental floundering, eventually managed, 'How's the book?' And she pointed at it as though they were in a bookshop and she had to distinguish it from all the others.

The woman finally looked at her properly. She had barely-there plucked eyebrows and Grace wanted to trace them with her fingers. She had a wide mouth and Grace wanted to reach forward and place her own mouth on it to see if they fitted together. Once again, she had to put her hands behind her back to stop herself reaching out. Why did she want to touch this woman so much? She didn't even know her name and yet she wanted to stroke her wrists and the undersides of her arms. She wanted to put her head into the crook of the woman's neck and her mouth on her clavicle. She didn't normally like tall blondes who looked vaguely Swedish. She went for the short and dark. And yet she felt as giddy as if she had just stumbled off the dodgems at a fairground.

'Do you read much?' said the woman, and Grace tried to remember how to speak.

'Is it a novel? I don't read them much. I mean I do like to read what I do read but I don't read novels. I like to read what I do read though.' If she had had an available hard surface to knock her inarticulate brain against she would have.

'That's a shame,' the woman said, and finally looked at Grace as though she was a human entity and not a piece of litter.

'Is it?' Grace asked, delighted that she'd got a response.

'Yes, I think so. Novels are realer than non-fiction, I think. I like reading about other people's ideas, all these strange ideas that then become your own. And later you can't remember where you got them from or if they're yours or not because everything gets all muddled up in your head.'

'It sounds confusing,' said Grace. It was approaching a conversation!

'I think it's magical,' said the woman.

'You're very convincing,' Grace said, although she wasn't

sure if she was because she was too busy looking at her to listen properly. 'Perhaps I should try reading some novels.'

'I'll lend you this when I've finished if you want. It's the umpteenth time I've read it but I can't give it to you now, I've got to get to the end.'

Was this a real offer? wondered Grace. Does it mean she wants to see me again?

'I've never read anything twice. Don't you get bored?'

'No. Never. It's my favourite book.'

And then, just when Grace thought the woman might be interested in what they were talking about, she went back to her book as if Grace was no longer there in front of her. Grace didn't know what to do now. She didn't want the conversation to end, although it hardly classed as a conversation, more an awkwardness. She wasn't ready to give up yet, though. I have social skills, she thought. I have social skills.

'What's it called then? The book?' she asked.

'*The Unbearable Lightness of Being* by Milan Kundera,' and the woman showed her the front of the book, perhaps to test if it was true that Grace did know how to read.

'He sounds Italian. Or Indian.'

'He was born Czech but then he moved to France.'

'Right.'

The woman started reading again. Grace found that she was standing on only one leg. She put her foot down.

'Are you waiting for somebody or are you getting the bus?' she said.

'Neither.'

The woman didn't look at her and Grace gave up.

'Sorry. I didn't mean to interrupt. Bye.'

'Bye,' said the woman with no enthusiasm.

Grace turned away thinking, I am a mature individual, I am not a teenager, so this cannot be a crush. This is not an embarrassing incident but a case of an unfriendly and border-line rude person who it is better I have nothing to do with. I have a job and a house and admittedly my life assurance is in favour of my sisters because I don't have anyone else to leave my life to but that does not make me an altogether pathetic person, just a sensible one. I am too old for this crap. She started off back to her car in her walk of shame, timing her steps to the refrain of the rejected, the stupid, the sad – idiot, idiot, I'm an idiot. She wasn't used to being rejected, let alone being rejected twice. Why had she tried again?

'What's your name?' the woman shouted after her.

Grace turned around.

'Grace.'

'What?'

'Grace!'

'Where are you going?'

'I was going to go home but I've just remembered my library books are overdue and I've lost my password and so I've got to go to the library. Do you want to come?'

It was a response she made without thinking. Dear God. Had any human being ever uttered such sad sentences? I am an altogether pathetic person and I never knew it, she thought.

'Sure,' the woman said, and jumped off the wall and came towards her.

'I was going to go to the library, I didn't make it up,' said Grace to the woman as they sat on the sofa in the front of the tattoo parlour. There was a strong smell of antiseptic which Grace found extremely worrying because it was what she imagined an operating theatre might smell like. She envisioned the back room as mortuary clean and filled with sharp stainless steel implements like a serial killer's preparation room and she shud-dered. It wasn't a good sign either that the shop went by the name of 'House of Pain'. She didn't consider it a good moment to be ironic. Although it probably wasn't ironic at all.

'And I thought you didn't read,' said the woman.

'I didn't say that,' said Grace. 'I read a lot for work.'

Grace waited for the woman to ask her about her job, which Grace was looking forward to because she always felt pride when she said her job title, even though she considered this vain.

'I think you should get your ears pierced,' said the woman.

'Are you joking?' asked Grace, and thought you must not know me at all and then remembered that the woman didn't know her at all and what is more who was this woman anyway? She could just be someone paid to lure the innocent into tattoo parlours and before you knew it you'd spent five hundred quid on having the Taj Mahal drilled into your back. It was a clever ruse, it had seemed such a casual decision on the woman's part. Grace couldn't decide if this place was interesting because it was unusual to her and because it would make a good story to tell her sisters or just frightening because of the possibility of serious mutilation involved. She remembered something she had read somewhere about people who got themselves 'branded' and felt sick.

'No, I think it would look nice, you've got pretty ears,' said the woman.

She leaned forward and gently pinched Grace's left ear between finger and thumb in the place where an earring would go, and Grace felt a shock that went all the way through her ear and then her head and then straight down her neck and down through her spine, as if she had been in contact with an electric fence. Bazam! Like the time she had walked into one aged twelve, while putting the horses in the paddock, having forgotten it was on. Then the woman let go of her ear and returned to the plastic file of tattoo designs. Grace checked her ear was still attached to her head and edged away from the woman because it suddenly felt too dangerous to be near her. What if she touched her knee or her arm? Would there be an electric chair jolt? The woman didn't seem to notice the effect she had had. She was flicking through the file.

'A mermaid?' she asked Grace, and Grace looked at the picture of a mermaid with enormous blue breasts to distract herself.

It was probably a good thing that the tattooist came out of the back at that moment because Grace had the urge to say something inappropriate about breasts, something seaside postcard smutty, to cover her discomfort. He looked like a tattooist should look – wiry, with plates in his ears and a vest that revealed his full sleeves of black skulls and crossbones to match the sofa. He was wearing shorts and up his legs the tattoos of mastiffs growled. Grace became acutely aware that she was wearing a raincoat from M&S. She wanted to tell him that she had, at least once, bought a drug, even if it had turned out to be oregano.

'What can I do you ladies for?' he said. 'I've got a good two for one offer you should take advantage of.'

'Only my nose pierced,' said the woman, putting the file on the table. Grace was relieved in case the woman had decided to go for something more extreme and she might have been asked to watch.

'Sure?' said the man, looking put out. 'I've got lovely flash. Have you looked at it all properly?' And he picked up the file and started to flap through it. 'Look at that one,' he said, pointing at a picture of a boa constrictor eating a naked woman with enormous breasts. 'That would look great on your arm.'

'Just my nose,' said the woman.

'And what about you then, lady?' said the tattooist to Grace.

'My ears,' said Grace. She was extremely surprised at herself – she had never considered having them pierced before.

The tattooist seemed disappointed and Grace wanted to take back her request. What if he avenged himself on her by doing it wrong? What if she ended up deformed?

'Gun or needle?' he asked with a sigh.

'Neither of those sounds like a good choice,' Grace said.

'It hardly hurts,' said the woman. 'It'll be over in a second.'

'Gun then,' said the tattooist. 'Marginally quicker. Come on, your friend can watch if she likes.' And he walked towards the back room.

The woman stood up and Grace stood up too. What on earth am I doing, she thought, and went with them as reluctantly as she would have entered a slaughterhouse.

Grace thought that the woman looked even more beautiful with her nose pierced, as though she might right now spread her arms like an Indian goddess. She stared at her own strange reflection in the tattooist's window and twiddled the small gold studs. It had hurt but not as much as she thought it was going to; at least, as they had told her, it had been quick. Now she would ask this woman out because this could hardly count as a date, could it?

'It hurts,' she said to the woman.

'It'll get better. Don't mess around with them too much. They'll heal soon and then you can wear nice earrings. I'll give you some of mine. Got to go,' said the woman. 'It was good to meet you, Grace. See you later.'

She walked away from Grace, who was too slow to think about what was happening because she was thinking about the earrings offer and how the woman seemed to want to share her things. Was this kindness or was it a casual approach to personal objects? Coming from a house where the detritus of centuries accumulated, she had always been reluctant to part with things. She was a hoarder by nature. What was the opposite of hoarder? Discarder?

'Oh,' she said, coming out of her reverie and looking at the woman's disappearing back. She was out of earshot and Grace had forgotten to ask for anything – name, phone number, where she lived, let alone a date. She didn't want to run after her and so she stood still, once again close to embarrassing and unaccustomed tears, trying not to fiddle with her sore red ears.

This is Violet and the wandering about

In Violet's knicker drawer, there were tucked eight pairs of vintage evening gloves. She had considered careers where they might come in useful. Torch singer. Hollywood starlet. Debutante. Unfortunately, none of these ever seemed to be advertised anywhere. Violet realized that she might well be many years out of date but she lived in hope that one day, if she ate all her vegetables, she would metamorphosize overnight into Rita Hayworth and then the gloves would be useful for her seductive piano-draping diva act. We all have dreams.

She had managed to get up and get dressed in leggings and an odd dress made out of blue felt, and she had eaten breakfast and washed her face and brushed her teeth and she felt a sense of achievement. Perhaps if she did things quickly enough 'the fear' wouldn't be able to catch up with her. She went to buy gloves because it was a relief to do something that was easy and because the shop was near enough to the flat to be able to scurry to it with her head down and her hood up. That way she could pretend she wasn't outside. It was the first time that she had left the house for a week. As she went down the road she rubbed her hand against the mossy wall to the side of her. Perhaps this had been a good decision. At least it was a start.

The glove shop sold vintage clothes too, mostly fifties stuff. Annie took her there the first time because she liked the clothes, although she was often too big for them, as most fifties clothes turned out to be surprisingly small.

Vera, who ran the shop, must have been in her sixties, and she dressed in her own stock, sporting pastel blue, moth-eaten twin sets with one button missing and stained yellow chiffon ball gowns. Since Violet was a regular, she made her Assam in a chipped bone china cup and saucer and told her about her youth. It always cheered Violet up to hear about youths.

'And to think what we used to get up to. We used oil for tanning, actual oil. We were one step away from basting ourselves in lard. To think about it now. It's a wonder we didn't burn to a crisp. Never mind the cancerous implications.'

And her faded blue eyes shone.

Violet, as far as Annie was concerned, had no friends at all other than her but that was not how Violet saw it at all. She regarded her many older lady acquaintances as her friends and yes, her choices were a bit random and you couldn't say that she was really close to any one of them, but so what? They were the only people she didn't mind talking to apart from Annie. There was Vera and there was Mavis from the dry cleaner's and Monica and Lorna in the hairdresser's. The checkout ladies in the supermarket and the lady who smelt of soup in Oxfam. It seemed to her that a 'friend' was whoever you decided it to be and that Annie's categorizations were much too stringent. True, she never went anywhere with them or visited their houses but she knew all about Lorna's impetigo and the soup lady's love of the later works of Trollope. Wasn't that enough?

Vera patted her hand and said, 'You're looking peaky today. What you need is a chocolate bourbon,' and went off into the back to fetch one. After Violet had eaten her biscuit and made use of a wet wipe that Vera had thoughtfully provided, she was very pleased to buy a pair of grey satin opera gloves with buttons all the way up that reached to her armpits, having been made to be elbow length for an average sized person. They cost twenty pounds even with her loyalty discount, which was pretty much all the money she had in the world apart from the change jar at home, but she felt better for her purchase, more solid and better able to deal with whatever life might throw at her outside the shop. Now she was protected. She put on the gloves, pushing them under her coat sleeves, and liked the contrast between the wool and the satin. She left the shop and stood on the pavement with her back to the wall and thought about what to do next.

Violet liked to do a lot of what Annie referred to as 'aimless wandering about'. She liked to sit on benches or in the windows of cafés eating chocolate cupcakes and watch people go about their business. She had a small black notebook with thick white paper, in which she drew miniature interpretations of things she had seen – moustaches, leaves, shoes, noses, dogs, lamp-posts, coffee cups and manhole covers. She liked to look at things that nobody else seemed to be paying much attention to. Along with Annie these were the things that kept her in the world. She was often jealous of dog owners and the purpose that dogs gave to their days; she considered dognapping, which, apparently, could be a lucrative business. There was one borzoi that she had her eye on but Annie would pass out if she brought it home because she thought dogs were unhygienic. She liked to make up names for the dogs too. Leon the bulldog with the white back, like the hitman in the film of the same name. That hideous drooling pug she had named Milly Molly Mandy after a childhood book she had particularly hated.

She would go to work, she decided now, she was halfway there anyway, and Annie would be pleased with her for going, but as she passed the leisure centre she felt pulled inside as if the half-dressed people on the treadmills she might find in there were exuding a magnetized force. For a while she stood on the balcony overlooking the swimming pool enjoying the wet tropical jungle warmth and imagining she was somewhere in the far east, until the screaming of the boys dive-bombing each other ruined this illusion. Then she went down to the sports hall. It was deserted at this time of day, cavernous and dark and redolent of the nightclub where she worked if she was completely broke; it could have been the smell of dried sweat. Although here it also smelt of the rubber soles of trainers that had squeaked across the floor and seemed sadder in its emptiness, as though it would never see human life again. She walked across to the trampolines and hoped that no one would come in. When she was a child she had been good at trampolining. It was the only time she had been grateful for being so tiny. Now she stood next to one and took off her shoes and her socks, remembering the feel of her tight white nylon leotard with the badges her mother had sewn on the front and the way the jumping reminded her of how she had once, when she was very small, it must have been nursery, by raising her coat over her head flown a foot or two across the playground in a high wind. Was that a real memory or only a dream? Suddenly she found it hard to breathe. She bent over and put her hands in the gloves on her knees and tried to catch her breath. Her eyes filled up with tears that wouldn't leave them properly, they seemed to have got stuck like the oxygen that was supposed to be entering her lungs. She sat down on the gym mat and breathed in great gulps down her tight throat. 'The fear' had descended. Her heart was hammering in a way that couldn't be good and her chest was tight as if iron bands had been wrapped around it. She sounded like an asthmatic or a man who had once sat behind her on a train who had had a tracheotomy. If only she hadn't left her mobile at home, she could have rung Annie to come and get her. Annie would have come for sure. But instead there was no one. Violet lay down on her side and tried to count her breaths. At that point, a voice interrupted her.

'You're not allowed in here, it's against regulations to go into the sports hall unless a registered activity is taking place.'

Violet looked up from her prone position and saw a young woman of the fit and athletic kind wearing the sports centre uniform. Violet got up with effort and panted. Her left leg had gone dead and when she trod on it pins and needles went through her foot. She limped across what seemed to be the giant expanse of the hall trying to breathe as evenly as she could and to look normal. There were tears in her eyes and snot on her gloves. She thought she might be going to be sick. What would her excuse be? She wasn't made for confrontation.

'Sorry, love,' said the woman, 'didn't realize you were, you know, physically challenged, come on, I'll help you, I've had my training for the differently able,' and she put out her arm and Violet took it with relief.

Outside again, having hobbled up the stairs clutching at the woman's arm and been carefully helped off the premises, Violet rubbed at her face and considered her options. She could try to get home as quickly as she could. Or she could go to work. Work was nearer and so she chose that. She would take refuge there for a while and then she could always say she had a headache when she had recuperated and see if she could make it home then. She walked down the street quickly, one leg still a bit numb, and then started to jog, hoping that the sports centre woman wasn't watching her. The air felt full of spikes. When she got to the shop, out of breath, Starchild was arranging wind chimes in the window against a backing of a purple Indian bedspread and a large statue of an elephant. The elephant was some kind of god apparently but Violet couldn't remember its name.

'Oh Violet,' she said, 'there's a full moon tonight and my

women's group is having a ceremony, so I'll have to leave at four. Is that all right with you?'

It was either a good thing about Starchild, aka Patricia, that she never remonstrated with Violet about the way she came into work whenever she felt like it, or a sign of her lackadaisical approach to the uneconomical business that her father funded.

'OK,' said Violet, taking her coat off and pretending that this was an average day in the shop. 'I'll make us a cup of tea.'

There was only herbal because Starchild thought that caffeine was evil, but Violet sneaked in her own Tetleys and pretended it was Rooibos. Shit, she thought, I just had a panic attack, but she chose not to share this with Starchild to avoid a holistic therapy suggestion. Her chest ached. She stood dipping her tea bag in and out of the cup in a trance until she had made it far too strong.

When she'd come back with the teas, Starchild had lit some incense and put a Ravi Shankar CD on. Violet put the cups down on the counter. Starchild had closed her eyes and was waving her blond dreadlocks in time to the music. Her large breasts jiggled along. Every time Violet saw her do this she thought of Annie, who said that Starchild was a trustafarian cretin who needed to fork out for an adequate bra.

'I'm thinking of stocking some menstrual cups,' Starchild said, swaying from side to side.

'What are they?'

'You don't use . . . tampons, do you?'

'Er, yes.'

'Oh no! You mustn't, you mustn't! They're terrible, horrible things. The environment hates them, and they interfere with your yoni's mucus ambience.'

'Oh,' said Violet.

'A menstrual cup, yeah?' said Starchild, and Violet automatically switched off. As Starchild wibbled on about a range of disgusting things that Violet preferred not to think about, she began to make one of the mental lists that helped her get through the day without spacing out entirely.

1. I think that 'the fear' is getting worse or at least more constant.
2. I just had a panic attack.
3. I should never have gone in there.
4. I should never have come in here either.
5. I don't know if I can last until the end of the day.
6. I don't know if I can last to the end of the hour.
7. How on earth am I going to get back home?

'So, yeah, then your feminine balance is restored!' said Starchild. 'Incredible, right?'

'Incredible' was one of Starchild's favourite words and with its pronunciation Violet began listening again. She needed to get a pen and paper and write down the list before she forgot it and perhaps that would help.

'Incredible,' she said.

'I knew you'd understand,' said Starchild, and hugged her. She smelt of musk, incense and damp, the exact same odour as the shop. Starchild began to twirl her hands in the air in time to the music.

'Now what do you think about genital piercing because I'm thinking about . . .' she said, and Violet began to look for a pen.

This is Annie and Laurence (II)

Annie cared about good etiquette so it normally didn't take long for a potential romantic interest to annoy her. It's probably not that I'm discerning, she thought, just easily riled. She didn't see that as a character fault, though. A meal was a good way to sound someone out, it got the job done much more quickly than a drink. So many men had poor table manners, she had found over the years. It didn't take a lot – elbows on the table, a wodge of food tucked into a cheek while talking, the inability to wait for another person to get their meal before you started yours, a lack of serviette control or flecks of food on the lips. That's that then, Annie would think. But this Laurence, his table manners weren't half bad, they might even meet her mother's standards. Moreover, he pulled out her chair, checked she wasn't in a draught, and suggested that she try the wine first. She was impressed but pretended she wasn't. No need to let him know that he'd passed that test, she thought, and considered sleeping with him when he asked for the bill and wouldn't let her see it. But she'd never slept with a man on the first date and she wasn't about to start now. She did however agree to going back to his flat for 'coffee'. Was that reckless? Her mother wouldn't approve of that and Annie felt a flutter of naughtiness that she found titillating. She did want him to kiss her, that much was certain. Just as well they'd both eaten spicy food.

When they got to his flat after the meal, she did a quick assessment and a surreptitious dust test with the back of her hand. There was none. 'A place for everything and everything in its place,' as her mother liked to say. And what's more he had proper wood floors and not cheap laminate. She couldn't abide laminate. She was surprised to see that he had an old upright piano in a corner and was also taken aback by the silver-framed pictures of horses which stood on top of it instead of the more expected family shots.

'Do you play that thing?' she asked him.

'It's out of tune,' he said. 'Sauvignon Blanc, Annie? Or would you prefer something harder?'

'What's with the horses?' she said when he brought her the wine. Much to her confusion he was also carrying a violin case. 'Don't tell me,' she said, 'you're a gangster.'

'Close,' he said. 'Royal College of Music. What would you like to hear?'

'What have you got?' she asked.

'Anything you like. Lady's choice.'

He took off his linen jacket and draped it carefully over the side of the sofa. Then he rolled up his sleeves and got out what looked to her like a battered old instrument you might find in a junk shop for a fiver and put it under his chin. He picked up the bow.

'"Come on Eileen",' she said, for a laugh, not expecting him to play it. But he did play it for her very slowly and she was surprised. She'd never met anyone else who could play more than Chopsticks on the piano. It sounded sad the way he did it and not like the song she had once danced to at her retro eighties-themed school disco with a lad she had later had to deck because he tried it on. Then he played a very fast piece that sounded like music a Russian gypsy would play. It was too show-offy for her tastes. Then he played something else that she didn't know because she knew bugger all about classical music but it was beautiful and it reminded her of churches. It brought tears to her eyes.

'Thank you,' she said when it was finished, and meant it. 'Isn't it great just to be able to do that?'

He smiled. He was sweating lightly and he smelled strongly of man. Eau de man, thought Annie, one of my favourite smells. He put the violin and the bow back into the box and took it away. He came back and handed her his clean white handkerchief. She wiped her eyes with it and hoped her face wasn't smeared. She should go to the loo to check.

'Pity you've put that thing away now, I was going to ask you if you knew any Johnny Cash,' she said.

He sat down next to her and made to put his arm around her.

'I've got to go to the bathroom,' she said, embracing her

mother's ban on the 'common' word 'toilet' and removing herself from his embrace. In the bathroom, she cleaned up her mascara and redid her lipstick carefully. Then she ran the water in the sink and looked in all his cupboards. His towels were clean and piled up neatly. His toothmug wasn't gunky. He hadn't chewed his toothbrush to bits. He had only two bottles of aftershave. She sniffed them both. Pleasant and obviously expensive. There was nothing dodgy anywhere. Was this a good thing? Surely, he must be hiding something even if it was only a giant packet of condoms. In her experience, they always did. She had run out of time to go and search his bedroom drawers and so she went back to him. He was sitting on his sofa with a body language so expansive that he looked like he wanted her to sit on his lap. She sat at the other end of the sofa and he leaned towards her. She leaned back.

'I'm not into one-night stands,' she said. There was no point beating about the bush. There never was in Annie's opinion.

'Technically this is night two, if you count the party, that is.'

'I don't, and I'm not going to sleep with you tonight.'

'What a pity,' he said.

'Well, at least you're honest.'

'Better to be, I think. What would you like to do instead? Shall I play you cockney standards on the old joanna or perhaps you would like to listen to a record? Or, if lengthy and acrobatic intercourse is unfortunately out of the question, we could go for a drive,' he said.

Annie had been expecting to be fending off his hand getting up her skirt by now and was confused.

'Why would I want to do that? It's cold out and we've only just got here.'

'You'll see,' he said, and he stood up and held out his hand. Annie didn't like being directed but swatting him away seemed rude. She could always let him take her home, now that she had ascertained he wasn't dangerous, just a musical bloke with a strange liking for horse pictures. She took his hand and he held out her coat for her and took her outside and helped her into his old Jag. Annie had a Mazda herself and liked to read *Autocar* and she had approved of the Jag when she saw it, not least because it wasn't middle age crisis red or drug dealer black but a practical racing green. Less naff than a BMW too. They drove some distance at perhaps too boy racer a pace and parked, looking down over the city lights. It was blowing a gale and a half, buffeting the car; it felt as if they might take off.

Now Annie was even more confused, and the Jag's heating was erratic and only making her knees warm and the rest of her was chilly and she had no idea what was going on.

'What is this?' she asked. 'An American movie? Are we going to make out? Or are you going to do away with me?'

That sudden realization made her retreat further into her coat. What if he was a murderer after all? Nobody knew she was up here. She had been pleased to see there were no other cars when they had arrived in case it was the kind of place where people indulged their curious sexual habits, but maybe the lack of others wasn't a good thing after all. She reached for the phone in her handbag. Let him try to overpower her, just let him try. But what if he had chloroform? Is it possible, she also wondered while she was thinking this, that I have watched too many films?

'No, I like to do this now and then,' and he turned to her with a serious expression on his face and leant towards her. She flinched back.

'I'm not going to hurt you, Annie,' he said softly and took her cheek in his hand and kissed her. It was a good kiss on Annie's kiss scale, not mind-blowing, but good and firm. She kept hold of the phone, though. Turning away from her then, much to her surprise, he wound down his window all the way to the bottom and turned the car stereo up loud so that the music blasted out into the night, Johnny Cash growling at top volume. Her hair blew right into her mouth. It was like being in a wind tunnel with follic whiplash.

'Relaxes me,' he shouted over the music. 'Work can be stressful. I expect you know what that feels like.'

And he sang along to the music and was perfectly in tune. It was 'Folsom Prison Blues'. Her favourite. She kept her mouth shut because she wouldn't be in tune herself. It was all very unexpected and Annie didn't normally like the unexpected, she liked to know where she was with things. He didn't try to kiss her again but felt for her hand and held it, stroking her palm with his thumb. After a while she wound down her own window and the wind blasted in on her side too and the music moved around them and through them in a way that felt to Annie like being purged. They said nothing after that, there didn't seem to be anything that needed to be said, and Annie felt the sense of time getting away from her that she had constantly, right from when she got up in the morning to when she got into bed at night, being sucked out of her by the wind. There was always too much to do, there was list after list after list, and yet here on the top of the hill the internal monitoring machine that maintained such a tight hold on her life seemed to switch off. It was the most relaxed she had felt in years. After another ten minutes of this he closed his window and she closed hers and they drove home in a silence that should have been uncomfortable with someone you had only just met but which was instead deeply companionable, as if they were old friends. After he had stopped the car outside her building and switched off the engine he came round and opened the car door for her. She got out.

'I must look a right state,' she said, trying to brush her hair down with both hands.

'You look beautiful,' he said and took her hands and held

them in his. 'It's been wonderful to spend time with you this evening, Annie. I hope you liked the music.'

'Do you do any rockabilly?'

'Does that mean I am allowed to see you again, because I would love to.'

She kissed his cheek. There was no lipstick imprint to rub off. What a state to get into she thought. She clacked in her heels up the steps of the building and found her keys and when she turned back he was standing there with his arms crossed looking at her as though she was a treasure he had found. She gave him a wave and let herself in. I could do with some adoration, she thought, it's very good for the skin.

This is Grace and the contact sport

Dolores said she did not know anything about that girl except her name was Sam and she worked in the park as a gardener. She looked gleeful about Grace having asked.

'You like her, no?' she said.

'I've only just met her and, I don't know, I wanted to see her. Tell her about my ears.'

Grace tried to underplay it but she still blushed. She fiddled with her studs, which had gone crusty. Dolores patted her cheek.

'Yes, you have done them. Very nice. I will try and find out for you but I think you should go now, go to the park and look for her. You work too hard, it's good for you to think about love for a change.'

'That would be weird! Going to the park I mean. She'd think I was stalking her.'

'Stalking? What is stalking?'

'Following someone about. In a bad way. Trying to find out about them.'

'Yes, that is a very bad thing,' said Dolores, tut-tutting and shaking her head. 'That happened to my cousin's sister-in-law. Very, very bad. But not the same at all. You go and look for her. I promise you it will be good. She is a pretty girl and you are a pretty girl. You will have fun together. Lots of fun.'

And Dolores winked in a lascivious way that nearly put Grace off completely. Sam, she thought, Sam. Now all the people she ever met, male or female or even dogs, would remind her of that name.

'Couldn't you find out her surname for me?' Grace said. Dolores had disappeared into her house but Grace stayed on the doorstep. 'Then I could try and find her on Facebook,' she called down the hall.

'You could stalk her on the net,' said Dolores, reappearing so suddenly that Grace jumped. In one hand was a packet of ham, in the other a packet of biscuits. She waved these items up and down like a market trader offering his wares.

'That's not what I meant.'

'My cousin's sister-in-law, she had trouble with that too. No, not good. Go and look for her. A lot more romantic. You need romance, I know it.'

'Probably,' Grace said under her breath.

'The jamón serrano or the polvorones?' asked Dolores. 'Or the two?'

Grace went to the park every day after work for a week as though she was there for the exercise. She wasn't looking for the woman called Sam, she was simply taking a stroll. Her sister Tess had rung her and asked if she wanted to go over to her farm in the Dales for the weekend but Grace had said no, without telling her why. It wasn't that Tess would have teased her, Tess was too nice a person for that, but that her own embarrassment stopped her. And what was she supposed to say anyway? Can't come and see you, am busy stalking the park. Then she went on Saturday after breakfast. This is ridiculous, she thought, this is creepy and sad, why can't I do this online? But how many Sams are there? Millions. And anyway, I'm not obsessive and this isn't stalking, I'm just perseverant, but she felt ashamed of herself and didn't admit to anyone what she wanted. What did she want? She wanted to have that woman lie down next to her so that she could caress her entire body. She wanted to tell her all her secrets, dull as most of them were. She tried to stop going but failed; it was as though there was a line stretched tight between her and the woman that couldn't be perceived by the naked eye. Had she fallen in love at first sight? Was this uncomfortable niggling pull what it felt like? If so she didn't like it much. No, she was better than this. Her past relationships hadn't all failed because of her, they hadn't worked out, that was all. It wouldn't be that difficult to find someone else to go out with, she'd done it before. She wasn't even sure if this woman was a nice person and anyway, if she had been interested in her, Sam would have asked for her number. This was a waste of her time. She would stop doing this.

It was the eighth consecutive time that Grace went to the park that she found her. She would like to have thought that she found her on the day she was going to give up trying, but this probably wasn't true. The woman called Sam was pollarding a tree with her back to Grace, there so casually, so easily, handling her clippers with skill. Thank God, thought Grace, and wanted to go straight up to Sam and hug her and say, 'I've found you. At long last I've found you.'

'Hi,' she said, hanging back. 'Well, this is a surprise! I didn't know you worked here!'

'Hi,' said Sam, looking round and resting her clippers on the ground. 'Nice to see you, Grace. How are you?'

'Would you like to do something?' Grace said. This time

Sam wouldn't be allowed to disappear on her. This time she would be the one in charge.

'What, now? I'm busy for about the next four hours. After that if you like? What do you want to do? You choose. How are your ears by the way?'

'Fine,' said Grace.

Grace tried to think of an activity more interesting than the library or a walk or a café and less painful than piercing. She liked swimming but it was too much for Sam to see her in a swimsuit before she got to know her better. She was ashamed of her ugly feet apart from anything. Badminton? Too wimpy? The cinema? It seemed dull but nothing else came to mind.

'The cinema?' she asked.

'We could go to roller derby,' said Sam. 'I go now and then.'

'OK,' said Grace, not knowing what roller derby was.

For this actual 'date' she tried to dress up by wearing a skirt that she had once mistakenly bought to go to a family wedding in, even though she never wore skirts. There had also been a matching fascinator, Grace was ashamed to recall. How her sisters had tried not to laugh. It was red, unlike the rest of her clothes which were grey or black or navy, and turned out to be so tight now she could get it on but not breathe well in it. Grace hated dressing up even more than liver but she felt she should try to show that she was taking this seriously. Was this serious? No, this was not. It was just a date. She was only showing she had tried, that was polite after all. She slicked on the red lipstick which an orange-tinged woman with long eyelashes like a cow had sold her to go with the skirt. Why had she paid fifteen pounds to look like a man on a stag night in drag? It reminded her of when she was a child and she and her sisters had plastered themselves with the dried-up palettes of eyeshadows and the worn-down lipsticks from their mother's dressing table; the effect was that of elderly colour-blind chanteuses who had put their make-up on drunk. They used to dance around the room pretending to be their mother complaining about the Russians. 'It's all gulag mentality, darling,' they'd say to each other, although they didn't know what that meant, 'work, work, work and the ice in the studios, darling. I'm permanently frozen! And don't even mention the rations! It's like Stalingrad all over again!' She wiped the lipstick off and leant her head against the bathroom mirror. Why was this so stressful? She'd never felt like this before a date before. She looked at herself in the mirror. Like a lady of the night who had recently eaten a very large burger. At least she wasn't tempted by the fascinator. It would have to do.

By the time she got to the rink she felt acutely uncomfortable, not least because her knickers kept going up her bum. She sat behind the barricade and rearranged herself surreptitiously. She adopted her best smile. The worst thing about this, she thought, was that she wanted Sam to like her. She hadn't felt this since school. Perhaps she could tell Sam that something had come up at work, yes, that was a good idea, a therapeutic emergency, and just give up on this. It was never going to work out. It felt, for whatever reason, too anxiety-inducing. Sam came on to the rink wearing the shortest of shorts. Grace found herself unable to move. Something went on inside her, something physiological. Her heart, her head and her groin all went thump, thump, thump at the same time. At first, she thought that this might be the signal for some kind of seizure.

To her surprise, roller derby turned out to be a violent sport involving women skating round and round and shoving and pushing each other, often until someone fell over. It looked highly dangerous, a fact borne out by the helmets and the knee pads and what must surely be impending bruises. Grace soon gave up leaning towards the action and started leaning as far away as she could. She sat watching Sam barge people out of the way in an aggressive fashion and was intimidated by her toughness. The only thing that she liked about it was the backs of the women's T-shirts. Marauder. Hammerhead. The Black Avenger. The back of Sam's T-shirt said, 'Tiger'. Everything else reminded her of being chased down the hockey pitch by girls who wanted to hurt her. To her great relief nobody suggested that she try it but one large woman did tell her, 'It's the best sport ever,' while spitting her mouthguard into her hand. Anything that involved a mouthguard, decided Grace then and there, will never involve me.

After the skating the other girls were going to the pub, but Sam refused and instead they went for a coffee in a nearby café before Sam suggested something else to her like hand-to-hand combat or knife-throwing. At the end of the date, if this was a date, was she supposed to kiss her? She had too much saliva in her mouth and had only brushed her teeth once before leaving the house. She didn't eat the cake Sam suggested because the skirt situation made eating impossible. Sam sat opposite her munching away. Grace was aware that if she budged forward her knees would touch Sam's but was that too intimate?

This is what Grace learnt about the woman called Sam: she came from Shrewsbury but she'd moved to Leeds five years ago. She thought that Yorkshire people were friendly and she liked the Leeds accent. She'd once slept in a cemetery for a dare as a teenager but had woken up at 4 a.m. scared and ran out. She liked mint tea. She liked chocolate cake. She didn't wear make-up. She didn't seem to ever wear a bra. Her T-shirt was tight and Grace could see her nipples but tried not to look directly at them and then had problems focusing on Sam's face. Sam was of course short for Samantha. She liked the park in the rain and all the ducks and geese swimming in it on the lake. She'd once seen a heron there. Grace memorized these facts for a future exam on Sam. She hoped it would be multiple choice because an essay question at this stage would be a stretch.

This is what Sam learnt about Grace: not very much because Grace filled every tiny silence with a question. It wasn't that she couldn't take silences, after all they were an important part of her job: the pregnant pause, the ill-considered gap, the long exhale before the crying started. What Grace feared the most was that Sam would walk out of the door and she would never see her again. Or that then she would have to re-stalk the park in an ever more embarrassing fashion.

'I'd better go,' said Sam, pushing back her chair.

'Yeah right, of course, yeah,' said Grace.

They both stood up.

'It was nice to meet you again, Grace,' said Sam.

'You too, great, thanks,' said Grace.

Sam turned away.

'Maybe,' Grace said, 'you might like to give me your phone number. Or I could give you mine. Whichever.'

'So that you can try roller derby?' said Sam and smiled.

'Please no,' said Grace.

'I've got no mobile,' Sam said, 'but you can leave a message on my home phone.'

Grace found a card in her wallet and wrote her mobile on it and put Sam's number into her phone.

'You're a psychotherapist?' asked Sam.

'Oh yeah, that,' said Grace.

'That's interesting,' said Sam, and Grace mentally cheered.

'Do you want a lift?' said Grace.

'I'll get the bus, thanks.'

Sam moved forward and kissed Grace on the cheek. Grace could smell the faint scent of coconut in her hair.

'I think the earrings look nice,' said Sam quietly into her ear and then, before Grace could react, took her face away and walked off. It seemed that Grace would have to get used to her back view, which admittedly was an attractive one. Sam strode with long legs, she almost loped. Grace stood still, thinking about the kiss. She was relieved about the lack of tongue action, she wasn't ready for that yet, but even when Sam kissed her that quickly she felt her heart lurch and wanted to put her arms around her and hold her tight. She resisted the urge to run after Sam and do just that.

Grace tried to wait a week before phoning but she managed only three days. Over the course of this time she analysed herself. Sam seemed an interesting enough person. She was certainly conventionally attractive. But nothing explained what Grace felt about her, which was both that she wanted to go around to her house and stand under the window and woo her Romeo style and that she wanted to lick her all over. The combination of these two urges disturbed her a great deal.

After three days she rang and left a message so full of ums and ers and digressions that she wished she could erase it. Sam didn't ring back. Grace rang again two days later, two days of pacing around practising her new message which she tried to write out so that she could read it aloud, but the sound of the beep made her panic and she couldn't prevent herself from saying, 'Perhaps you didn't get my message?' Sam didn't ring back. Grace was not surprised, considering the incompetence of the messages, and so she pretended to herself that she didn't care anyway. She didn't mention Sam to any of her friends as an amusing anecdote, she didn't ring Eustacia or Tess to ask for advice. She tried to ignore the desires that wouldn't go away and bury herself in work, she tried to go back to the contented sort of life she had had before but she felt constantly on edge. What if she met Sam in the street? It would be typical now that she wanted to avoid her. Because she had been rejected and, as it turned out, being rejected was shit. Had she been right to be the one to ring? Maybe it should have been the other way around. If only she had waited. One of her straight friends had once had the stupidity to ask her, 'But who is the man?' 'What do you mean, who is the man?' 'Who, you know, does the asking? You know, rings up, suggests places to go, pays?' Grace thought that this was the most ridiculous thing she had ever heard. 'It doesn't matter,' she said, 'whoever, whatever.' God, was being hetero-sexual that rigid and old-fashioned? Apparently so. How horrible, she thought, how boring. But possibly there were rules about these things that she still didn't understand. Well, there's nothing else I can do now, she told herself.

'And the girl?' asked Dolores. 'The girl Sam. The one with the nipples sticking out of her T-shirt at my party. Yes, yes, I saw. How is she?'

'Oh, I met up with her once but it didn't work out. Not my type,' said Grace.

'Shame, shame,' said Dolores. 'Do not worry, I'll find you another girl quick.'

'Please don't,' said Grace.

'Yes, yes,' said Dolores, 'don't be shy now.'

And yet Grace spent far too much time imagining various romantic and carnal scenes that were never going to occur, and at night she dreamed repetitively that Sam was following her down the long upstairs corridor of her childhood home but that every time Grace turned around she had disappeared. She had got into Grace's head and there was, it seemed, no getting her out.

This is Violet and her mother on a Tuesday afternoon

'Steve has lost all interest,' said Violet's mother, as she precision-chopped carrots for a stew. The kitchen was large and bright, full of 4 p.m. July sun, and Violet was half blinded, rocking back and forth in a kitchen chair and waiting for her mother to tell her to stop doing that. She had made an enormous effort and gone what seemed to her a very long way from Leeds to Cheshire on the train to see her mother in the hope that it might help. She had managed this feat of endurance by listening to loud Beethoven on her headphones, eating far too many wine gums and drawing tiny pictures of the scenery in her sketchbook. It seemed to have been a good decision because not only had it not induced a panic attack but she also found her mother's home comforting when she got there. Annie's flat, while expensively decorated, did not have the same cosiness factor; nothing was worn down or old as it was here. The journey had exhausted her, and she wanted no more than to go and lie down in the room her mother still referred to as 'Violet's room' even though she hadn't lived in this house for ten years, the room with the candy-striped wallpaper and the shelves full of trampolining trophies.

'Are you listening to me?' said her mother.

'All interest in what?'

'He's gone off it.'

'Gone off what?'

'Sex.'

'I didn't want to know that,' Violet said, catching her fall from the chair just in time, blushing and turning away towards the window. She had avoided any mention of sex near her mother since 'the sex talk' when she was fourteen. She still couldn't think of that now without extreme embarrassment. 'The lawn needs mowing. When's Steve coming back?'

'I know it's hard for you to talk about these things,' said her mother. 'God knows I could never have spoken to my mother about sex. But I don't know who else to turn to.'

Violet turned around at the sound of her mother's voice. And it was true, her mother, who never cried, not even at her own parents' funerals, was crying. She was standing in the middle of the kitchen with a Heineken apron on, the one Steve used for barbecuing in, Steve, who was not, and never would be her father, but who was the only substitute she had for the one in France whom she had never met. She didn't mind Steve, he was a good enough replacement for someone she didn't know and didn't much want to. The apron was much too big for her mother and hung down to her ankles and she was crying with her face down into her navy polo neck and the dog was licking her floury hands. Violet had always liked her mother's hands; she had got fatter as she got older and now they were dimpled and her wedding ring was entrenched in the skin of her finger, but they were hands that Violet associated with placing a cold flannel on her forehead when she was ill or tucking her into bed at night. That was why she was here – she wanted to be comforted and patted and told that everything was going to be all right.

'The dog seems to be licking your hands, Mum.'

'Bad dog. Don't do that. Go out. Go out. Can you put him outside? He takes no notice of me. He's Steve's dog.'

And she went to wash her hands and Violet shooed the dog out and shut the door to the hall. Her mother's pink lipstick was off centre and her mascara had rubbed, and it made Violet feel sad. She would have liked to leave the room or better the house. She shouldn't have come.

'What about your GP? What about if you told him a bit about it?' she asked, sitting back down.

'No,' said her mother, blowing her nose on a tissue from her apron pocket. 'No, I couldn't talk to him. I've got no sexual problems myself,' and she swayed slightly.

'Did you drink before I got here?' asked Violet, shocked both by the possibility of maternal afternoon drunkenness and the horrible nature of the discussion.

'Only a glass or two. I feel so unwanted. He won't even touch me any more. He doesn't seem to want to. I asked him if he was having an affair but he denied it.'

And her mother put her face into her hands and started to cry again. Violet saw that her mother's dark hair was slightly matted at the back and wanted to go and get a brush but didn't.

'Do you believe him?' she asked instead and went to get her mother another tissue from the box on the oak dresser that had been hidden away in the attic when she was a teenager. Gradually, over the years, her mother's things had crept out into Steve's house, which they had moved into when Violet was seven. That was a good thing, Violet thought, her mother finally having her own things around her. She touched the blue and white Chinese teapot she had loved as a child. Her mother had pretty things.

'Of course I do. I'll say that for him. He is utterly, utterly trustworthy. Always has been. But he's gone all monkish recently.'

Her mother was still sniffing. Violet gave her the tissue and put her hand on her mother's shoulder.

'OK. Look, Mum, I do understand. I mean I don't think about it but I suppose I always did presume that you still did. You know.'

'Did what?'

'Did you know. It.'

'Call a spade a spade, Violet. Sex is a wonderful, natural thing. Well. Used to be.'

'I know, you told me that when I was fourteen. What are you going to do about Steve?' Violet said, putting on the penguin-shaped oven gloves and opening the oven door. A wave of heat rushed out.

'What can I do? I've tried buying new underwear. And very expensive it was too. I'll have to take it back. I wonder where I put the receipt,' said her mother and got up and went to look in a drawer in the dresser.

'What about some counselling?' Violet asked, closing the oven door.

'Do you mean marriage guidance? I'd be too embarrassed.'

But apparently not too embarrassed to talk to me, thought Violet. Her mother had her back to her and was stirring her hand around in the drawer.

'Well, something like that. Because if it's as bad as you say it is I don't think black lace is going to help,' said Violet, sitting back down at the table.

'Pale pink silk. Black lace isn't very tasteful. No, I can't find it.'

'Maybe he'd like not very tasteful? I can't believe we're having this conversation.'

'Yes, and you're not being very helpful,' said her mother, and came and sat down next to her.

'What do you want me to suggest?'

'If I knew that I wouldn't have asked you. I've got all het up about it. Is the stew in?'

'Yes, the stew is in. Have some more wine, Mum.'

'What are you here for anyway?'

'That's a little bit rude,' said Violet. Her mother was never rude.

'I'm sorry, yes, it was. But you rarely come here and so I wondered if something was wrong,' said her mother, doing her concerned face which always made Violet want to laugh.

'Sort of,' said Violet and started to twiddle with the pepper grinder.

'Are you feeling unwell again?'

'Sort of.'

'Has Annie been helping you at all?'

'Yes, I suppose so.'

'It's just that she can sometimes seem . . . I'm not sure if she is the ideal person for you when you feel . . . like that. You could always come and stay here with us for a while. Steve would love to have you.'

Violet thought about this. Steve would be the jolly giant he always was – teasing Violet about her size, calling her 'Mousie', patting her on the head. And her mother would try to keep her occupied with baking and walks by the river. She wanted to tell her mother the truth. 'I'm tired of being scared all the time and everything is so much effort. It's like I'm underwater,' she wanted to say, but how could she say that? Her mother wouldn't understand, she never lacked impetus, what with the house and Steve and her work in a soft furnishing shop she never stopped. She couldn't possibly understand Violet's feeling of having completely stalled.

'Perhaps you are coming down with something?'

'Maybe.'

'I know what. I'll run you a bath. I've got this lovely new raspberry bubble bath.'

'I'd prefer to get pissed, to be honest.'

'Violet! Do you think that's a good idea? If you are feeling low.'

Her mother would never use the word 'depressed', it was a swear word. Her mother liked things to be nice.

'I've got "the fear", Mum,' said Violet and tears rose into her throat.

'What fear?'

'I'm afraid all the time.'

Her mother stood up.

'I'll just check the oven,' she said and walked over to it and while she was turned away Violet took the screwed-up tissue her mother had left behind on the table and mopped her eyes.

'It's probably hormonal,' said her mother brightly without turning around. 'I'll run you a bath.'

This is Annie and her sweet tooth

Annie loved her flat even more since she had had the big clearing-out session. She stroked the black marble top of her clean kitchen counter enjoying the cool smoothness of it and looked in the ordered cupboards with the neatly lined-up tins. She was toying with the idea of getting a cleaner, which her mother would totally disapprove of. She was fed up with doing it all herself and Violet was useless and anyway why shouldn't she when she could afford it? I won't tell her, Annie thought. Like I won't tell her that I've met a handsome man either. She'll only get over-excited.

Later she stood outside Manfred's wondering yet again at the faded cards in the window advertising badly grammaticized services and badly spelt objects. She had more than once suggested to him that she correct them but he had said that this was tinkering with the freedom of the customer and everybody had the right to make mistakes. She didn't agree with him but brought it up sometimes for fun. Now she went into the shop hoping to enjoy a chat and buy some baklava if he had any. Annie had the sweetest tooth of anyone she knew.

'Annie,' Manfred said, putting down his book and smiling. 'Beautiful as always.'

Manfred was reliable in his compliments.

'What are you reading?' asked Annie.

He showed her the cover. *Japanese for Beginners*.

'Is it hard?' she asked. 'I was no good at languages myself.'

'The pronunciation is very straightforward. Bit like Spanish.'

'You speak Spanish?'

'Yeah. Did Spanish and French at school, I was good at them, and I've got German and Turkish from my mum. I thought I'd learn something different. Then I'll go for Mandarin. Working up to that. I can now get directions to any hospital in Japan, should I ever need to do that.'

'That's useful.'

'I can also get to a massage parlour.'

'That sounds dubious.'

'It does that. Where's Violet, then? How is she?'

'Not great. In bed most of the time.'

Manfred reached under the counter and got out a packet wrapped in silver foil and opened it out. It contained shortbread.

'Sorry, Annie, run out of baklava. This is all I have. My mum made it. I told her that my favourite customer likes a freshly prepared pastry or biscuit item.'

'Thank you very much.'

Annie took a piece and put it into her mouth. I probably take Manfred's kindness too much for granted, she thought. She munched while he looked on expectantly.

'Delicious. Please thank your mum for me. It was very kind of her.'

'No worries.' He busied himself with his extensive chocolate display. 'Are you all right, Annie? You look perturbed. You can tell me all about it if you want.'

Annie hesitated and then she said, 'Violet's got this thing she calls "the fear".'

'Sounds nasty.'

'She's scared all the time but she can't tell me what about. She's had it for years but it seems to be getting worse. I try to understand but it's not in my nature.'

'Never get scared?'

'Not that I can think of. You?'

'Only in dark alleys. My mum gets that, I reckon. "The fear". She's agoraphobic. Will hardly leave the house.'

'I can't get Violet to leave the house either.'

'Maybe she could go see someone.'

'I do know a therapist who's supposed to be good.'

'There you go then.'

'Would your mother see a therapist?'

'Would she heck! But Violet's more modern, if you see what I mean. Worth a try, don't you think? She's nothing to lose. Except a few quid.'

Annie took another piece of shortbread.

'With all those languages you could do something else if you wanted to.'

'I don't mind it in here. And it's my dad's business, isn't it? We make a good enough living.'

'What did you want to do? When you were younger.'

'Simultaneous translator. Like for the UN. That must be brilliant.'

'You could work towards that.'

'No, way too late. And I'd have to fork out to go to university, wouldn't I? And we'd have to pay someone to run the shop while I wasn't here.'

'You can do anything if you want it enough.'

'That's what I like about you, Annie. You've got a lot of ambition. That's good. I wish I had your drive.'

'Why don't you go to Japan on a holiday?'

'It's hard to get away. And, to be honest, my mum needs me. Between me and my dad, we don't like to leave her on her own for very long.'

'Why haven't you ever told me that before?'

'Never came up.'

'This shortbread really is very good.'

'Anything for you, Annie,' he said, with a large smile. 'Anything at all.'

This is how Grace got Sam to kiss her

Sam phoned and left a message on Grace's mobile. In it she invited Grace to her flat. To her flat! Grace felt as if she had been awarded a prize for good behaviour. She ignored the fact that she had more or less given up and that it had been fifteen days of anxiety and torture. There was an entrance exam. She had passed. She listened to the message seven times.

She rang the doorbell and Sam came down to open the front door for her and Grace went in after her and fell over a pile of junk mail in the hall and twisted her ankle and had to be helped up the stairs. She loved being helped up the stairs because it meant that she had to drape an arm over Sam's shoulder and Sam put her own arm around Grace's waist. Sam's shoulders felt strong and her arm taut, it must be all the digging, thought Grace. She wanted to kiss her but she was in too much pain.

'I've just moved in,' Sam said as they struggled upwards slowly one step at a time.

'When?' Grace said, gritting her teeth.

'About a week ago.'

'I remember you said that you liked these houses but it was a shame that they'd been made into flats.'

Grace was not sure how she managed to get that many words out of her mouth without hyperventilating.

'Did I? I don't remember,' said Sam.

On the landing outside Sam's door there was a huge jungle plant. Her living room was full of plants too, plants Grace couldn't name but which were so lush they were menacing. She wondered if Sam also had them in the bedroom. She hoped not.

'How's the leg?' Sam asked.

'Better,' Grace said, although she was lying.

'I think you should sit down.'

Sam lowered her gently on to the sofa and Grace managed not to pull Sam down with her although she wanted to very much. She was sad that the physical contact had ended. She could hear noises coming through the ceiling. Guitars.

'What's that music?' she asked.

'The man upstairs plays in a band and he practises,' said Sam.

Standing there, with her hands on her slim hips, she was as beautiful as Ingrid Bergman and Grace considered telling her that but it seemed over the top.

'What kind of band?' said Grace, even though it wasn't that easy to speak.

'Heavy metal country. I've got a flyer that he gave me.'

Sam went over to a table and ruffled through a pile of papers. That at least was familiar in this strange new country of infatuation that Grace had emigrated to. Everybody in the whole world had those piles of papers. They must be a feature of being human, like having two eyes or going out without a coat when you should have worn one but being too lazy to go back and get it. Grace decided to give herself up to her tangled emotional state, her preceding two days of twisted nerves and inability to digest food and the extreme pain in her ankle. She closed her eyes and listened to the guitar. A whole new musical fusion. When she opened her eyes again she was lying on the floor and Sam was kneeling next to her.

'You fainted,' Sam said, looking alarmed. Grace liked the fact she could elicit this emotion in her because up to now Sam had always seemed such an even-tempered person, if you ignored the roller derby aggression.

'What?' Grace asked, trying to sit up. The room spun. She lay back again.

'You fainted. Do you need to go to hospital?'

'No, no, it's OK.'

'Is it your leg?' said Sam.

'It hurts a lot,' Grace decided she might as well admit.

'Why didn't you tell me?'

'I didn't want you to send me home.'

'I wouldn't have. Can you sit up, do you think?'

'I'll sit up if you kiss me first.'

It must have been the pain that inhibited Grace's until then strong inhibitions in Sam's company.

'What?' said Sam, although she had probably heard.

'Kiss me Hardy. I know it's emotional blackmail but I don't care.'

Sam's kiss took away the pain. Her kiss was the one Grace thought she would remember until her deathbed. The cold floor under her back. The ridiculous music coming down from above. Sam's long body almost touching her but her sweet mouth on hers. She opened her eyes to see that Sam's eyes were closed so she closed hers again. Mouth on mouth. Nothing more. Bliss. It was like falling slowly through cool water on a hot day. Then suddenly there came a loud noise that interrupted this reverie. To her dismay Sam's mouth moved away from hers and she opened her eyes to see Sam's face was above hers, looking nervous. The noise came again, and it wasn't guitar.

'What's that?' Grace asked.

'Ruth,' Sam said.

'Who's Ruth?'

'My ex-girlfriend. I must have left the downstairs door open,' said Sam.

'Where?'

'It's OK,' she whispered, 'lie back down. Sssh.'

Grace lay back down again parallel to the coffee table. Under it there was a screwed-up piece of paper. She reached to get it. It was

70

a Fry's Chocolate Cream wrapper. She had a moment of nostalgia, she thought they had disappeared. Wagon Wheels. Curly Wurlies. Her grandfather Cyril had had a thing about them. I must ring him, she thought. Walnut Whips. Wrigley's spearmint gum in sticks. Then voices came back into her consciousness.

'No, I'm not going to let you in,' said Sam in a voice that seemed both calm and kind.

'Please. I want to talk to you,' the other voice shouted. Ruth. The ex-girlfriend.

'Well, I don't want to talk to you,' said Sam.

'Have you got someone there?' shouted Ruth.

'Go home. I'll ring you tomorrow.'

'No, you won't. You say that but you won't ring.'

'Yes, I will. If I say I will, I will.'

'Swear.'

'I swear. Now will you go home?'

'You've got to swear on something.'

'Have you been drinking?'

'No!'

'You have.'

'Well, I've had a couple.'

'Right.'

'Let me in, Sam!'

And the banging started again. Ruth. The ex-girlfriend. Grace felt smug. She was the one on the inside of the door. She was the one being kissed. She tried to imagine what Ruth looked like. Squat. In a baggy red checked shirt. Moustached. Then Sam reappeared crouched by her side. Grace put her hand on Sam's trainer.

'Are you OK?' Sam asked her, putting her cool hand on Grace's forehead.

'I'm fine,' she said, loving to have it there. Sam was her idea of a dream nurse.

'Sure? Are you cold? Do you want a blanket?'

'How long have you been split up?' Grace asked, because now she wanted to know everything.

'Not long. But she can't seem to accept it's over,' said Sam, and shrugged.

'Is it over then?' Grace's stomach twisted.

'Yes. Completely. But Ruth, she's insistent.'

'I can hear that.'

Sam stroked her forehead. More banging. The guitar bloke started again.

'I'm sorry about this,' said Sam, and she did look sorry. Grace wasn't, though, she was jubilant.

'Do you want me to talk to her?' Grace asked.

'In a professional way? No. Definitely not. That would make it much worse.'

'You could ring the police?'

'I don't want to get her into trouble. It's not her fault. She's drunk.'

'What about the neighbours?' And Grace pointed to the ceiling.

'What about them?'

'Do you think they'll call the police?'

'There's only the guy upstairs. The girl downstairs is away. And that guy isn't the sort to call the police.'

'Ah. That's all right then,' said Grace.

Sam sat on the floor cross-legged next to her.

'He's got loads of skunk growing in the attic apparently,' she said.

'That'll be why.'

'But I've got to get you to the hospital.'

'No, I'm OK, honest. My leg hurts, that's all. Don't worry about the fainting. It's nothing to do with the leg. Blood sugar thing. Cup of tea would do the trick. And a biscuit. I like being down here to tell you the truth.'

'I'm so sorry. I feel so embarrassed.'

'It's entertaining. My life isn't that exciting, you see.'

'Wait a minute,' Sam said, and moved away. The guy upstairs started to play a tune that Grace recognized even through the banging and kicking. What was it called, though? Sam came back and put a blanket over her and lay down next to her. She took her hand.

'This is bliss,' Grace said.

'You're crazy,' said Sam and she smiled and squeezed Grace's hand.

'I'm easily satisfied.'

'Here. Open your mouth and close your eyes.'

Mint and chocolate. Hard cold dark chocolate and creamy mint.

'I love you,' Grace said through the mouthful.

'What did you say?' said Sam.

Grace felt Sam's arm go around her waist, her mouth on her ear.

'Yum,' said Grace.

'Black Rock,' said Sam.

'Mmm?'

'The name of the band.'

'Stupid name.'

'Yeah and the guy wears an all leather outfit.'

'Cool.'

'He's very fat.'

'Not cool then. I've got it!'

'Got what?' Sam asked.

'"The Ace of Spades",' said Grace, feeling ever so pleased with herself. A snog, chocolate, and a memory that functioned – she was having a great, if strange, day. '"The Ace of Spades". I knew, I knew it. He's playing the bloody "Ace of Spades". Such a good song.'

This is Annie and the family question

Annie had never told her mother about the men she had been with; as far as she was concerned it was nothing to do with her. There had been more than one and less than ten. That seemed like a reasonable number but she doubted her mother would think so – she was probably still getting over the shock of finding out that not only was Annie no longer a virgin but that she had lost her virginity in her mother's bed while her mother was at a coffee morning. At least her misadventures hadn't been as disastrous as Violet's. Like the time Violet had had to crawl out of a room clutching her clothes when the man she'd gone home with had left her stranded in a darkened room while he made noises by himself in his bed.

Also, her mother had seen off a teenage hopeful or two, or rather made her father see them off. It was not uncommon for Annie to come down the stairs after hours of getting ready to find that the lad had gone, frightened off into the night. Her mother's say was final. 'Chubby.' 'Overlapping teeth.' 'Will never amount to anything.' Then there was Michael Alexander Wrigley, the only one she'd ever loved, whom she'd got engaged to aged seventeen, two days before they moved out of their terrace. At first Michael came around all the time to the new house, rolling up the drive in the Triumph Herald he was doing up with the dodgy exhaust that blew black smoke wherever it went. Annie's mother seemed to have accepted the engagement even if she had frowned pointedly at the small silver ring with a garnet that Annie wore on her left hand.

'Not what I'd call much of a ring that, is it? But then he's only a mechanic I suppose, can't earn much. Well, I know how headstrong you are, Annie, so I'll not try to stop you. But you are still going to university.'

The word 'university' had started to hang over Annie's head like an approaching prison sentence. She knew she had to go, she did want to be a lawyer very much, but she couldn't square it with being away from Michael and so secretly she had slipped in Manchester on to her UCAS form. That way he could come at weekends. She didn't tell her mother, whose heart was set on Exeter or Bristol, 'somewhere where you'll meet a nice sort of person'. How her mother knew that those places were where a nice sort of person lived was beyond her because her mother had never been further south than Chester, but she knew she meant 'a nice sort of man'.

Her mother had at least left them to it and they had now done it in every room in the new house, but it seemed to Annie that Michael's enthusiasm was waning even though when she asked him about it he said it wasn't. He kept saying that he was up to his eyes in work, that this car needed doing and then another one, even at the weekends. One day, after she had gone round to his house for once, and they had had sex in his tiny single bed, she asked him.

'Do you not like me any more?' Said not in a whining tone but as a demand because Annie was developing, along with her 38E bust, her mother's forthrightness.

'I love you, Annie. You know I love you. Look.' And he picked up her hand to demonstrate the ring. 'I asked you to marry me, didn't I?' he said but he dropped her hand with a casualness she couldn't tolerate.

'What's wrong with my house then?' she said.

'What do you mean? Nothing's wrong.'

'You don't like it there, do you? Or you don't like me? One or the other, or perhaps both. Tell me the truth for once.'

'I think . . . I don't know . . . you've changed since you've moved,' he said, and looked out of the window and picked at the duvet cover.

'How have I changed?' asked Annie quietly.

'You know . . . you're different,' he said, still not looking at her.

'How?'

'I don't want to talk about it.'

'Well, you've got no choice now, have you? Tell me. And would you look at me while you're talking to me.'

He turned his head to look at her. It was a funny thing about Michael Alexander Wrigley but he had got uglier as he grew up, like a reverse Ugly Duckling. Once he had been a pretty little boy with blond hair, but every day now his ears seemed to stick out more and his skin was stippled with acne like someone had thrown pink paint and spattered him. Meanwhile Annie, an ordinary little girl, was going in the other direction and becoming beautiful.

'You've got . . . you know . . . stuck up. Looking down your nose at me like your mum does.'

'What?'

Annie got out of bed in a hurry and yanked her knickers back on and then her bra.

'Don't pretend, Annie. I don't know if it's the house or what. Like you're better than me now you live there.'

'When did I say that, you pillock?'

'There's no need to call me names.'

'There bloody well is.'

Annie put on the rest of her clothes.

'You can shove it,' she said.

The thing is he always came after her. She stormed out every now and then but he was the one who always apologized although he normally hadn't done much wrong, she'd just got aerated. But this time he never came around or rang, he left her to it, left her to sweat. There was no way she was backing down, how dare he say that about her, but a week went by, and then it was two weeks and he still hadn't called and she'd bitten her nails off and she didn't know what to do. Her mother said nothing, she didn't seem to be aware that he hadn't appeared, but Annie knew this wasn't true, she was just keeping out of things for once. She knew that her mother was hoping it was over. Was it over? It was three weeks on when she went to see him. His mother answered the door and told her he wasn't in.

'I'll wait then,' said Annie and barged her way in and up to Michael's bedroom. Among the car mags on the floor there was a pair of knickers, a pair of small pink nylon knickers that would hardly have fitted round one of her legs.

'Tiffany Jones,' said Michael's mother from behind her. She didn't like Annie.

She never spoke to him again. A broken heart, she found, had nothing to recommend it. It kept you up at night crying so hard that your eyes got swollen and needed ice cubes. It encouraged you to forget to use conditioner or shave your legs. It made your revision seem so pointless that you only just got the grades you needed. She vowed never to let that happen to her again.

As an adult, there had only been that one semi-suitable bloke whom she'd met at one of her brother's horrible parties. Simon was a quantity surveyor. They went out for three months but he wasn't the most exciting person ever. He wore striped pyjamas to bed and driving gloves to drive, he played golf and wouldn't kiss her unless he'd brushed his teeth first. She always had to initiate the sex, which she'd thought she liked doing until she had no other choice in the matter. Then she took him home for Sunday lunch. As she left the house with him later, her mother took her to one side. 'Quite a nice lad,' said her mother. 'But not good enough for you.' In retrospect Annie had known that. It's why she had taken him.

But this man Laurence, he pressed all her buttons. She saw his self-assured face looking up at her when she came down the steps outside her flat and she thought about whether he would, in her mother's take on things, make a good dad. Solvent, good-looking, too charming by half, posh, parents who lived in Surrey, courteous, kind, clean, not prone to halitosis or dandruff. Did not, as far as she knew, pick his nose. Not a ball-scratcher either. Clothes from labels she approved of, although that shouldn't mean anything at all. How superficial. An interesting past playing violin before he moved into copywriting. He sent her well spelt texts and properly punctuated emails. He always rang when he said he would, was always on time. He opened doors for her, gave her his jacket if it was cold. He brought her big bunches of Stargazer lilies and small boxes of expensive chocolates. He did everything right, as though there was a 'how to charm women' manual and he had read it cover to cover. He ticked all the boxes if there were boxes to be ticked. She could have made herself a spreadsheet; she liked Excel.

And she'd come outside, and he'd tell her how beautiful she looked, and she didn't even say, yes, I know that, like she usually did. She spent even more tedious time over her appearance and she knew that was for him. He was a handsome fairytale prince with fresh minty breath, almost too good to be true. She kept waiting for him to slip up but he never did. She hadn't taken him home in case her mother started putting pressure on her; she feared he might be considered 'a good catch', which was one of her mother's highest compliments. In bed with him she made louder noises than she would normally have made. Annie loved sex but she thought that it was a quiet and private activity that should be done in the dark. The only language that was needed was sighing and heightened breathing. Not squeaks. Not, on more than one occasion, a grunt. At times, when she caught herself making these noises, she felt embarrassed, but he seemed to like it. When she looked in the mirror afterwards she saw that he'd made a mess of her make-up by kissing her so much and that she'd also got burn from his stubble. She didn't even mind when he started to want to leave the lights on. After all, when had she ever not enjoyed being looked at? But it worried her that she didn't mind, like it worried her that she liked him more than anyone she had ever met apart from Michael. She'd told herself that after that disaster, she would never again get so involved. She wanted to be adored, that was all well and good, but she didn't want to have to rely on anybody else for anything. She didn't want to be dependent in any way. But she liked this man. She liked him a lot. And wasn't it about time she thought about getting married and having a baby just like her mother wanted?

Annie had expected that the office would be pink. Pale pink like the kind little girls were supposed to like but which she'd never had. She hadn't been a girly girl, that came later, she had been a fighter with permanent bruises and constantly torn dresses. The school bully Stu Patterson had sat on her once and nearly broken a rib until she punched him in the whatsits. All the kids cheered and even the teachers tried to hide their amusement. But the office wasn't pink, it was cream like the good stationery her mother liked to use for thank-you notes. The oatmeal carpet looked brand new. There was a completely empty desk, not even a computer, and there was nothing on the walls apart from a calendar showing flowers, and a clock. Annie responded well to minimalism. It felt soothing.

'Annie, nice to meet you, please come and sit down, I'm Grace.'

Annie sat down. The chair was well supported at the back. Annie approved of this too. She appraised the therapist. Tall. Long fingers. Early thirties. Dressed neutrally in black trousers and a blue shirt. Not beautiful by any means but kind-looking. Yorkshire but posh.

'Now what can I help you with?' asked Grace and she held a silence.

Annie was good at silences herself and recognized Grace as a fellow professional with them.

'I don't think I want children. Well, certainly not right now.'

'Is that a problem?'

'I've never told my mum,' said Annie. 'And I don't know how to.'

'Then let's go into that further perhaps.'

This is Violet's secret outing

Since the unhelpful visit to her mother, Violet had, apart from the occasional foray to the shop, stopped going out again, but she had had an idea and had decided that she would, for once, follow through with it. It might help, it might not help, but it was worth a try at least, wasn't it? It was just as well that Annie owned the flat where they lived and that the rent she charged Violet was about half market prices, because Violet was always in arrears. It was due next week and Violet only had three-quarters. Surely it would make little difference if she used some of it. It was only 'borrowing'. It was a Friday afternoon and Violet was at work, except she wasn't at work, and would have to lie to Annie when she got home about that. She'd never told a lie to Annie before, not least because Annie would be able to spot one a mile off, but she didn't have any other option. Everyone has secrets, Violet thought, even Annie must have them. She looked up at the lamp-shade. It was purple with dirty gold tassels, the sort of thing that both her mother and Annie would be horrified by. Oh well, I'm not here as an interior design judge, I'm here as a . . . what exactly?

'You're a seeker,' said the woman who was sitting across from her, 'I can tell that.'

'Am I?' said Violet and the woman smiled in a conspiratorial way as though this was something only the two of them knew.

'And someone doesn't want you to be here,' said the woman.

The photocopied flyer had been attached to the front door of the shop with Blu-Tack along with a range of other cards advertising healers, shamans, herbalists, spiritual retreats, yoga, and a man called Barry who apparently had a van. Violet had pulled the sheet of paper off when Starchild was out. It wasn't one of the new ones anyway. There was a faded photo of a rainbow on the front. It had only taken her two weeks to decide to go. Positively speedy by her standards.

'I'm Susan, by the way,' said the woman, which surprised Violet because she'd been expecting she'd be called 'Rainbow' and not something so sensible.

'I'm Violet.'

'A lovely flower.'

Susan spread her cards out on the red tablecloth that clashed with the lampshade. They were so pretty that Violet reached out to touch the nearest one but Susan put her hand over hers and looked at Violet with her big brown eyes like a cartoon deer.

'You're afraid of dying,' she said, which seemed to be the most obvious thing she could say to anyone. Violet decided that from then on in she would cut off the soundtrack in her head of her own doubts and Annie's withering remarks.

'Yes,' said Violet, 'I am a bit.'

'Yes, I can see it in the cards, they never lie.'

I wonder if she has a script for this, and Violet cut off that thought too.

'And your mother has had a very big influence on you. And you have three brothers.'

'Er, no, no brothers at all actually.'

'No, three, I definitely see three. And your father is very

81

small. And both of your parents like old things. You often feel left out. Different from other people. As though something is missing. And once, many years ago, you were left behind somewhere. Oh yes, a dark place. You will have more than one lover but only one true love. And one child, only one child. An only child like yourself.'

'But I thought you told me that I have three brothers.'

'Essentially you are on your own. Inside yourself. Ow.'

'What?' said Violet. 'What did you see?'

'I get chronic cramps,' said Susan, 'when it's my time of the month. I've got a TENS machine but it's run out of batteries. Now I think of it I could have taken them out of my vibrator. Except they are probably just about done. Silly me. Now, where was I? Were you in a dark place?'

'I am in a dark place, I think,' said Violet.

'I can tell. You are lost in a dark wood. But where are you heading, in what direction must you go?'

'I was hoping you could tell me something about that.'

Susan flipped over the last card. It had a tower on it.

'What does that mean?' said Violet.

'It means that even if everything comes crashing down, you will be OK. Don't worry about a thing because every little thing gonna be all right.'

'Isn't that Bob Marley?'

'I love him, don't you?'

'But which way should I go? Out of the dark wood?'

'Towards the light.'

'But I can't see any light,' and Violet felt desperate.

'The cards never lie,' said Susan, sitting back. 'There's a cash machine in the Co-op if you haven't got enough cash. I'll come with you and buy some batteries.'

Violet traipsed home and didn't tell Annie where she'd been. She felt ashamed of her stupidity, of thinking that a thing like that might help. It had been a complete waste of money and now she couldn't even pay the rent. What should she do now? How would she stop 'the fear' from consuming everything? She had no idea. She went straight to her room and got into bed.

This is Grace waking up in Sam's bed

When Grace was twelve, normal was Susannah Lewes, the girl who sat behind her in their first year at school. Normal then was having your hair in a French plait and wearing clean clothes and having neat handwriting. Normal was eating a roast on Sundays and sitting with your family in a row on the sofa and watching TV together. Then when she was fourteen, normal was a different thing altogether. Normal was having the right jeans and having boys want to snog you and you liking Strongbow. It was not the thought of snogging a boy making you feel physically sick and being in love with a girl who was in the Sixth Form and didn't even know your name. At seventeen normal was going out with the head boy and having a decent tan. The paraphernalia and the language changed but normal didn't.

'Normal is so boring, normal is so average, who wants to be like everyone else?' said Great Aunt Beatrice as she pruned the 'Maiden's Blush' roses while *La Traviata* blasted out of the open windows at maximum volume. Grace and Eustacia and Bella and Tess were playing croquet on what they referred to as 'primo lawn' to distinguish it from the others. 'I don't,' said Bella, which was all very well for her because she was the coolest one of them, she had no trouble at school at all, all she had to do was shorten her skirt to above the knee and it became a new craze. Grace, however, was suffering. What Beatrice didn't understand was that normal was advantageous as camouflage, that normal was the ease of being in a world into which one naturally fitted without the need of an adaptor plug. The word 'lezzer' was thrown at Grace like a hand grenade. Girls shielded their bodies from her view in the changing rooms. An alternative form of bullying to less popular girls was to say that they fancied her or worse that she fancied them.

'What is a lezzer?' she asked Beatrice and Cyril when aged twelve.

'It means that you like girls better than you like boys, which seems eminently sensible in my book,' said Beatrice.

'Male homosexuality was of course very much tolerated, and, one could argue, more than tolerated in the ancient world,' said Cyril. 'I'll find you some literature.'

The Spartans however were of little help to her at all.

What is normal? Grace now knew that it was a word that needed air parentheses around it. It didn't, after her years of investigation into the strangeness of the human state, seem to exist in the adult population and she was grateful for this knowledge. She was grateful too to have escaped the prescriptions of childhood, its narrow conventions and petty divisions, to live in a world where she could now move about more or less freely. Grace had had sex with twelve women before in her life. Was that 'normal'? She'd never asked anyone else except Eustacia, who had looked at her and said, 'Two,' and Grace had had to laugh. She had not ever had sex with a woman she had been in love with before, and she was, she realized, when waking up in Sam's bed, most certainly in love. She felt stupidly happy, face-achingly so. She couldn't stop grinning, and then her heart would rise suddenly like an out-of-control lift as she remembered things from the night before. The way they had got so sweaty that they had stuck together and only laughed about it. The way Sam had pulled her knickers down her legs slowly. Grace felt finally that she had reached a state that everyone else had talked about but which she had not been able to imagine clearly. This is what it felt like to be in love as people had always described it. 'It feels like my vagina is pulsing and that I've got tachycardia,' she considered saying to Sam, but decided against it.

Sam wasn't in the bed, which had a wooden headboard and a footboard but wasn't big as doubles go. The duvet cover was green. Grace sat up. Opposite her was a chest of drawers with a mirror on top of it, draped with a black and white scarf. Grace was grateful not to be able to see her morning complexion. In front of the mirror was a large rectangular wooden box. Maybe it was where Sam's earrings lived or where she kept letters from old lovers. Grace wanted to open that box and see what was inside it. She pulled back the duvet, knowing that this was completely the wrong thing to do.

'Are you all right?' Sam asked, making Grace jump. She was standing in the doorway. Even in her faded towelling bathrobe she was beautiful.

'Yes, I'm great,' Grace said, trying not to look guilty. She had an urge to lick her thumb and check for sleep in the corner of her eyes but she stopped herself in time. She wanted to ask for a kiss but she didn't want to appear demanding. She wanted to say come back to bed with me but she'd missed the opening.

'What would you like for breakfast?' Sam said, which should have pleased Grace. Being offered breakfast was, in her experience, a good sign. It meant that the person who was suggesting it had some modicum of politeness, and that even if all it resulted in was half a stale croissant the offer indicated kindness. Better than the time someone had offered tea and Grace had said she preferred coffee and the woman involved had said, 'I don't have any coffee,' and simply stared at Grace until she was forced to leave.

'I'm fine, thanks. I've got to get home,' Grace said, and she picked her clothes off the floor and put them on as quickly as she could with her back to Sam. She sat on the bed to put her socks and boots on and she could tell that Sam was looking at her but was remaining silent and the silence made Grace's face go hot. She got up and faced Sam.

'Thanks for a nice time,' she said.

'I had a nice time too,' said Sam. 'Call me.'

Was that the brush-off? Was that the end of it now?

'OK,' said Grace. 'I will.'

She went into the hall, Sam following her. Grace opened the front door of the flat and without looking at Sam again she said, 'Bye,' and moved quickly down the stairs even though her leg still hurt. She let herself out of the house and the door clicked shut behind her and she wished it hadn't because she wanted to turn around and go back upstairs and say, 'What did you mean when you said, "Call me"? Did you mean that or was it your way of saying, "Go away, you unpleasant woman, I'd rather sleep with anyone in the world than sleep with you again."' Am I being completely and stupidly paranoid? thought Grace as she unlocked her car door. Her teeth were unbrushed and the inside of her mouth tasted like fur. She looked at herself in the car mirror and flattened down her sticking-up hair and gave her unwashed face a once-over with her hand. She looked rough. That's what Sam must be thinking – that rough-looking woman, thank God she's gone now. Grace sniffed under her armpits. Why did one armpit always smell worse than the other? I want to be there always, at Sam's, she realized. I want to belong there. I want to find out everything about her that there is to know. I want to have sex with her that keeps me up all night until I am begging for sleep. That is not good. I've only just slept with her once and she probably doesn't even like me. What would I tell a client to do under these circumstances? I'd say go home and get some rest and deal with it later. She got out of the car, relocked it, and went back to the house and rang the doorbell. After a while she could see through the opaque glass panel Sam's shape padding down the hall. Sam opened the door and seemed pleased if surprised to see her.

'Did you forget something, Grace?' she asked, smiling.

'What did you mean when you said, "Call me"?'

'Do you like eggs?' said Sam, and put out her hand and pulled Grace inside.

This is Annie and her suggested night out

'Violet?'

'Yeah?'

Annie's manicurist was on holiday and so she was sitting in the living room giving herself a pedicure. 'Slumming it', as Violet would put it. Violet, having got up at a reasonable hour for once, especially considering it was Sunday, came out of her room in a mini red kimono and mustard yellow cords. Annie raised her eyebrows.

'You look like you were on the game in Japan but then got confused and decided to go hunting.'

'It'll have to do,' said Violet, 'there's nothing else that's at all clean. Do you want some toast?'

'Do you like Laurence?' asked Annie.

'He's OK.'

Annie watched Violet move into the kitchen and look in her cupboard. Well, she'd get no joy there; Violet's cupboard was always half empty apart from useless tins like pilchards. Why did she buy them? Who likes pilchards? But she knew that Violet found shopping overwhelming and was easily seduced by pretty packaging.

'What does that mean – he's OK?'

'Did he go to public school?' asked Violet. 'I haven't got any bread. Have you got any bread?'

'Of course I have. Look in my cupboard.'

Violet came and slumped next to Annie on the sofa and Annie moved the pot of varnish away before Violet could attack it, because Violet had once got polish on the top of the coffee table and it had caused Annie no end of effort to get it off.

'Yes, he went to public school,' said Annie.

'Eton?'

'"Minor" is what he said.'

Violet harrumphed and picked at her fingernails and went to put her thumbnail in her mouth but saw Annie was about to slap her hand down and stopped herself in time.

'Does he know how to sail?' she asked.

'How would I know?' asked Annie.

'I bet he does, though. And I bet he pronounces the names of wines properly. You know, like I bet he rolls his "r" on Rioja.'

'He doesn't drink rioja. He drinks burgundy,' said Annie.

Violet snorted.

'Would he drink warm Lucozade if pushed?' she asked.

'What kind of question is that?'

'Would he?'

'No, definitely not. And neither would I,' said Annie.

'Yes, you say you wouldn't but I know, in an emergency, you would. Laurence would prefer to drink his own urine. In fact, he probably has on one of those trekking through the jungle expeditions that posh boys do on their gap years. How come all posh boys want to be explorers?' asked Violet.

Annie finished her toes and looked at them with satisfaction. Violet reached for the pot of polish but Annie quickly put on the lid and placed it back in her extensive manicure kit. She hadn't even got any on the newspaper which she had carefully put out to catch any accidental drips, not that Annie was a person prone to accidental anything.

'You forgot about the bread,' said Annie. 'Do you want toast?'

'Do you want toast?'

Annie knew that Violet felt guilty about eating her food. She also knew that she did it while she was out anyway and carefully repositioned the cupboard's contents afterwards to hide the gap. To pre-empt this, Annie encouraged her to do things out in the open.

'No. But you have some. There's half a loaf.'

'I bet he wears deck shoes that have seen actual decks. I bet he knows how to turn about a boat. I bet his family dress for dinner.'

'You're being ridiculous. You know nothing about him.'

She watched Violet put the bread in the toaster. Soon there would be crumbs everywhere, including in the Flora, and jam smeared on the counter top, but Annie was so used to clearing up after Violet that she hardly thought about it any more. She wondered if Violet was jealous of Laurence because she wasn't paying as much attention to her as usual. That would be strange; she hadn't thought of Violet as the jealous type.

'No, you're right,' said Violet. 'I don't know anything about him.'

Violet stood watching the toaster.

'A watched pot never boils,' said Annie. 'Come here and sit down.'

Violet slumped next to her. Annie had been thinking carefully about her next suggestion. It was easy to spook Violet, she was like a very shy pony. You had to introduce ideas in a casual way, as though the outcome wasn't very important to you.

'I was thinking we could do something together.'

'Like what sort of thing?' asked Violet, looking alarmed. She had put her feet on the coffee table. Annie looked at her. She put her feet down again.

'Let's go out somewhere. The three of us. Would you like to do that?'

'Dunno,' said Violet.

'How about tomorrow?'

'Dunno,' said Violet.

'It'll mean going outside and interacting with a stranger and so I'll understand if it's too much for you. You can say no,' said Annie. It was important both to acknowledge 'the fear' and offer a get-out clause.

'You don't like me saying no,' said Violet. 'You get cross.'

'You can say what you want. And I don't get cross.'

'I am fighting my way through the thicket.'

'I have no idea what that means. Could you explain it to me?'

'Dunno.'

Annie was pleased with her own patience.

'Look, we'll have a good time. As long as we don't go to that terrible club you used to work at.'

'I'm sure that Laurence is used to the smell of urine.'

'You keep using that word. It's worrying me.'

'We could take him to the shop. He could buy some angel cards. Yes. OK. OK. I'll come if I must. Where do you want to go?'

Annie had already made the decision long before she had suggested anything.

This is Grace and her new definition of happiness

Grace's world suddenly expanded. It was amazing what a difference having one new person in it could make. Except it wasn't just any person, it was Sam. Sam – the woman I am in love with – Grace wanted to introduce her with this honorific.

She had presumed that if she ever had anything like a girlfriend she would want to show her to all her friends immediately, to shout it from the rooftops, but no, it was the opposite, she wanted to keep the thing secret. The what – the affair? Grace liked that word, it sounded forbidden and exciting. And Sam didn't seem to want to go public either and that pleased Grace. Being with Sam felt like a secret only they shared, as though they were creeping around together in the dark holding hands where no one else could see. No, I can't play badminton this weekend, she told her friends Marcia and Sally, a gay couple she knew from her badminton group, I'm coming down with something. No, I can't come to the cinema, she told her friend Andy, with whom she had formed a two-person Sandra Bull-ock fan club, I've got people coming to stay. She was aware that she was a cliché – dropping people when you were with some-one new. But she was thirty-two, and so she felt that she was allowed to do that for the first time. No, I'm studying, got a lot of reading to do, I'm thinking of doing a PhD, she even lied to her sisters. And yet she didn't feel ashamed of the lies as she probably should have done, instead she felt protective of her and Sam. It was such a small thing that it was like a seedling that needed shade to grow in, somewhere out of the harsh sun-light of the gaze of others. And what were they to each other anyway? Was someone you had slept with five times your girl-friend? Was someone whose mouth you thought about when you were supposed to be listening to someone complain about their husband your lover? Just because knowing it was her knocking on your front door made your knees shake. Just because you got out of their bed and went to work so crumpled from being awake half the night with them that you probably looked like a bag lady. Just because they let you use their tooth-brush. It didn't mean anything. They could say, 'No, I don't want to see you again,' at the drop of a hat. And this insecurity was so frightening to Grace that at the same time as her world expanded it contracted like a fist grasping her heart. What if she changes her mind? What if she says it's over? I never knew I was so insecure, thought Grace, but maybe I never had something to be so insecure about before. The way Sam placed her hand on Grace's belly and it contracted. The way she bent to kiss her breast. It was all wonderful but it was all so tenuous. This new way of being could be taken away at any moment. She couldn't tell anyone and yet she had to.

'Can I come over?' she rang Eustacia to ask.

'Of course, come any time. You know I love having you here. Come for the weekend.'

'No, I'm busy, I'll just come for lunch.'

'Is anything wrong?'

'No, everything's fine. I just fancied a chat.'

Eustacia was a painter, although you'd never know it to look at her. She didn't look arty or bohemian. Eustacia was a thirty-year-old woman with smart clothes and a neat brown bob. She didn't wear dungarees or smell of turps. You couldn't imagine her spattered with paint. She looked like one of those good English-women who are headmistresses or who head committees – clever, capable, in charge. She was the next sister down from Grace but she had been the motherly one – she cooked for them on the ancient Aga, she cleaned the house as best she could, she tried to keep up with the enormous quantities of laundry, she even washed herself. True, Cyril's personal hygiene was unimpeachable, but Beatrice didn't believe in bathing, she favoured liberal splashes of eau de Cologne, including over the dogs, and there was only a freezing bathroom with a bath that took an hour to fill up with lukewarm water. Only Eustacia bothered, the rest of the sisters used grubby flannels. But it was to Eustacia's credit that she never told the rest of them what to do.

Now and then, in need of her sensible advice, Grace drove

too fast from Leeds to the coast near Filey in a car about to fail its MOT, to eat Eustacia's complicated recipes learnt from French cookery classes, many of which seemed to involve pigeons and chestnuts, and listen to the quick movements of her brush across the canvas, which had always been one of the most comforting sounds that Grace knew. Eustacia painted in oils – seascapes mostly, she marked the long beaks of the birds on the shoreline, the brightness of fishing floats, the colours of the rising tide. Her paintings were sold in a small shop in the village near where they lived in a house like a white cube at the end of a beach of the windswept kind that always reminded Grace of seaside trips from her childhood. Cyril shouting Xenophon to the waves. Thalassa, Thalassa, the sea, the sea. A house which, the first time you saw it, might as well have THIS IS AN ARCHITECT'S HOUSE written in fifteen-foot-high letters across the front. Her husband Jeremy was twenty-two years older than Eustacia, a kind, quiet man with a grey beard clipped as neatly as a yew hedge and a love of world music. He went to Womad and he lent Grace strange CDs, undeterred by years of total lack of enthusiasm for any of the things he liked.

'What did you think of Blunderwein then?' he asked.

They were skiving while Eustacia saw to lunch.

'It was OK,' Grace said, trying to avoid looking him directly in the eye, because she'd only been able to stand five minutes of it.

'I don't know why you insist on plying her with music every time she comes up. She's a lost cause,' said Eustacia, giving Jeremy a beer and Grace a glass of white wine.

'I don't want wine, I want beer,' Grace said.

'You'll have what you're given,' she said, and Grace took the glass.

'There's hope for everybody,' said Jeremy.

'Not for her, matey. She's too set in her ways. Aren't you?' asked Eustacia.

'Yep, 'fraid so. I'm sorry, Jeremy.'

Grace's answers, her lack of interest, made him look gently puzzled. Not annoyed or anything, he wasn't that sort of man, but perplexed in a 'darling, I can't get the clue for three down' way. He couldn't understand why Grace loved the Stones and Nirvana and tolerated Bach but couldn't stand anything else.

'Wait a minute, Grace, come to think of it something did cross my mind earlier this morning. Now what was it? Do you remember, darling? I was walking to the shop and I thought of something. Something for Grace. Something for Grace.'

'Is that a mantra?' Grace asked.

'I beg your pardon? Yes, that was it. Off the wall but it's worth a try. Always worth a try.'

And off he pottered in his immaculately ironed (by Eustacia of course) chinos.

'That Blunderwein thing?' Grace asked.

'Yes,' Eustacia said.

'It had cowbells and a bloke playing the sitar in it. Which is not that weird compared to some of the awful stuff he's foisted on me. What does Jez mean by "off the wall"? Off whose wall? It must be off the planet, more like. Have you got any olives?'

'Don't call him Jez please. He hates it. Be nice. He is trying.'

Eustacia looking stern was a face which Grace associated with order and calm; it was as reassuring to her as a lullaby. Now it was accompanied by a sound like whales mating coming over the integral speakers.

'Jesus,' Grace said, 'that is horrible.'

'I've got olives or peanuts.'

Eustacia was possessed of every grown-up skill imaginable including the filling of food cupboards with suitable supplies.

'I want both.'

'You're being petulant today. And stop following me,' she

said, because Grace had trailed her into the kitchen. The doorbell rang and Eustacia went to answer it; she was followed into the kitchen by Tess. Now she did look like an artist. Tess had ridiculously long brown wavy hair that touched her bottom vertebrae and which she washed with rainwater from the butt. Tess had a handful of silver rings and an aromatherapist for a best friend. Tess grew her own tisanes for period pains. She wove baskets voluntarily. She was a Persian cat of a person with the same naturally indolent, purring nature. She should have been an artist's model reclining next to the stove in a Paris studio. Unfortunately for her natural vocation she took up with a farmer and had two kids and so she worked around the clock. But she was still the same girl who used to sit on one of the lawns in a rickety deckchair and eat ripe cherries on summer afternoons. She was a hugger and attacked Grace to Grace's great reluctance. Then she let her go and picked a long brown hair off her front.

'Sorry. The hair. I had to wash it this morning. It was full of straw and I thought washing it might wake me up.'

She yawned, stretching her arms up over her head.

'Have you been sleeping with the sheep then?' Grace asked.

'Mike has been sleeping in the barn the last couple of days.'

'Most people go to the spare room after an argument.'

Her twins Rowan and Linden came in after her. They were stick-like, wraith thin, with matching blond hair and skin that you could almost see the blood moving through. Small ghost children versions of their robust father, nothing to do with their side of the family at all. Grace had never told Tess but her children gave Grace the spooks. She herself had never made a negative comment about them despite what Grace regarded as constant provocation on their part.

'We want to use Jeremy's computer,' said Linden.

'You are being inaccurate,' said Rowan. 'Jeremy has a Mac.'

'Well, technically speaking a Mac is a computer.'

'I think the word you were looking for was "please",' said Tess.

'You always say that, Tess,' said Linden. 'Can't you just accept that it is implied?'

'Go and find Jeremy and ask him,' said Eustacia and the twins disappeared in the direction of the study.

'I'm beginning to think I should buy them a computer and a telly,' Tess said.

'I've met a girl, someone, a woman,' Grace said to her sisters as casually as she could. She shuffled her socked feet on the warm floor and wished that she had under-floor heating.

'Really, Grace?' Eustacia turned towards her, olives in one hand, peanuts in the other, like a fifties advert for being a good hostess, and smiled her lovely smile. 'That's wonderful! Really?' she asked.

Another person might have been insulted by the enthusiastic level of her surprise. Grace wasn't. She was pleased that she cared.

'Yeah, really. An actual human woman.'

'Tell us all about her,' Tess said.

'I think I might perhaps be in love with her,' said Grace, as though this was an affliction that had come upon her like warts.

'Hmm,' Eustacia said, and her expression changed to one of reserve.

'What?' Grace asked, quickly on the defensive.

'I don't want to say this.'

'Yeah, you do. Go on. Get it over with. It's too soon. I'm too old. I have no idea about anything.'

'Why would we say any of those things?' said Tess.

'I wanted to say there was no "might" about it. Might is a qualifier to protect yourself.'

'And I thought I was the therapist.'

'It's hard to see your own foibles.'

'Oh well then. I am in love with her.'

'Good God! That's amazing!' said Eustacia.

'That's fantastic,' said Tess.

'And so when are we going to meet her?' Eustacia said.

'Sometime.'

'That's very vague,' said Tess.

'It's early yet, we've only been going out for a couple of weeks. I don't think I should inflict my family upon her right now. Not you two obviously. You're nice.'

'Why haven't you told us about her before?' said Tess.

'Well, just, you know.'

'Why don't you bring her down here!' said Eustacia. 'Or I could come over?'

'Come to mine,' said Tess. 'Next weekend.'

'Not yet,' said Grace.

Her sister Bella might have taken umbrage at this but not Eustacia and Tess, who never took umbrage at anything.

'Then let's have a toast! To Grace's girlfriend! Is that the right word? Would you prefer "partner"?' said Eustacia.

'Girlfriend is fine.'

'What's her name?' said Tess.

'Sam.'

'To Grace's girlfriend Sam!' said Eustacia. 'Long may she be loved!'

'Hear hear,' said Tess.

'I liked that,' said Grace.

They both hugged her and she let them.

This is how Violet met the woman (I)

Annie and Laurence and Violet went to a club with drag queens because Annie liked them, possibly because their beauty maintenance levels rivalled hers. Violet found them sad. The tragic songs they sang about love and loss made her eyes water. She hoped that they had happy lives and worried that they didn't. It had been ages since she had gone out anywhere at night and it was horrible. The music and the lights were migraine-inducing and the noise of strangers shouting at each other was too much. There were so many people here and the crush made her feel panicky. She wanted to go home. To her annoyance the club didn't seem to concern Laurence, and Violet realized that she had underestimated him. That didn't mean she had to like him, though. She awarded him half a bronze star for lack of homophobia instead of a whole one. She was making him an imaginary star chart in her head. He had lost three stars already because he had spent most of the evening boringly braying on in that voice of his that made Violet feel like a minion who should tug her forelock whenever he deigned to glance in her direction. He was solicitous to her too, wanting to please Annie obviously. Like an over-attentive waiter. 'And what can I get you, Violet? And how do you like your job, Violet?' My jobs are crap, she wanted to tell him but didn't. She was trying to be friendly for Annie's sake but she was bored with it. She excused herself and went to the loo and sat in there for a while, feeling marginally protected from the hubbub outside by the cubicle walls, even if they were only made of plywood. For entertainment she read the graffiti on the back of the door. Apparently, someone called Alison would do all sorts of things for money. She went into a reverie. Would she do any of those things for money? She thought not. She would hold hands for a fiver. That was about it. Someone banged on the door and she had to come out. She was washing her hands, impressed that there was soap in the dispenser and hot water coming out of the tap, when the tall woman at the sink next to her asked her if the big woman with her was her girlfriend.

'Yes,' said Violet, taken aback.

'That's a pity,' said the tall woman, looking Violet right in the eyes.

'Why is that a pity?' asked Violet.

'Well, if you hadn't had a girlfriend, I was going to ask you out.'

'Oh, you mean girlfriend,' said Violet, shocked.

'Yes, that's what I said.'

'I know, yes, it's that I didn't understand you. I thought you meant was she my girlfriend, you know, my friend, so I said yes. I'm not gay.'

'I am,' said the woman.

'Well, yes, I suppose you would be.'

'What's your name?'

'Violet.'

'That's a nice name. Are you having a good time?'

'Not very.'

'Would you like to come home with me then?'

'I was going to go home with my friend/not that kind of girlfriend Annie and play Scrabble.'

'Come home and play with me instead.'

And before she knew it, there she was. She had been drunk so it was like drunk driving in that respect, one minute you're in one place and the next another and you can't remember the journey. She felt sober now though, standing in the living room while the woman was in the kitchen, which was a tiny room off the living room with a swing door that she had pulled across behind her. Violet found this touchingly polite, as though tea-making was a ritual that should be conducted in private. It looked like she had shut herself into a miniature saloon. The living room was large and in one corner there was a small tiled fireplace that had been blocked up and postcards of famous paintings were stuck around it. Violet walked over to it and touched the tiles. Cold. The paintings were all by Impressionists. It made her interested in the woman. It was warm in the room, too warm. She took off her coat but didn't know where to put it.

'Cézanne,' Violet said, and it must have been loud enough for the woman to hear because Violet listened to her say, 'Yes, Cézanne.' The way she said it, it sounded like 'Shazaam.'

'Abracadabra,' Violet said to herself.

The five drinks she'd had were wearing off and she felt increasingly nervous. Probably this had been an extremely stupid decision based on a desire to get away from Laurence. She had a history, much to Annie's disapproval, of going home with strangers. Men liked her, she wasn't really sure why. Perhaps because she was small, and it was true that men liked small women like Annie said? She enjoyed the fact that she was the one who got to change the balance of the evening every time. She was pursued and then she was the one who got to say 'yes'. It wasn't as if her shyness wore off around men but that she found it made her feel powerful, that moment of acceptance, it was the only time that she ever felt that way. It made her feel better, although it was sometimes hard to distinguish if the man was flirting with you because he liked you or because he was just a flirt. It stopped her, at least for a night, being the one on the outside looking in; she was an essential part of the story. Annie said she was 'easy' and Violet knew she was right.

The woman was standing there in front of her with two art deco cups.

'Do you want to sit down?'

She put the cups on the coffee table and took Violet's coat and went away with it. She's stolen my coat, thought Violet, now I'll never be able to leave. I'll be trapped here for ever like an abducted princess held by an evil witch. Not that this woman looks like an evil witch. In fact, she is very pretty. Why have I noticed how pretty she is? What am I doing here?

The woman came and sat on the sofa next to her and put her hands on Violet's.

'Your hands are cold,' she said, and she rubbed Violet's between hers as though she was going to start a fire there. There was a silence that felt intense, like the oxygen in the room had been condensed. Violet's heart beat faster. The woman moved in to kiss her, closing her eyes, and Violet watched her doing it. It reminded her of a scene from a film but she couldn't remember which one. She returned the kiss and closed her eyes too. It felt softer than with a man. Smoother lips. Not too wet. She'd done a lot worse. She didn't feel anything else though, no tingle, no rush of lust. The woman stopped kissing her. Violet opened her eyes.

'Now what do we do?' Violet asked. 'I don't really know what happens now.'

'There are no set instructions,' said the woman, smiling and moving her head away.

'OK,' said Violet and she sank back into the sofa cushions. She felt flushed. It could be that she was still drunk. Or maybe it was adrenalin.

'You don't have to stay. You can go home if you want to.'

Violet said nothing; she was trying to consider if it would be a good idea to stay or if it was better to go now before things accelerated and the choice overwhelmed her.

'What normally happens next? With a man,' said the woman.

'Well they . . . probably at this point they put their hand up your shirt and try to deal with your bra.'

'Shall I do that then?' said the woman.

'OK,' said Violet, at a loss as to what else to say. It seemed only reasonable. The woman put her hand up Violet's shirt slowly and on to her breast on top of her bra and Violet felt as if this was some sort of medical examination, but then the woman started to gently stroke her over the bra with her thumb. Violet was glad that she was wearing her best lacy one and not one of the grubby ones. It felt soothing. Violet closed her eyes again.

'Nice bra,' said the woman. 'Like this?'

'More or less,' said Violet, still with her eyes closed. The stroking combined with the alcohol was hypnotic. For the first time since she had left the club she relaxed. 'A man almost strangled me with my bra once, he tried to go from underneath.'

'Rooky,' said the woman. 'Would you like to touch me? I'm not wearing a bra.'

Violet opened her eyes. Strange as it was, she had nearly forgotten that she was with a woman. 'OK,' she said, since it seemed rude to refuse.

Violet put her hand up the woman's shirt and it was true, she wasn't. Her breasts were downturned, not upturned like Violet's own, and warm. Avoiding the nipple area Violet started to stroke her with a thumb so that they matched.

'What's that like?' asked the woman.

'Nice?'

They sat with their hand on each other's breast and the woman moved forward to kiss her again and pushed her gently back against the arm of the sofa. Violet felt the light pressure of her legs against her own. This is not unpleasant, thought Violet, it is actually nice. She took her mouth away from the woman's and whispered, 'I've never seen a live naked woman before apart from my friend Annie and briefly in changing rooms, but that's different.'

'We don't have to take our clothes off if you don't want to,' said the woman quietly with her mouth on Violet's ear, 'we can do whatever you want,' not knowing of course that this was the worst thing she could have said to Violet.

'Can we stop now then?' asked Violet, who had goosebumps all over her upper body.

'Yes. Did you not like it?'

They withdrew their hands from each other's clothes. Violet crossed her arms over her small chest and one leg over the other.

'It's a bit like the first time I ate an artichoke. I couldn't really work out what was going on. But what you did did feel . . .'

'Nice?' said the woman, raising her eyebrows.

'Yes.'

'What would you like to do now?'

Don't give me choices, Violet started to panic, and the woman must have been sensitive to that because she said, 'We can keep kissing if you want, nothing else.' Violet felt grateful to this woman whom she had only met an hour ago but who yet seemed to understand her in some small way.

'Can we?' asked Violet.

'Sure.'

'I do mean it. When you say that to men they say yes but they don't mean it.'

'That doesn't sound good.'

'I don't mean, you know, that anything nasty happens. It's only that they seem to be overtaken by something they don't want to stop,' said Violet. 'They always want to go that little bit further.'

'Unpleasant.'

'More annoying really,' said Violet. 'I have a theory though that they quite like the tension. The "will she won't she" bit.'

'That sounds both unpleasant and old-fashioned.'

'Now that you say that . . .'

'Well, I'm not going to do that.'

And Violet felt relief. She put her hand out and touched the woman's face in gratitude.

'You're pretty,' Violet said.

'Not as pretty as you,' said the woman and leaned forward

and kissed her again. They slipped down until they were lying on the sofa together side by side and she held one of Violet's hands and kept the other one on Violet's cheek. To Violet it felt adolescent because it was on a sofa not in a bed, like the time she had gone babysitting with Thomas Green when she was fifteen and they had lain just like this, pausing only to eat peanuts and to half watch an old episode of *Baywatch*. It didn't have the sense that things might change any minute as it had with him, as if some urgency might start in him and he would move on top of her, although he never did. She waited for the woman to prove that she had been lying and try to do something more but she didn't. Instead they kissed for what seemed to Violet like a long time and she got lost in it so that it became not many kisses but just one that went on and on. The woman didn't try and put her hand on Violet's breast again and it made Violet trust her. She began to entertain a half dream that butterflies were landing on her lips. It was different, the lack of stubble or beard. She put her hand on the woman's smooth cheek again and stroked it. Then the woman stopped kissing her and reached up to the back of the sofa and pulled down a red blanket.

'Are you tired?' she asked. 'Do you want to go home? Or you could sleep here?'

'Here,' said Violet, realizing that the energy required to call a cab and get all the way home was too much. The night air would be such an assault and nothing more alarming seemed about to happen. The woman pulled the blanket up over them. There was just enough room on the sofa for them to lie next to each other. She put her arm around Violet's waist and her nose against Violet's hair.

'Night night then,' she said and soon she fell asleep.

Violet lay in the dark thinking, this was a stupid idea, I'll never go to sleep here, she could feel the woman's body so close to hers it should have been uncomfortable but it wasn't, it was drowsy and soft. She suddenly felt sleepy and she yawned and when she closed her eyes soon she was dreaming about her hair growing and growing, so that she became Rapunzel and the woman was standing far below her window being the prince wearing chainmail calling up to her.

When she woke up on the sofa the woman's arm was still around her and her body was curled around Violet's and Violet felt safe, as if she was still in her dream. Carefully she man-oeuvred her mobile out of her pocket. She switched it back on. It was seven ten. She had a headache. She thought of Annie and how she hadn't told her anything more than that she was going away with this woman. Annie was going to be angry. Annie was probably going to be furious. There were eight missed calls on her phone and one text. She opened it. 'WHERE THE HELL ARE YOU?' She'd better go, although she didn't want to. It was warm here and quiet. She crawled out of the woman's arms and stood up. The woman opened her eyes.

'Are you going then?' she asked without moving.

'I think so.'

'Bye then. Nice to meet you, Violet.'

'You too. Bye.'

She closed her eyes again. Violet stood there to see if any-thing else would happen but nothing else did. The woman seemed to go back to sleep. Violet let herself out of the flat quietly and walked home. Another one-night stand, she thought, another stranger. Except even stranger than normal. She realized that she felt tired but remarkably OK. 'The fear' was not following her home and that could only be a good thing. She saw a miniature poodle with a pink ribbon in its topknot and she smiled. Maybe when she got home she would try to draw it from memory. Or the woman's mouth. Maybe she would try to draw her mouth.

This is when Annie goes ballistic
(from the Greek – scrotum)

'So?' asked Annie. She had been sitting on the sofa, waiting for the flat door to open for what felt like hours, although it was only just past 8 a.m. She had slept on the sofa and had a crick in her neck. That wasn't helping her mood.

'So,' said Violet, edging into the room.

'Come and sit right here. You're not getting away with it that easily. What happened?' said Annie in what she knew to be her best reasonable lawyer's voice, the one that came out automatically in stressful situations. She had always prided herself on it.

'Are you angry?'

'Angry? Why should I be angry?' said Annie.

'At me going off like that.'

'Well, one minute you've gone to the loo, and the next you come over, say you're going, and then this Amazonian lesbian drags you out of the club. I was gobsmacked. I've hardly slept waiting for you to come home. I've kipped on the sofa. Why didn't you answer your bloody phone? Why didn't you answer my text?' Annie heard her voice start to rise in an unappealing fashion.

'I switched my phone off.'

'Typical. And what happened with that woman then?'

'I slept with her. Well, sort of.'

'I knew you would. I knew it.'

Annie turned away from Violet. She felt an urge to lie down again under her duvet and stay there for some time. All night long, as she tossed and turned, an internal version of her mother had been haranguing her. 'Well, it doesn't surprise me she's a lesbian. I've always thought she was you know, unusual. Not like other people. Not that I mind them. Lesbians that is. That's fine by me. Whatever takes your fancy,' and Annie was so exhausted by that damned voice.

'Do you mind?' asked Violet.

'No, why should I mind?' said Annie.

'You seem strange.'

'Strange?'

'Strange,' said Violet.

'Well, let me put it this way,' said Annie, getting right back on track and going for the jugular, 'as far as I know, my best friend who I've known for ten years is heterosexual. How do I know this? Because she's told me about every useless man she's ever had. Of which there have been far too many. Then one day we go to a club, she cops a girl, and goes home with her. It's like I know nothing about you. Nothing. Who are you?'

'I'm Violet Amelia Mayweather.'

'I should have known you'd say that! Well, you can take your stupid name and shove it where the sun don't shine!'

And with that Annie got up and left the room. She slammed her bedroom door to drive the point across. Then she opened it again and came back for her duvet, which she pulled off the back of the sofa, the end of it missing the vase on the coffee table by inches. And that would have been Violet's fault. Then Annie stamped back to her room, slamming the door so hard this time that it bounced. She threw off her dressing gown and got into bed. She had done the door-slamming for effect mostly, since she felt less angry now; instead she felt a sense of satisfaction at having expressed herself so clearly, even if it had been partly non-verbally. In her family what might have been called 'theatrics' had been openly encouraged. She had made her point, let that be the end to it. Maybe her mother would shut up now. She sighed and closed her eyes. Her heartbeat, which had been jacked up on rage, slowed. She heard her door open and felt Violet lie down on the bed next to her and decided not to push her on to the floor. She had only been worried and confused, it was only natural, why could Violet never see how much it bothered her when she went home with strangers? And why would she go home with a woman stranger? What was going on? She found herself too tired for this right now.

'You can stay here if you're quiet. I want to go to sleep.'

'Annie,' Violet said, 'don't be cross with me. I hate it when you're cross with me. You go all operatic. We kissed and it was, weird, and then she said stay anyway, so we had a cuddle on the sofa and then we fell asleep. I didn't sleep with her, sleep with her. We didn't you know do whatever it is lesbians do. It was like sleeping next to you.'

'Since when did I try to stick my tongue down your throat?' Annie said.

'You once tried to manually force me to eat asparagus. Annie. Annie. Annie. I love you, Annie. I love you more than I love . . .'

'What?'

'I love you more than you love *Breakfast at Tiffany's* and Cary Grant and margaritas put together. I love you more than the word "diplodocus" and much, much more than whirligig washing lines. You are my bestest bestest best best best best . . .'

'Are you still drunk?'

'Perhaps a bit.'

'Shut up and go to bloody sleep.'

'OK.'

'And don't snore,' said Annie.

This is Grace head over heels

Grace doodled on her pad as she sat in work, drawing hearts around Sam's name as though she was a teenager. She thought about how it was a funny thing that Sam looked a little like Barbie. Tomboy Barbie; she looked like the Swedish au pair/ porn star/exchange student that boys dream about. And girls too. And yet she had had some very ugly girlfriends. Ones with thick glasses and big ones with acne and ones with odd hair and terrible teeth and all the other things we are supposed not to like. Grace got to see some of their photos by accident. Well, not by accident. She had a constant urge to go through Sam's things that she'd never had with anyone else before. When she was out of the room Grace looked in her coat pockets but never found anything. She couldn't say that she enjoyed this, and Sam would have gone mad if she'd found her doing it; Grace thought that she would have herself. Or would she? Grace couldn't imagine Sam going mad about anything. It was one of the many things she liked about Sam. The list grew all the time.

One day, Grace was looking in a kitchen cupboard at Sam's and when Sam surprised her, a box fell out on her head from the cupboard above. Grace said that she had been looking for egg cups which, ridiculous as it was, was the first thing that came to mind. Sam didn't seem annoyed and didn't question her. Grace added that to her list – a trusting nature. She wasn't sure that she had one. The box had spilled out photos all over the floor and Grace started to pick them up; there were women in every single one.

'Who are they?' Grace asked.

'Friends,' Sam said, but Grace didn't believe her. Some of them at least had to be exes. Grace sneaked glimpses at the photos as she put them back in the box. Not that bad, she thought, as she pawed one after another, I'm not that bad-looking at least. The photos seemed to prove that Sam was attracted to the oddness of ordinary people. It was yet another character asset not to be so hung up about looks, especially when you were so beautiful yourself.

How was it going? It was going well, Grace thought. All

right, the sex was great, and yes, it was better than it had ever been before. All right, she had more orgasms in the first months than she had had in years. They stayed in bed for days at a time, whole weekends, having sex, talking, drinking cold tea they had forgotten about and eating jam sandwiches for sustenance. It had never occurred to Grace that sex was fun, it had always seemed like such a serious business, such an uphill struggle to a higher goal. But it didn't feel like that with Sam, it felt like an adventure where anything might happen – Grace's toes might fall off, her skin might set on fire. She was entranced by Sam's body, which she could touch any part of without having to ask permission first. She could kiss the mole on the nape of her neck whenever she wanted, she could stroke her hair, interlace her fingers with her own, tweak her nipples, run her fingers bump by bump down her spine, she could do anything she felt like doing and Sam, it seemed, enjoyed this. Grace even liked Sam's feet, and she normally found other people's feet disgusting. All the physical boundaries that Grace had arranged around herself were crossed, and she hadn't even known how many there had been. How reticent she had been with other women, how afraid of touching them wrong or being too invasive. And in turn she could let Sam do whatever she liked to her, and she loved this more than she thought she ever would, she realized that she had longed to be touched in such an intimate way. It felt so good to be wanted, to be properly wanted, and she lost a shyness that she wasn't aware she had had. They had baths together. They shared cups and combs and clothes. One of them weed while the other one brushed their teeth. What made her separate from the world, her edges, were slipping away as she blurred into Sam's body. And the mental walls she had had too. She had thought that she was a relaxed person but this turned out not to be the case, at least not in comparison to Sam. Sam did it all so easily.

The first time that Sam went to Grace's house for tea, Grace was on edge. She wasn't that into housework, but she'd even mopped the kitchen floor with a mop she'd had to buy specially. She feared Sam criticizing the house but of course she didn't, instead she plonked herself down on the floor next to a bookshelf and began to pull books out. Grace left her to it and made them cups of tea. She dropped milk all over the kitchen floor and had to use the mop again.

'I've never read any of this stuff,' said Sam. 'It looks interesting. What's Jung like?'

'Difficult to explain. A lot of it is very off the wall. I'll lend you that book if you like,' said Grace and smiled despite herself, remembering Sam's first offer to her.

Sam crawled across the floor to Grace, who was perched nervously on the edge of the sofa. She knelt in front of her.

'Do you have a nice bed?' she asked.

Grace's legs twitched.

'It's soft,' Grace said.

'That's OK,' said Sam, and ran her hand up Grace's legs and pushed herself between them. 'Don't mind soft.'

Grace believed that what she was feeling was that thing called joy. She hadn't felt it, she realized, since she was a child when she and her sisters galloped the horses after the lurchers across the stubbled fields. She felt like this all the time now – a feeling that came from being almost, but not quite, out of control, like she was going too fast downhill to catch her breath. And yet strangely for her, work, which had always been such a motivating force in her life, was becoming less so. She was, although she hated to admit it, almost irritated by some of her clients. Perhaps it was because now she was fulfilled by something else, somebody else, that work had faded into the background. Perhaps this was normal, this relative disinterest. Yes, that was it, she was too busy thinking about Sam to think about anything else with any degree of seriousness. She was pretty sure her clients hadn't noticed, however. Soon she and Sam would be out of this intoxicating stage, she imagined, and into something less overwhelming; she would steady herself and then she would be able to concentrate again.

'Mary, I'm afraid time is almost up,' she said now in her understanding therapist's voice after she'd finished doodling. She hadn't been listening properly. Something about the husband. Her therapist's voice was one of calm and interest and so she doubted whether Mary was able to tell that she was so distracted.

'Oh no,' said Mary, looking genuinely upset, as though the session was a lifeboat she was desperately clinging on to. Tears had carved a path into her thick foundation like car tyres through slush.

'Yes. What do you think you've got out of today's session?'

It wasn't a real question, it was Grace's signal that the hour was coming to an end and that Mary needed to leave. How often do I not ask real questions, Grace wondered?

'Well. I don't know. Um. I think I feel a tiny bit better?'

Mary's hands were still gripping the sides of the chair and it seemed doubtful that she could be detached without the aid of force. Her nails had been industrially chewed.

'Mmm hmm.'

Grace was good at the non-committed hum.

'I feel calmer. I think so. I've got things clearer in my head now. Not so worried. I hope I can go to sleep tonight. I haven't been sleeping well. Yes, I think I'll sleep better now. I'm glad that I came today.'

Mary tried a pinched half-smile and Grace rewarded her with one of her special therapist half-smiles in return. She reserved the full ones for major breakthroughs. She had only once, as she remembered it, clapped her hands, but that was a mistake as the client was back on the whisky two weeks later. But was this smile therefore an artifice? Before she had thought of it as professional.

'Yes, much better. Thank you so much. Can I come back next week?'

'Of course,' said Grace, half leaning out of her chair to encourage Mary to move, but realizing that she looked like an elderly person trying to rise she sat back down again. 'Make an appointment with Lesley as you leave.'

'Oh, thanks,' said Mary, still attached to her chair. 'Thanks a lot. Thanks for being so kind and listening to me rabbiting on and on. You must get so bored with it all.'

Yes, is what Grace could have said, I do a little. I didn't ever use to but now I do. Sometimes what I hear is still as involving as it ever was, but now some of the time at least it's the same old self-hatred and general disgruntlement that I've heard so often and you are no exception to this. You're not the worst client I've had by many miles, not least because you wash, but you're not exactly the most riveting, are you? No wonder . . . but there Grace stopped herself before she thought something that she was ashamed of.

'See you next week,' she said.

'OK. Bye then,' said Mary.

'Goodbye.'

Mary finally stood up, and Grace stood up after her and ushered her out of the door without touching her. Grace did not touch her clients although she knew they wanted her to. They wanted a hug, a kiss on the cheek, a pat on the back, an everything is going to be all right, a strong cup of tea, and possibly a biscuit. But she wasn't like that. The only person she liked physical contact with was Sam. Is that what they used to call a character failing, Grace wondered? Now they call it an attachment issue. Perhaps, now she thought about it, she was only so distracted today because she was going to Dolores's house for her supper with Sam. It was official now. They were 'dating'. Sam was her 'girlfriend'. It was real.

Grace had a cup of coffee and the caffeine perked her up. Her last client today was Annie Barnes. She found her an interesting woman, glamorous and forceful, with a degree of self-confidence which was impressive. Of course, behind the make-up there were cracks, but that, in Grace's experience, was the case with everyone. Even with Sam? Where were her cracks? If she had any Grace was yet to find them. And she didn't feel like looking for them anyway.

Grace watched Annie sit with her legs neatly crossed. She always wore tights and heels. Grace had never got on with tights; their crotch never reached hers.

'I'm not perfect,' said Annie.

'In my experience nobody is,' said Grace.

'I agree with you,' said Annie, 'but people seem to think that I am.'

'And why is that do you think?'

'My aura of impenetrable self-belief.'

Grace smiled and so did Annie.

'And is that difficult to maintain?'

'You bet it is. But nobody knows that.'

'Nobody at all?'

'I don't think so. But sometimes it gives me a headache.'

'I'm not surprised.'

'The nearest I get to being my real self is with my best friend. But even with her I can't let my guard down all the way.'

'What would happen if you did?'

'She needs me to be strong for her. She can't always cope well on her own. She suffers from depression and I try my best with her but it's hard.'

'Depression is hard to deal with. Especially when it's someone you care about who is suffering from it.'

'I care about her a lot and I'm worried about her. She keeps sleeping with idiots. And now she's gone and done it with a woman and as far as I know she's never done that before.'

'And do you find that a problem?'

'That it's a woman? No. I don't care about that, it was just a surprise, that's all. I do care about her going off with strangers all the time, though. It's dangerous but it's like she can't help herself.'

'Have you considered that it might be a way for her to alleviate the depression?'

'Of course I have. It's a distraction, isn't it? We've never talked about it but it must make her feel better about herself. It worries me no end.'

Annie frowned.

'Have you tried talking to her about it?'

'I keep trying to cheer her out of it. I find myself saying the sort of rubbish my mother would say, you know, pull yourself together, pull your socks up, that sort of thing, even though I know those are useless things to say and I feel bad about saying them. But she won't get help and what the hell else can I do?'

'That must be very hard for you too.'

'Nothing on how hard it is for her. I know that, even if I don't tell her. I speak my mind you know, all the time, I'm known for it, but with her I don't know what to say or do any more.'

This is Annie taking Laurence home
to see what would happen

She gave in and took him to see her parents for Sunday lunch. She knew this was probably a mistake. Her mum would in all likelihood be dismissive, which would be depressing. On the other hand, she might be enthusiastic, which would be strange because her mum rarely showed enthusiasm for anything outside proper grouting and new hosiery. Annie was surprised to find that she felt nervous but Laurence was impeccable. She watched him shake her father by the hand and she watched her mother appraising the handshake.

'Mrs Barnes,' he said, 'a handshake doesn't feel right, does it?' and he kissed her on one cheek. 'What a lovely home,' he said. 'Now I know where Annie gets her good taste from.'

'Annie, show Laurence around then, don't just stand there gawping. I've got gravy to be getting on with, and your father has to find where on earth he has hidden the wine to stop himself drinking it.'

And Annie noticed in her mother something that she had never heard before, it was a slight change in accent, an elongation of the vowels. Well I never, she thought, and Laurence took her hand and she let him.

'I'd love to see the house,' he said.

'Seriously,' Annie said to him when they were out of earshot, 'you don't have to look around. Nobody's expecting you to buy it.'

He kissed her cheek.

'Lead on Macduff,' he said.

Half of her was expecting him to mock them. Half of her wanted him to. Go on, she dared him mentally, muck this one up, but he didn't.

'That's very nice,' he said, about the colour scheme in the lounge. 'I wouldn't have thought of putting that there,' he said about a piece of fake marble statuary in the conservatory.

By the time they had circled back to the kitchen she felt the unfamiliar sensation of having wanted approval and having got it.

'It's a charming home,' he said to Annie's mother as she dished up out of the hostess trolley. 'And who knew these still existed? What a brilliant idea! I'm going to get one for my parents for Christmas. Perhaps you could advise me?'

Annie found herself wanting to nudge her mother, look, look, table manners. Laurence talked to her dad about property development and the wine he had brought, and to her mum about his love of real gravy and the glory of her cooking. He mentioned football in a way that seemed knowledgeable and asked about what was of note to visit in the local area. He was nothing but courteous, pulled out her and her mother's chair to sit down, praised Annie as the most intelligent woman he knew. Her parents were themselves throughout – her dad relaxed, her mother over-observant, but they were charmed, she could tell. Her mother said nothing on the doorstep, only smiled and patted Annie's arm and Annie didn't know what to feel about that. Relieved? Happy? They drove home with the windows down, Annie with a scarf round her hair and her Chanel sunglasses on and the breeze blowing on her face. She pretended he was Cary Grant. She didn't want to be Grace Kelly though. She would, of course, be Sophia Loren. Halfway there Laurence pulled over to the side of the road and stopped the car next to a hedge with bits of plastic bags stuck in it.

'Annie, Annie, beautiful Annie,' he said. 'Aren't your family great?'

He reached and took her hand.

'That's one way of looking at them,' she said.

What was going on? Oh no! Maybe he had taken the whole going home for lunch thing too seriously. That hadn't even occurred to her. What if he was going to pop the question? She bloody hoped not. Apart from anything else it hardly made a romantic story did it – he stopped by the side of a B road. Bloody stop it, she said to herself. Calm down. She withdrew her hand and took out her lipstick and tried to put it on without making a wobbly line. Her face in the mirror looked composed.

'They were very kind indeed. Thank you for taking me to meet them. I felt honoured.'

'I wouldn't go that far.'

'I have a thing to ask you?'

'Right then,' she said, and put her compact back in her bag, as though she was now calm, and she turned towards him and looked him in the eye. He looked, to her surprise, furtive.

'It's kind of a delicate matter. I wouldn't ask if it wasn't very, very important to me.' And he coughed.

'OK.'

Am I blushing, she thought? I'm bloody blushing. I'm not ready for this, I'm not ready at all.

'It's . . . well . . . this is embarrassing I know, but I have a cashflow problem. I would ask my friends of course, but you know what Rex is like with money, and the rest of them aren't any better. And there's Ma and Pa of course, but they've bought that second place in the Dordogne and it's eating up cash. And as for my brothers, what I'd give to have a family like yours. Respectable. Stable. Sensible, if you understand what I mean. There's not much of that in my family unfortunately.' And he did look embarrassed. She had never seen him look like that before.

'How much?' asked Annie, trying not to feel surprisingly disappointed.

'Not that much. A couple of thou. Two perhaps? I'll sit down with the figures with you later if you'd like? Would you think about it?'

Annie turned back to face the windscreen and watched the cars overtake them. She thought about it; she had always been good with money, careful to the point of tight. Even her mother had had to borrow out of her piggy bank now and then when she was a child to pay the milkman. That was the only time she had lent anybody any money before; she had never even lent to Violet, who spent money as soon as she got it and often survived on change scrounged from pockets to the end of the month. But, she thought, everybody becomes unstuck now and then, and there was a small voice inside her head, a voice of pride that said but not me and she felt superior and magnanimous.

'OK,' she said, and looked at him. 'I'll lend it you. I trust you.'

'Thank you, you don't know how much this means to me. I'll set a date with you to pay it back. Do you want interest?'

'No, it's all right.'

Was it good that he looked so grateful or was it pathetic? No, it was nice to see that he wasn't completely perfect after all. He was flawed and that made her like him more. She smiled at him.

'Thank you. Thank you so much,' he said.

She felt that she should have asked for more details, but that would seem like she didn't trust him after all, and she never liked to go back on her word.

Laurence kissed her on the mouth and looked at her with such relief that she felt like she had made the right decision.

'Shall we go home and I can make love to you?' he said.

And Annie giggled, although she was not a giggler by nature. I must not have my head screwed on right, she thought, and took off her scarf to let her hair whip in the breeze.

This is Grace's girlfriend Sam

Dolores was the most curious person that Grace had ever met, and, since Sam hardly knew Dolores, this was going to come as a shock, Grace assumed. She had to watch Sam being grilled over the mussel stew.

'And how did you get here?' said Dolores.

'On the bus.'

'Were there many people on it?'

'Not that many.'

'Oh, that surprises me, I would have thought that this time of day there would be many, many people. How long did it take you?'

'I'm not sure. Twenty minutes?'

'Did it go the long way or the short way?'

'I'm not sure.'

'What number was it? What time did you leave home? Is it far to the bus stop from your house?'

To Grace's relief Sam didn't seem irritated by Dolores's love of detail. She felt that the evening had been a success; they had all drunk a large quantity of red wine and this had resulted in Dolores showing Sam her varicose veins and then wanting to discuss the failed operation she had had to get them removed. Sam didn't seem to mind. How tolerant she was. How nice.

'I'm sorry about the veins,' Grace said as they sat in bed later.

'She's funny,' said Sam.

And Grace felt like this was a minor test that either Sam had passed or she had passed. Or perhaps both. Next stop was her family.

Grace sat in her office and wrote their names over and over on pieces of paper in different scripts, which is one of the most stupid things that you can possibly do with your time and which, when you are in your thirties, should probably result in community service. But she did it anyway. And she kept them in a drawer and got them out and put them in lines on her desk and they made her smile.

Sam and Grace.
Grace and Sam.

She had changed all her passwords to a variant of Sam's name. Her pin number had become Sam's birthday. She had bought liquorice tea and nettle tea and tea made from goat droppings that tasted like wasps. She had bought spider plants and cyclamen and most of them survived. She had experimented with the crop top type of bra that Sam occasionally wore, but rejected it for its pancaking properties. She had also bought three blue T-shirts and a pair of blue trousers because she had borrowed a blue T-shirt of Sam's one day and Sam had said that it suited her. She went to the strange hippy shop she had never been into before to buy a wind chime because Sam had one, even though she thought wind chimes were awful. She hung it in her backyard and the clinking noise annoyed her so much she had to take it down. She even cooked, although cooking was an alien concept to her. Eustacia was the one who had cooked when they were young, because Cyril and Beatrice were incapable of anything more than anchovy paste on water biscuits, porridge, and stale brandy snaps. Grace had never learnt how, she couldn't even cook spaghetti without it sticking together. She tried her best, though, ringing Eustacia for suggestions, but while Sam was complimentary about her efforts Grace found most of it horrible and when on her own she returned to piccalilli on toast and whatever else she had recently foraged from Manfred's.

These were delightful days. She was still not that interested in work but who cared? No one was monitoring her levels of enthusiasm after all and it was probably a good thing that it no longer occupied so much space in her head – she was a normal person now, a person with a girlfriend, and work could be pushed into the background; it was a thing she did that was worthwhile, and which made her money, and that was all. Probably this was the same for most people. She had better things to do with her time.

Everything, as seen in the company of Sam, no matter how ordinary, was interesting. The compromises involved in going to the Co-op and chucking things into a mutual trolley became a form of entertainment. Reading out stories in the papers to each other in bed with their legs kicked over each other replaced proper books. The time Sam's washing machine went on strike and Grace had to wash her clothes and they hung them on her radiators together and, since they weren't dry the next morning, Sam left them behind and Grace had the later pleasure of stroking them and folding them neatly. And for days afterwards Sam's clothes smelt the same as hers. The way that Sam mispronounced the word 'fenugreek' and this becoming code between them in public situations for 'come to bed with me'. The morning Grace tripped on a book and threw muesli all over the floor and over herself and how the memory of this made them laugh every time it was mentioned. The evening they went to the theatre and both thought the play was rubbish and they left in the interval and went back to Sam's and stayed up all night playing backgammon. How it felt naughty, like Grace imagined skiving school must have done, not that she ever had. Even when Grace woke up in her own bed on her own she remembered the fact of Sam's existence and reached over and touched the pillow on the other side of the bed. She put her nose into it to see if it smelt of Sam's hair and it did and it delighted her.

She had often found herself analysing the most ordinary of interactions. Now, mostly what she did was feel. Feel her skin prickling, her belly shaking, her legs going wobbly, her heart pounding away. Every time Sam kissed her she felt faint, came out of the kisses swaying, felt that she needed a wall to rest herself against, and had to hold on to Sam's arms to stand up straight. Sam laughed at this and Grace was very pleased, she had never known that she was funny.

Sam got her to go running, which was something Sam did now and then but Sam was fit and ran like a gazelle and Grace was not and ran like a wheezy hippopotamus. She watched Sam run away from her in a tight top and leggings while Grace had only managed to find an old T-shirt and some falling-apart shorts. Sam had proper Nikes but Grace had Converse and her feet hurt every time she slammed them on the ground. Her thigh bones seemed to be grinding on her shin bones. That couldn't be good. Sam came back to her and said, 'Are you OK, Grace?' and Grace couldn't speak because she was trying to breathe. She sat down heavily on the grass. Sam jogged on the spot next to her.

'Could you keep going, do you think?'

Grace leant back and closed her eyes and to her surprise felt Sam nuzzle her neck. She opened her eyes and Sam was lying on the grass next to her with her head propped up on her elbow.

'But didn't you want to run more?' asked Grace when she could speak.

'I want to be with you more than I want to run,' said Sam, and leant forward to kiss her. Grace had never kissed a woman in public before. She looked around. There was a man walking his dog that she could hear muttering, 'They think they can just do anything they like whenever they like. It shouldn't be allowed.'

'Did you hear that?' asked Grace.

'Stupid old man,' said Sam, and touched her arm. 'We should have sex right here and see what he does,' she said.

Grace felt elated by Sam's attitude. She reached over and traced her jawline.

'We can do anything we want,' said Sam.

'Yes,' said Grace, 'yes,' and kissed her again.

When they got back home and after they had showered together, Grace put on one of Sam's T-shirts and went into the sitting room. She saw the light on Sam's retro answerphone flashing. Sam came in. She was grinning.

'That was good,' she said.

'You've got messages,' said Grace.

'I'll get them later,' said Sam. 'Shall we have a fry-up?'

'Yes,' said Grace, even if she hadn't had one in years.

How many times a day do I say yes now, thought Grace as she drove home. All the time, all the time. She felt so happy she wanted to do something to demonstrate it. Like throw confetti or hand out flowers to strangers in the street. She parked next to Manfred's and got out.

'Well, hello Grace,' said Manfred. 'Haven't seen you for ages. You look flushed. Anything I should know about?'

'I've got a girlfriend,' said Grace.

'Well, well, congratulations,' said Manfred. 'I'm very pleased for you. Is she fit?'

Grace blushed.

'I'll take that as a yes,' he said. 'When's the wedding then? Do I hear the ding dong of bells?'

'I think it's too early for that,' said Grace.

'Not by the way you look, you've got that glow. I'm pleased for you, love. I think you should celebrate with some tinned peaches.'

She drove the hundred metres home and parked but didn't get out of the car. She sat clutching her tin. Marriage? She had never even considered it. But maybe it was possible. Maybe everything was possible.

This is Violet's discussion with Annie on the nature of sexuality

'What are you then?' asked Annie.

They were having lunch in the local Italian, outside which

very optimistic people were on the pavement pretending that they were somewhere European with sun. Annie had said she would treat her and Violet reckoned this was because Annie felt bad for shouting at her the other day. It was the first time in a long time that Violet had eaten a meal in a café and she was impressed with herself for being in a venue designed for the purpose of social interaction for the second time in a week. Hopefully it meant that 'the fear' was in abatement, albeit temporarily, or perhaps it just meant that Annie's 'forcing her out of the house' technique was finally working. Whichever one it was, she didn't feel too bad and didn't want to hide under the table as she had been tempted to do in the past.

'What am I what?' asked Violet. Pizza or pasta, she thought, pizza or pasta. It was a perennial problem and the portions were always too big and then she'd feel guilty about leaving half of it. Plus, Annie was paying, and would therefore feel obliged to eat the leftovers to get good value and complain that she had eaten too much.

'Easy choice, I would have thought, easier than trying to work out which salad is best. Straight or gay? You choose,' said Annie.

'I didn't know they were salads.'

'That waiter there or the girl with no hair in the corner?'

'How do you know she's gay?' said Violet, looking up at the girl, who had short hair and big black glasses.

'I didn't say she was gay, that was your presumption because she looks like she could possibly be, based on your assessment of what a gay woman looks like. Neither was that the question I meant, as you well know. Are you hetero or homo?'

Annie crossed her arms under her bosom so that the waiter would pay them attention. It didn't work. Violet knew that Annie would now be convinced he was gay.

'Um. I haven't thought about it yet,' said Violet, who was

lying because she had of course, although not in such a worried way as might have been expected, but she didn't want to tell Annie this, although Annie probably already knew.

'Don't dither. It's unbecoming. Are you a lesbian?'

'I hope not,' said Violet.

'I don't think that's the right attitude. Don't let the thought police hear you saying that,' said Annie.

'No, I don't mean it like that, I just don't like that word. I wish that Sappho had been from another island. Do you know the names of any other Greek islands?' asked Violet.

'Corfu. Crete.'

'Corfucian.'

'I think you'll find that's "Confucian".'

'That's a religion. Cretan. I'll have to get out the atlas,' said Violet, trying to concentrate on the menu again but only getting as far as prosciutto.

'You haven't got an atlas.'

'No, but I wish I did have. Why haven't you got one? Do you want to have a dessert as well?' said Violet.

'Are you having one?'

'That wasn't my question.'

'As if you ever give a proper answer. You haven't even answered my first question properly.'

'Which was?' said Violet, who had completely forgotten. This happened to her all the time – her mind wandered off, even in the middle of important or pressing conversations. At least, she thought, I'm not losing my memory, I never had a good one in the first place.

'You mean you can't remember? I despair of you.'

'You despair of me frequently. And you know what my memory's like,' said Violet. 'It's a pathetic memory, it's like it's a toy poodle puppy and yours is a Great Dane.'

'I asked you if you were a lesbian and you started off about

Greek islands. I'll change the terminology if you prefer. Are you gay? A dyke?'

Violet tried to think about it properly. At times being with Annie was like an exam and she wanted to try her best.

'Gay's all right. Sounds happy. I suppose because that's what it means.'

'And dyke?'

'It reminds me of that bit in *Good Morning Vietnam* where Robin Williams is reading the news and he goes something like "A river broke through a protective dyke today."'

'Are you going to see her again?' said Annie.

'I don't know,' said Violet.

'You could phone her. Do you have her phone number?'

Annie's inability to stop her questioning techniques was often exhausting. Violet wanted to lay her head on the table.

'No, but I know her surname,' said Violet, who had seen it on a letter. Not that she had been looking.

'Then why don't you look her up, see if she's got a landline. What's her surname? I'll do it,' and Annie got out her phone.

'I can't,' said Violet.

'Why not?'

'I just can't.'

'Why not?'

Violet bit her lip and considered the question.

'I'm thinking. I'm a slow thinker, you know that.'

'Perhaps you are bisexual,' said Annie.

'Dunno,' said Violet.

Violet was uncomfortable and had started to fidget with her cutlery in a way that she knew made Annie want to slap her hands. Annie sighed and put her phone back down on the table and looked at the menu again. Violet stared out of the window. She saw the borzoi she liked but decided not to point it out to Annie. She would have the pasta; there, a decision.

On their way home Violet stubbed her toe on the pavement because she was distracted by a man cycling down the road with juggling clubs sticking out of his knapsack. She mostly bought her shoes from a children's shoe shop that sold Startrite, the old-fashioned kind where they would still measure your feet with that sliding machine. It had a rocking horse that she always wanted to get on. Violet's feet were what she considered to be an embarrassing size two, embarrassing because whenever in the past she had mistakenly entered an adults' shoe shop and asked for that size, she was greeted by reactions ranging from a fetishistic interest in a salivating salesman to complete indifference from bored shop girls counting the minutes to home time. 'No two, we haven't a two.' 'But you haven't really looked,' Violet had tried beseeching. 'Couldn't you go in the back and look a bit?' 'We haven't got any. We never have.' Then Violet would give up and leave the shop with her head hung down, feeling ashamed for being so minuscule. I wish I was Annie, she'd think, then I could tell them to eff off, or at least ask to speak to the manager. Or even shove them aside with my bum. Violet had never complained about anything in her life. She wondered what would have happened if she had grown up in China years ago and had her feet bound. What size would they have been then? So small she would have been walking en pointe, like a ballet dancer? And the crippling pain. She stopped and put her hand on the wall next to her.

'Annie! I've stubbed my toe!' she called out but Annie was way ahead of her by now, wincing at every step like the Little Mermaid because her expensive shoes were too tight as always. Violet limped down the pavement towards her.

'What the heck have you done?' Annie called out to her.

'I stubbed my toe! Didn't you see the man with the juggling clubs? I nearly fell into the road.'

'Hurry up,' said Annie as Violet came towards her and, with

unexpected solidarity, linked her arm with hers, and together they hobbled home like a pair of old ladies.

Back in the flat Violet went to her room. She had already found what she thought was the woman's phone number in one of the plastic-wrapped phone books she had discovered on the top of the electricity cupboard in the downstairs hall. She had forgotten such paper evidence of your whereabouts even existed in this digital age. But she hadn't dialled it. Did she like her? Was it possible to like a woman the way she had sometimes liked a man? Was it allowed to call her? And what, what, she wanted to know, was it like to have sex with a woman? Would it be very weird? What if halfway through she didn't like it and wanted to stop? She could hear Annie making coffee with her complicated Italian coffee maker and found the noise as reassuring as she found Annie herself. She looked at the drawing of Sam's mouth that was lying on her desk. She put her finger on it.

This is Grace not taking Sam home to Ravel Corner

Great Aunt Beatrice rang her. Cyril had had a fall. Could they come? Grace said yes of course, straight away. It would never have occurred to her to refuse Beatrice or Cyril anything. She considered things. She and Sam had been going out for three months now; was it too early to ask Sam to come with her? She dithered. Her family were mostly nice. Sam was nice too and so why shouldn't they get on? But what if they didn't like her, how would that make Grace feel? And what if Sam didn't like them; there were so many of them, and all so full on. She decided in the end to be a grown-up about it and let Sam decide.

'No thanks,' said Sam, who was washing up in her flat while Grace stood behind her. Why have I chosen to ask her now, thought Grace, and therefore miss the chance of seeing her face. Now what am I supposed to say? I don't want to grill her on why she doesn't want to come, I don't want to show her how disappointed I am, maybe it is better that I'm standing behind her.

'Are you busy this weekend?'

'Not particularly.'

'Then come, they're nice, you'll like them.'

'I don't do family.'

'Oh. Why not?'

'I just don't do them.'

'Will I meet your family?'

'They're a long way away, so probably not.'

'Right,' said Grace. 'Well, you'll like my sisters, I think, they're great. Well, Eustacia and Tess are. Bella not so much, she's an acquired taste but she's entertaining at least. Please come.'

'No thanks.'

'OK,' said Grace in a way she hoped didn't sound passive aggressive. 'I might be a couple of days. It depends on how my grandfather is.'

'OK,' said Sam. 'Do you want some tea?'

'I'm pretty worried about him.'

'Yes, I expect you are. Tea?'

Grace didn't understand. Sam wasn't a callous person, she was nothing but kind. Grace had seen her helping children in the park to find their lost mittens.

'He's very old, you see, and unsteady, and this isn't the first time he's fallen. And Beatrice is very old too and she shouldn't really be caring for him on her own. And so I've got to go.'

'Sure,' said Sam.

Would you just listen to what I am trying to tell you, thought Grace; she decided on directness, none of this pussyfooting around.

'I would like you to come. It would help me.'

'Sorry, Grace,' said Sam, turning towards her at last, 'I've got things to do.'

Grace fought back a sudden urge to take Sam by the arms and shake her. Why the hell wasn't she listening properly? Instead Grace put her hands in her pockets.

'OK, well, I'll ring you.'

'Fine,' said Sam.

There wasn't any more that Grace could do or say, it seemed, but it was the first time that she had ever felt angry with Sam.

It was funny going 'home'. Everything was the same, a time warp. The long potholed drive the car struggled along that they had used to swerve down in the Land Rover. The first view of the house, the gothic nightmare tacked on to the seventeenth-century main house. She tried to look at it subjectively; it looked as if bats might fly off out of the chimney at any moment. It looked like there were mad women in its attics and that the threshold shouldn't be crossed, that there were beasts within.

Beatrice answered the creaking front door after Grace and Eustacia had rung the bell for ages and ages. She was wearing jodhpurs and slippers and pulled over her dowager's hump what looked like one of their school lab coats and over that a filthy apron. In her hand was a grey stringy mop dripping water. The wrinkles on her face were etched in deep to her papery skin and there was a hint of a beard on her chin.

'I've been mopping!' she said and shook the mop and they were sprayed with dirty water and they stepped back but she didn't notice. 'I thought I would make an effort for your arrival, dearest girls.'

They made their way slowly upstairs. The banisters were shaky, the wood panels on the walls were splintering, and, as they emerged into the upstairs corridor, a plume of smoke drifted towards them.

'Oh dear,' said Beatrice, not now able to move at any speed, 'I was perhaps over-enthusiastic with the fire. Do run please, girls.'

They ran to the room at the far end and opened the door. The grate was full of smoke but luckily it was such a big room that it hadn't spread far. Cyril was sitting up in a four-poster with shabby curtains half hanging off around him, calmly eating a boiled egg off a tray.

'Girls!' he said.

'Had you not noticed, Cyril,' Grace said, 'that your room was on fire?'

Eustacia was trying to damp down the grate.

'I was otherwise engaged,' he said, and Grace noticed that the bed was covered with a layer of books and papers. He was even older than Beatrice, in his late eighties as far as they could work out because of his vagaries, but his eyebrows were still startlingly black and abundant in comparison to the lack of hair on his freckled head.

'You could have gone up like a torch,' Grace said.

'Never mind, dear,' said Beatrice, who had hobbled in behind them. 'Let's open the windows.'

Cyril, as it turned out, was healing better than anyone might have thought. He was now Emeritus professor and only went to the university for the occasional lecture or to go to the library, and seemed happy at home writing in bed.

'Like Descartes,' he said. 'This being bedbound isn't at all bad. I've got through a lot of work, Grace. Only it's a strain on Beatrice with the stairs. I'm thinking of moving to the drawing room.'

'Girls,' said Beatrice, 'could you possibly help with the bed? I think there's a portable jobby in the attic.'

Once they had found their way through the large cobwebs and the alarming examples of stored taxidermy up there and got the mildewed camp bed downstairs, they went back for Cyril and moved him down to the dark drawing room, which looked like it hadn't been used for years. They piled his books, many of which were frangible, on the imposing sideboard. The green William Morris wallpaper looked mouldy.

'You haven't sold this then?' Grace said, patting the sideboard, because during her childhood every so often items had disappeared to auction, and, in the case of the Ming bowl used for putting used tea bags in, to Sotheby's. 'Needs must,' Beatrice used to say, sadly waving goodbye to whatever it was. 'Is it teak?' asked Grace.

'Ah, we came into some luck,' said Cyril, in his camp bed, tucking down his army issue blanket that had probably been inherited from some distant relation in the Bombay Boxers. Everything in this house had a story about where it came from. His pyjamas were from Harrods, monogrammed of course, but were about fifty years old and fraying at the neck.

'Wonderful,' said Beatrice, 'wonderful.'

Eustacia, who couldn't help herself, was swiping at the furniture with tissues. 'You know that Jeremy and I would be glad to help you out if you need us to. I mean that.'

'It's all right, dear. Two thirty at Catterick. Go Baby Go,' said Beatrice. 'Simply awful form, hence the odds. Always been pulled up. But I saw him in the paddock and his ears were pricked and his tail was up, and I thought, aha, and rang my little man.'

'Paid for the electricity,' said Cyril. 'We were in danger of falling into permanent Stygian gloom.'

'What were the odds?' asked Grace.

'Ah,' said Beatrice, tapping at the side of her nose, 'a lady never reveals her age. I think I hear a car.'

Tess arrived first, battling up the incline of the drive in her disintegrating Land Rover and stopping before nearly taking out one of the stone dogs on the front steps.

'That was a good stop,' Grace said to her.

'At home, it's better because it makes the gravel spin and once she broke a window,' said Rowan, climbing out of the car.

'Well, she didn't exactly break it but there was a big crack,' said Linden, getting out the other side.

'Who's she, the cat's mother?' asked Tess, hauling a huge canvas hold-all out of the front seat.

'You've started saying that way too much lately, Tess,' said Linden.

'Yes, it's irritating and not at all necessary,' said Rowan.

'It's supposed to show that we are being rude calling her she,' said Linden.

'Well, why doesn't she say that then?' asked Rowan.

'I have no idea,' said Linden.

'Is Bella here yet?' Tess asked Grace.

'If she was here, her car would be here. Obviously,' said Linden.

'Is Sam here?' said Tess.

'No, she couldn't come,' said Grace.

'Shame. How are the oldies?'

Up the drive then came Tess's car's antithesis – a Range Rover with tinted windows.

'Ah, here we go,' said Grace.

Bella threw herself out of her car and rushed towards them, stopping only to kiss them both on either cheek. This always surprised Grace and they bumped noses. Bella wiped lipstick off her aggressively with her thumb. She swept her long dark brown (fake from Russian virgins apparently) hair off her beautiful face. Cheekbones that could have sliced cheese. One of those spindly figures that turns out to be a marvel of yoga stretch. Clothes so understated and uniformly grey and black that they reminded Grace of East Germany but probably cost more than her entire wardrobe put together.

'You're looking peaky. I know a great spa. It's pricey but they'll give you a discount if you say you're my sister. Augusta! Augusta! Damn that child. She's still in the car. Can you go and get her out, Grace? She's sulking.'

She grabbed Tess before she could protest and hurled herself through the door in her high-heeled boots. The twins trailed them. Bella rushed about as though busy was an ideal to live up to. To think she used to be so laid back, so can't be arsed. Grace went and opened the passenger door. Augusta was still strapped in. Grace kissed her. On one cheek only. She needed normal influences. Augusta scratched at the tight plaits on her head (Grace expected the nanny did them). She had her grand-mother's sly grey eyes and it always disconcerted Grace to see them in the face of a child. Augusta started to pick at the back of the seat in front of her.

'I've got cellulite,' she said sadly.

'You are eight years old.'

'On my leg. Look.'

She pulled up her trousers to above the knee.

'That's not cellulite, that's your thigh. It's a normal eight-year-old thigh.'

'I'm fat, like Daddy.'

'You are not fat.'

'I'm nearly the most popular girl in my class. Heidi Fair-shield is first most popular because she has an indoor and an outdoor swimming pool. We only have an outdoor one. It is heated, though. Have you got a swimming pool?'

'No,' said Grace.

Augusta looked at her with great pity. Bella was a vet in York and so was her husband Ray, and they must have been loaded but it didn't seem to have done this poor child any good.

'Why haven't you got any children?' said Augusta. 'Did you forget?'

'No, I didn't forget.'

'Perhaps it's because you don't like boys very much. You need a boy to have one, Mummy told me. I don't know why you need one but you do. I don't like boys either.'

'I don't dislike boys.'

'But you haven't got a boyfriend, have you?'

'This is very true.'

'Why haven't you got a boyfriend?'

'Perhaps you should ask Mummy.'

Augusta reached her hand out and put it on Grace's cheek and patted it softly in the manner of a friendly grandmother.

'Never mind. I drew you a picture,' she said. She handed Grace a piece of paper. 'It's you.'

A wiry scarecrow with articulated limbs like a puppet and tangled hair stood in the centre of a field surrounded by a flock of crows. Another crow was sitting on the figure's head. Grace smiled.

'I like it,' she said. 'Thank you.'

'I didn't get the hair right,' said Augusta, 'but I ran out of brown felt pen and then I scribbled on it too much to change it.'

'I see. Let's go inside, shall we?'

'Is there Diet Coke?'

'I doubt it very much.'

Augusta got out of the car and Grace closed the door. Augusta put her hand in hers. She loved Augusta far more than Rowan and Linden and frequently felt guilty about this. She would never tell Tess and certainly not Bella, who was likely to boast about it as if she had won a best child competition. They climbed the steps. This was the nearest she would ever have to a child of her own. The thought made her sad. At least there were children in her life, that must count for something. Many people didn't even have that. But what if she had been straight – would she have been a mother by now? Would she have expected to have a child

136

because that was the natural order of things? Would she have imaginary baby names like some of her friends had? Would she be considering calling a child Tiberius or Fluella? These were thoughts she had had more than once. The other day she had found an old book from her childhood with the alphabet spelt out with animals. The twins and Augusta were too old for it now. It would have been nice to have someone to read it to. And all for want of a boy.

'Am I too fat to have a piggyback?' asked Augusta.

'You are not fat!'

Grace crouched down and Augusta climbed on top of her back. Grace stood up. Augusta was, it had to be said, a solid child.

'It's a secret.'

'What is?'

'That you're my favourite aunty.'

Grace felt very, very pleased. Augusta interlocked her hands around Grace's neck and Grace slipped her hands under her knees.

'Tally ho!' said Grace.

This is Annie and Laurence on their mini-break

'Annie,' said Laurence, 'I've got that money I owe you. Sorry about the delay.'

He handed her a cheque. It had only been two weeks since she had lent it to him and she was surprised to get it back so quickly.

'I didn't know people still had cheque books,' said Annie.

She felt a surge of satisfaction. It wasn't the money that mattered, it was the principle of it. He was a man to be trusted. She had been right all along and now she had the proof in paper form. Perhaps she should frame it. She kissed him hard on the mouth.

'Don't worry, it's not going to bounce. And I was thinking, perhaps we should go away for the weekend. Would you like to?'

'Yes,' said Annie decisively, still relieved by the cheque and not considering the full implications of this, 'I'd love to. But only if we can go Dutch.' How modern I am, she thought, and how much that would annoy my mother.

'Are you sure? I don't want you to think that I am taking advantage of your generosity.'

'Where are we going?'

It was Annie's first ever romantic mini-break. Michael Wrigley had once taken her to a Harry Ramsden's in Wallasey but that hardly counted. He had wanted to take her away to Blackpool for what he termed a 'dirty weekend', but the words 'dirty weekend' offended her and she had rejected the offer. Her world was different now. Sophisticated. Exotic.

'Paris? Rome?' he asked.

Annie imagined herself in a Parisian café sipping Sauvignon Blanc or perhaps champagne, wearing Dior. She imagined herself sitting in a Roman piazza sipping Chianti wearing Armani. She didn't want to tell him about her fear of flying and how, on her only ever flight to Amsterdam with Violet, she had been sick.

'Or we could rest chez nous. The Dales? The Lakes? I know, how about Edinburgh? We could drive. The borders will be beautiful this time of year.'

'Yes,' said Annie, 'yes please.'

She wanted to ring her mother to tell her but after the lunch success knew that this was a very bad idea. Every time her mother rang she asked after 'that Laurence'. She knew exactly what her mother would say. 'He's a nice young man but he hasn't asked you to marry him yet so just you make sure he keeps his hands to himself.' She knew, without anything being said, that Violet wasn't keen on Laurence, and her reaction to the mini-break idea was disappointingly muted. Annie decided, for once, not to get into a discussion about this, it would only ruin the experience. She was very excited, and she didn't do very excited as a rule. She splashed out on a new extremely tight dress in which her cleavage protruded as if she was a fig-urehead on a ship. She looked all va-va-voom. If this time he did ask her to marry him, she would be prepared for it sartori-ally at least. This dress would not need to be Photoshopped. She had also now completed her mental Excel spreadsheet with, at the very top – to be trusted. If he asked her she would at least now be able to consider it with logic on her side.

Edinburgh, as it turned out, was more beautiful than she had expected, all hills and secret alleys, and Annie might have loved it but it was also grey and cold and very wet. Oh well, you can't have everything, thought Annie, who was trying not to be annoyed about having to wear her coat over her new dress and getting her shoes splashed. I should have worn my Bur-berry and my boots. I forgot we are still in the north. There was no sitting outside to be had unless you wanted to drown. Her dream of a sunny square had perhaps been unrealistic. All right, stupid. She was peeved, which wasn't a good start.

'I was going to make a reservation,' said Laurence as they left the hotel, which at least was a decent hotel with a superior brand of shortbread next to the kettle, to go to what he called 'supper' and she called 'tea', 'but I thought this would be more fun.'

They turned up a side street, hardly able to see in front of their faces because of the drizzle. They had had to borrow an umbrella from reception and it had giant scottie dogs on it, much to Annie's annoyance. Her mood was not improving.

'Here we are,' said Laurence.

It was a fish and chip shop.

'Wonderful place,' said Laurence, 'you'll love it.'

The table was Formica and the seats were plastic and bolted to the floor. There was one of those tomato-shaped ketchup bottles in front of her and white pepper and salt in shakers the shape of men in kilts. It was a disaster. She'd never get the smell out of her hair or her clothes. The food would be awash in grease. The waitress brought them cod and chips. On a plate, so Annie supposed that was something. And then, to her surprise, the waitress plonked down a bottle of champagne on the table with two glasses. Laurence grinned.

'Only in Edinburgh,' he said and poured her a glass. I am being a stuck-up cow, thought Annie, and took the glass he offered her.

'To us,' he toasted.

The fish and chips were delicious, Annie hadn't eaten them in years. She began to feel better. There were people in proper evening dress coming up to the counter. It's all a bit of fun, she thought, he just wanted to surprise me.

'My mum does a good chip,' she said, tucking in.

'I bet she does,' said Laurence. 'They also do the famous deep-fried Mars bar in here.'

'They do what?'

'Deep-fried Mars bars. Bloody fantastic.'

I do like this man, Annie thought.

'I love you, Annie,' he said, and reached across and took her greasy hand in his greasy hand. Annie had never known what to say to that. She knew what was requisite obviously, but since that was out of the question, how did you respond? The best she could think of was, 'Right you are then, I'll just get back to my chips,' and he didn't seem offended but smiled and started to eat his too.

This is how Violet met the woman (II)

It wasn't too cold in the park and the sky was blue. Violet and Annie were eating barley sugars from a paper bag. Annie called them shirley buggers. Annie looked extremely happy as she sucked on a sweet and swung her bag. All she had said about her weekend to Violet was that Edinburgh was beautiful, and frankly Violet wasn't interested in hearing about Laurence anyway.

In a nearby flowerbed there was a gardener digging, her T-shirt stuck to her back, her hair to her forehead with sweat.

'Hi,' said Violet, blushing.

The woman unbent herself, dropped her spade on the ground and came over to Violet and kissed her on the cheek.

'Sorry,' she said, 'I'm all sweaty.'

'That's all right,' said Violet, 'I don't mind.'

'Just as well,' said the woman with a huge grin, 'I'm like this a lot,' and she wiped her face with the sleeve of her T-shirt.

'This is Annie, she's my flatmate, you know, the person who I said was my girlfriend only she isn't that kind of girlfriend,' said Violet.

'I'm Sam. Pleased to meet you, I won't shake hands.'

'No,' said Annie.

'This is where you work then,' said Violet, thinking that Sam was a nice name.

'Yeah,' said Sam.

Then they stood there staring at each other and grinning. Annie stood there too, one hand on her hip, the other one swinging her handbag, watching them.

'Do you want to do something later?' asked Sam.

'Yes, I mean, yes,' said Violet.

'What would you like to do?'

'I don't really mind. You can choose.'

'I'll have a think. I think better when I'm digging. I'll give you a ring later. What's your number? You forgot to give it to me. Have you got a pen?'

'No,' said Violet, 'but Annie will. Annie is really organized.'

Annie reached into her bag and got out a fountain pen and a leather-backed notebook.

'Annie always has a pen,' said Violet, 'and paper. Not any old biro either.'

'I'm impressed,' said Sam.

Violet went to give Sam the piece of paper but Sam said, 'Put it in my pocket,' and Violet did. Violet went back to where Annie was. Annie swung her bag and looked at the trees.

'I'd better go probably,' said Violet.

'See you later,' said Sam. 'Enjoy your walk.'

'Thanks,' said Violet.

'Nice to meet you, Annie.'

'That was Sam,' said Violet.

'Yes, I got that,' said Annie, striding across the park, which meant that Violet could hardly keep up.

'So?' asked Violet.

'So?'

'What did you think? And could you slow down a bit? Why are you marching so fast anyway?'

'Tall. Blond. Female. Dirty. Has the hots for you.'

'Really?'

'Which piece of information are you saying "really" in relation to?'

'Annie.'

'At least it's reciprocated,' said Annie, who had speeded up if anything. Violet had always envied Annie her purpose on outings, her straight and directional lines in contrast to her own easily distractible meanderings, but it did make her feel like a snotty child trailing after a parent on an urgent errand to somewhere important.

'Is it? I mean, do I?' she asked.

'Why are you asking me? Don't you know? You nearly kissed her back there.'

'Did I? What did you think of her then?'

'I told you.'

Violet was running now, only to collide with the aggressive swing of Annie's handbag. It was shiny like a chestnut. Did she polish it? With shoe polish? The kind that came in a squeezy bottle or the retro kind that came in a tin and you had to apply with a duster?

'Ow!' Violet was winded and stopped. 'I mean, did you like her?'

'No.'

'Why not?' asked Violet, who tried to keep the look of hurt off her face and failed.

'She's only after one thing,' said Annie, who kept going.

'You sound like your mother!'

'But I'm right.'

Annie was getting further and further away.

'How can you possibly know that? You met her for two minutes.'

Violet was incredulous, not for the first time, about Annie's ability to make up her mind.

'Trust me, I know. Call it the voice of bitter experience.'

Annie stopped and turned around. She wasn't even out of breath. Violet found that she had sagged, that her back was arched like an old woman's. She tried to stand up straight and had a sudden flashback to her two whole lessons of ballet aged four. She'd hated ballet. Annie snapped her fingers at her and Violet came to.

'I'm sorry, Violet, I know you want a different answer from me but I can't give you one. You like her. I don't. I don't need to like her because I don't want to go out with her. You do. That's fine. We have a difference of opinion. End of story.'

'You never like anyone I go out with,' Violet said.

'No, I don't.'

'Why not?'

'Do you want to know the truth?' asked Annie with a sigh so tired it made an immediate nap seem like a good idea.

'Do you ever tell me anything else?' Violet asked.

'No.'

'What's your answer then?'

'Because I think they're all twats.'

There wasn't a lot you could say to that, Violet found, although she searched for adequate words. Meanwhile Annie strode off. Violet wasn't going to run after her, she wasn't going to go back to Sam. She was at an impasse. She sat down on a bench to wait for help that was completely unlikely to come. A number of dogs came up to sniff her before deciding she wasn't even interesting enough to use as a pissing post. In the end, she got up and went to the car park but of course Annie's car wasn't there. God, she must be in an even fouler mood than I knew, thought Violet. She began the walk home and started to sing a song her mother had used to sing to her about maresy doats and dozy doats. A date, she remembered, an actual date. She couldn't remember the last time she'd had a proper one. Let alone one with a woman. She was surprised to find that she didn't feel scared but instead had a buzz of excitement. Curiouser and curiouser. She sang all the way home.

This is Grace and her family at Ravel Corner

'How wonderful to have you all here,' said Beatrice as she presided over the dinner table.

Eustacia had cooked the supper, having brought the ingredients with her, for fear of the sell-by dates in the pantry and the resulting salmonella. She had also got her sisters to help her to disinfect the kitchen. There was far too much feral cat hair on the surfaces for her liking.

'Too many women at this table,' said Bella, 'and yes, Augusta, you are eating that and no, it's not fattening. Jesus. Will one of you please tell my daughter that she needs to eat because she certainly doesn't want to listen to my advice on the subject.'

She bit on her knuckle and leant back in her chair. You'd think it would be good to see the chinks in a person's armour when they are that together, but mostly it was sad, Grace was surprised to feel.

'Augusta,' said Eustacia, 'eat your food please,' and miraculously Augusta did.

'I have to disagree with you, Bella,' said Linden, eyeing his carrots with distaste. 'I'm male, Rowan is male, Cyril is male, Kite is male.'

'Kite is a dog,' said Rowan, who had pushed his carrots to the rim of his plate.

'That's Aunt Arabella to you,' said Bella.

'But he is male,' said Linden.

'I think you will find that Aunt Arabella said there were too many women here, which is technically true because there are. There is only one man. We are children. Kite is a dog. QED,' said Rowan. He started to do what looked like sums on the notebook next to his plate.

'Do you want any more potatoes, Grace?' asked Eustacia in her best hostess way.

'Your potatoes are the best,' said Grace.

'Yes, dear,' said Beatrice, 'cooking never was one of my strengths.'

'Speak up,' said Cyril from the end of the table, 'I can hardly hear you, Beatrice.'

'Deaf,' she said, 'you're getting deaf, dear. You need an ear trumpet.'

'My mummy can't cook either, except disgusting lentils and my daddy can only make hot dogs but it's OK because our nanny knows how,' said Augusta, poking at her food.

'Tess doesn't believe in cooking. She believes in macrobiotics,' said Linden.

'Yes, it's an interesting set of theories,' said Rowan.

'You are a little bit weird,' said Augusta.

'That's inaccurate. We're not "a little bit weird", we're "special and gifted",' said Linden.

'We're fast tracking for Cambridge of course,' said Rowan.

'It's better than Oxford for maths,' said Linden.

'Good God, Tess,' Bella said, 'Augusta is right, your children are weird. Nothing wrong with being weird of course, but they are.'

'That doesn't mean that Augusta is right to say that to them, does it?' and Tess's eyes went all fiery.

'Would you all please calm down,' said Eustacia.

'Piss off,' said Bella.

'Tess,' says Linden, 'Aunt Arabella is using inappropriate language for our age group again.'

Come nightfall and 'the girls' were standing outside the French windows at the end of the palm house. It was cold in there because of the broken panes and the palms were all dead. They were sharing a spliff that Tess had produced, except for Eustacia who was sweeping the floor with a broken broom.

'I worry about them a lot,' said Eustacia.

'Me too,' Grace said, 'they're so unsteady now. One of these days . . .'

'We all worry about them,' said Tess.

'One of these days what?' asked Bella.

'They're not going to be able to manage any more,' said Eustacia.

'What about a home?' said Bella, inhaling deeply and passing the spliff to Grace, who took it and said, 'Are you mad?'

'I did once suggest it,' said Eustacia.

'Cyril went mad, didn't he?' said Tess.

'I can't imagine Cyril going mad,' said Bella.

'He went a shade I must describe as magenta,' said Eustacia. 'He was furious. I mean absolutely furious, and I got a long lecture on the importance of the independence of nation states.'

'And Beatrice said she was going to burn down the house if you ever suggested it again, didn't she?' said Grace. 'And I don't think she was joking. She nearly set Cyril on fire by overfilling the grate before we got here. Imagine what she could do if she went to it with a will.'

'It doesn't bear thinking about,' said Eustacia, 'but I'm afraid we must.'

'Well, what are we going to do?' asked Tess.

'What can we do?' asked Grace.

'I don't think very much,' said Eustacia.

'It's impossible,' said Tess.

'Bugger,' said Bella.

'I don't think that we should involve our mother whatever we do,' said Grace. 'Please can we all agree on that.'

'I wouldn't douse that woman if she was on fire,' said Bella.

'I think that's going rather too far,' said Eustacia.

'I know that Mum's not great but she's not that bad,' said Tess.

'She is pretty bad though,' said Grace. 'She couldn't care less about any of us, least of all Cyril and Beatrice.'

'And then,' said Bella, 'while she burnt, I'd stand over her and toast marshmallows.'

'Bella!' said her sisters.

'What?' said Bella.

This is Violet looking at Sam

When Violet got home, Annie was out which was good because Violet didn't feel like any more fighting. She stood in her room and looked at her clothes. Mostly they were on the floor. She took the clothes she was wearing off and put on the things nearest to her, which turned out to be red velvet trousers that were too long so she had sawn lengths off the bottom with scissors and a blue cotton top ringed with horizontal ruffles that she liked because it reminded her of flamenco dancers. Both of these things felt familiar and soft and were of comfort to her. She stirred her way through the clothes sea until she found a purple mohair cardigan that, according to the felt pen marks on the label, had once belonged to someone called Poppy. Violet wondered who Poppy was and if she had jettisoned the cardigan because she had grown out of it or because she had gone off it. Violet liked her clothes to have some sort of imaginary history. The only full-length mirror was in Annie's room. She was tempted now to go and look in it but couldn't make herself. She never looked in the mirror at her outfits; she never looked in the mirror full stop, apart from a quick glance at her face when she brushed her teeth and now and then when she put on eyeliner. Her energy level dipped, and she sat on her bed. Her excitement had waned. Did she even have the strength to go out with someone? Did she want to get to know a new person anyway? She considered giving up on the day and getting into bed and staying there. It would be so much easier. She could only now anticipate that the date might produce anxiety rather than pleasure. Yes, she would do that and pretend this afternoon hadn't happened and when Annie got home she might be able to rouse herself enough to talk to her. She hadn't the strength to cope with anything else. Her phone rang with an unknown number and she picked it up but didn't answer. Her thoughts wheeled around in the opposite direction, as frequently happened to her. Maybe she should try something new, maybe it would be good for her. She had enjoyed the kissing, she might enjoy something more. How would she know if she never tried? Why was she such a wimp? She considered switching her phone off altogether but it rang again and this time she swiped to accept the call.

'Hello,' she said.

'Hi Violet, this is Sam.'

They went to the cinema. Then this is a real date, thought Violet, who watched the film with such little concentration that, if asked, she could have told you that it was set by the sea and nothing more. She was far more concerned about the pressure of Sam's thigh against her own coupled with the worry that Sam would try and take her hand, which was inexplicably clammy. What if she did this and other people saw? What if the secret straight police were watching? But Sam's hands remained in her own lap and Violet was both relieved and disappointed. After the film, Sam invited her back to her flat for coffee and Violet felt the way she had when, after a particularly good trampoline performance, the applause started, a combination of phew, I didn't muck that one up, and hurrah, they like me.

This time they graduated from the sofa to the bedroom.

'I don't want to do anything yet,' said Violet and expected Sam to sigh with impatience but she didn't, she took off her clothes matter of factly as if she was going to bed and then got into the bed.

'Have you got a torch at all?' asked Violet, who had turned her eyes away for propriety's sake, although how propriety might come into this situation she hadn't the faintest.

'Sure,' said Sam and got out of bed and left the room, still naked. Violet slipped a glimpse. Sam had a white bum and brown arms the colour of tea, what her stepfather called a 'farmer's tan', well, not the bum bit, and she tried not to giggle. Wasn't she supposed to feel a frisson, because she felt nothing but a blush. Sam came back into the room and passed a small torch to Violet, who had again found a profound interest in staring at the wall.

'Could you switch off the light, please?'

Sam went and did this, and Violet got into bed on the far side, still fully clothed. She was impressed that Sam could find her way back to her bed in the dark because she never could and always banged her shins. Sam got into the bed.

'And could you lie on your side perhaps?' Violet asked.

'Like this?'

Violet switched the torch on underneath the covers and lit up a cave in which Sam's body lay on its side like an odalisque by Matisse. She ran the light up and down Sam's body, trying to memorize it as though for a land survey. There was a mole on her ribcage underneath her left breast. Bigger than mine, thought Violet, which isn't saying much, and with browner nipples. She had slight stubble on her lengthy legs that reminded Violet of a field of corn near her childhood home after it had been razed, and knobbly knees. She had visible ribs and a flat stomach but wasn't painfully thin. Her pubic hair was fluffy and not wiry and was blond like her head. She might try to draw Sam when she got home. She had no memory for words but a good visual one. When she came up for air, she switched off the torch and reaching over Sam set it on the bedside table.

'I think I could probably draw you now,' she said.

'Another time,' said Sam, and put her hand on Violet's stomach over her trousers. Strangely for such a tiny woman, hers was convex. She ran her hand down between Violet's legs.

'Would you like to take your clothes off or shall I take them off for you?' she asked.

'You,' whispered Violet.

Violet had often been surprised in the past by the ardour of men. Their enthusiasm, their drive. The way they pushed and pulled. Sam didn't do that. First of all, she removed Violet's clothes slowly as though she was unwrapping a Christmas present. Normally Violet didn't like to be naked around a man, she tried to keep at least something on, but by the time Sam pushed down her trousers she was thinking the opposite. Sam unhooked her bra deftly and pulled the straps down. Now Violet was wearing only her knickers, which were her very best ones and violet like her name. Sam started to run her fingers slowly all over Violet's body, as though this was her way of memorizing. Violet lay on her back, her head under the covers, and Sam touched her face, her neck, the line of her arm to her fingertips and back, and then across her breasts, touching each nipple in turn, and down to her stomach. The feel of her fingertips looping over Violet was like being drawn on. After a while she stopped being nervous and started to enjoy the touching and to try and anticipate where it might go next, and by the time that Sam replaced her fingers with her mouth, all of Violet's body was straining up to meet it.

'Would you like to take your knickers off or is this enough?' asked Sam.

For once it was an easy decision for Violet to make.

It was all extraordinary and yet all ordinary, Violet thought afterwards as they went to sleep. It was all artichoke and also all potato. It was nothing like she had expected and yet so familiar, because you were not dealing with the alien anatomy that was a man's body but the same mechanics as your own. Sam did things to her and she did things back, it was reciprocal, their bodies worked in the same ways. It was easier to anticipate what Sam would like, based on Violet's own experience. She knew not to rub a nipple round and round, harder and harder, as though it was a malfunctioning button that would finally function correctly if you managed to work up enough friction. She knew that clitorises did not respond well to the same kind of treatment either. When she came she saw colours – red, blue and green – and when, copying what Sam did, Sam came, Violet felt a sense of achievement that she had never known with a man. Now I know what my own body feels like to be touched, she thought, and I didn't know what that felt like before. How soft we are, how intricate. You would have thought that I would have grasped this already but I never have. It was more sensual and less pornographic, less about parts and more about skin on skin, more like a painting and less like a film. Yes, it felt like a painting, as though it was a long afternoon in June in the shade on a riverbank and we had all the time in the world. And Violet remembered the book of Klimt she had at home, the women entwined around each other, and understood now how accurate that was. For once she hadn't felt embarrassed by her smallness either; although Sam was much taller than her it had been sex between equals, compatriots and not enemies engaged in a battle for an orgasm. She had liked it very much. And she hadn't felt the need to run away home afterwards either, quite the opposite; she had stayed the night, her back against Sam's front, Sam's arm around her, and she would have happily stayed past breakfast if Sam hadn't had to go to work. I need to tell Annie about this, she thought, I must get home now and tell her, she will definitely want to know, having forgotten that Annie had left her in the park the day before.

This is Grace and the goodbye

Back down the long drive, the monstrous house receding, and Beatrice, standing on the doorstep, getting smaller and smaller. Nearly all of her family had kissed her goodbye in various combinations of single and double kisses and Grace had felt bombarded. Augusta had even hugged her round the thighs and told her she didn't want her to leave. The twins had shaken hands.

'Well, Cyril was much better than I thought he would be,' said Eustacia.

'That's something,' said Grace, trying to avoid the potholes, and thinking that it was unimaginable that one day this would no longer be 'theirs'. It was impossible to think of it belonging to anyone else, impossible not to imagine Cyril and Beatrice still tottering around its draughty hallways. She remembered the depths of winter there, how they would run in layers of unravelling jumpers from grate to grate and bed down next to them with the lurchers for warmth.

'Remember "bogging with the dogging"? What happened to that home help you got?'

'Beatrice frightened her off as soon as she could. She thought the house was haunted.'

'It is haunted.'

'They need help. We need to do something but I don't know what.'

Grace had never heard her sister sound so frustrated.

'It's hard to help people who think that help is the enemy. At least the horses have all gone now so there's not that to worry about any more.'

'I suppose so. I was thinking. What about if one of us moved in?'

'You what? Are you mad?'

'I've been thinking about it. Jeremy and I could rent our house out, move here.'

'You are mad,' said Grace.

'You already said that,' said Eustacia. 'And I was thinking that well, you might like to come too.'

'Then you have reached the point of insanity and I, even in my professional capacity, can do nothing more to help you.'

'Well, there's no way that Bella is going to move, and Tess can't what with the farm, and after all they've got families and it's too hard to uproot them. We haven't. It's our responsibility.'

'No, it's not. Well, not just ours. And it would never work!'

'Why not? You could even bring Sam if you wanted to. I'm sure you could both find jobs somewhere. We don't have to talk about it any more now. Just think about it. Please say you'll just think about it.'

'I think you're insane. It would be like an eccentric commune.'

'No worse than our childhood. And there's so much room, it's not as if we'd be bumping into each other all the time.'

'Have you mentioned this whacked-out idea to them?'

'No, of course not, I wanted to talk to you first.'

'Humph.'

'Does that mean you'll think about it? Because honestly, Grace, I can't think of anything else.'

Grace puffed air out of her mouth in the way of someone bamboozled by life.

'Grace,' said Eustacia, 'can I ask you something else without you getting offended?'

'You couldn't offend me if you tried.'

'It's about Sam. I haven't met her yet and I would like to. Is there some kind of problem?'

'We've just been busy, you know how it is.'

'I know you've got a lot on but couldn't you come for an afternoon? Or I could come to Leeds, we could go to that arts café we went to last time. Have you taken Sam there?'

'No. I mean no, I haven't taken her there. I'll ask Sam about visiting. I promise.'

'Lovely,' said Eustacia but Grace felt guilty.

This is Violet and her decision to go un-operatic

When Violet got home, Annie was cooking curry even though it was only 10 a.m. on a Saturday and normally Annie would still be in bed and when she did eventually get up would eat toast like she always did. Annie's cooking style was incomprehensible, as it seemed to involve making loads of mess for little result. The honest evaluation that Annie expected after the event could also be traumatic. She was fine when she stuck to roasts or pasta, but then she got it into her head to do things involving bok choi or pine nuts and she didn't seem to be able to follow a recipe but always said 'bugger it' halfway through and started chucking in random items. Violet couldn't understand how Annie, famed for her logic, could cook like this.

'How come you're cooking now?' asked Violet. Annie ignored her. 'Any for me?' asked Violet, who found that she was starving and therefore willing to face the inevitable weirdness.

'No,' said Annie, stirring the saucepan full of bubbling things and switching off the burning rice.

'You always make too much.'

'Not this time,' said Annie, spooning dollops from the saucepans on to her plate, leaving most of it behind. She got a knife and fork out of the drawer and went to the sofa and switched on the TV. She never ate in front of the TV and Violet knew that was because Annie's mum thought it was common and that you might drop things on the carpet or God forbid the sofa. She never watched it in the daytime either.

'What's the matter?' asked Violet.

'There's something I want to watch,' said Annie, changing channels.

'Annie, I . . .' said Violet.

'You what?'

'I went to the cinema.'

Annie was always interested, it was one of her best characteristics, and she always listened properly and analysed everything and so everything that Violet did was witnessed and repeated back to her and she could look at it more dispassionately and attempt to make sense of it. She was so used to having Annie's opinion that she took this for granted. But this time Annie didn't even look at her. Violet considered her options.

1. She could go and stand in front of Annie and force her into a conversation.
2. She could pick up the saucepan and empty the contents over Annie's pretty head.
3. She could leave the flat with a degree of operatic intensity completely alien to her. But where could she go? She couldn't go back to Sam's and she was too tired to go to a café and she didn't like pubs and wasn't it too early for them anyway? Back to the park bench from yesterday? But then Sam might think she was stalking her. I want her to like me, Violet realized.
4. She could go to her room.

There seemed to be only one viable option open to her personality type, so she went to the fridge and looked at her shelf for something to do. A jar of capers and two yoghurts, all out of date. She took the jar and crept off to her room. Now instead of feeling good she felt rubbish, as if 'the fear' was creeping up on her again. It had seemed to be a bit better. The woman seemed to help. Or maybe it was just having something else to focus on. That was good. Why couldn't Annie see that? After the capers, which she ate even though she didn't want to, she put on Leftfield, but only quietly in case it upset Annie, and listened for a while and wondered why Annie, who was never weird, was being weird. She found a pencil and drew a picture of Sam's back from memory. She pushed it into the piles of other drawings on her desk. Then she got into bed and pulled the duvet right up to her ears. I have slept with a woman for the first time, she thought. This could be counted as a momentous occasion except that I have no one to speak to about it apart from Annie who is sulking for some reason I don't understand and who therefore won't listen, and my mother who I can't bear to tell. It was all so strange. She closed her eyes and fell asleep.

This is Grace and the problem of the inability to mix

'I don't believe in this patriarchal hegemony,' said a friend of Sam's called Ned. He had a man bun which evinced immediate distrust in Grace and wore braces over his shirt. He looked like he was in a folky sort of band but he was a graphic designer/ hairdresser apparently. Sam's friends seemed heavy on the 'I'm a freelancer', or 'I do something digital' or 'I have multiple occupations all of them cool'. To be honest she wasn't that keen on Sam's friends – they were what Grace would have described as 'trendy', even though 'trendy' wasn't a word she had heard used since school and was a word she was sure they wouldn't ascribe to themselves. She might also have gone for 'pretentious' if pushed.

'Yeah, it's all like very non-representational,' said another of her friends whose name was Ellie, a girl with greyish-pink hair in plaits. She too was a slasher – some sort of florist/website creator. 'I'm a floral designer,' she said, and looked at Grace as if she couldn't possibly know what one of them was. Grace found that when she was asked for her opinion by these people she had the same sort of stomach pain as when asked by a nun in geography exactly where Jakarta was. 'Um,' she found herself saying a lot, 'er'. When did she get so tongue-tied? After a while she noticed that if she said nothing at all, no one seemed to care, and she was ignored completely, as if she wasn't even sitting there. This was probably better but made her very uncomfortable. Occasionally Sam would try to bring her back into the conversation but sometimes she seemed to forget, leaning across her to make her point and Grace felt completely invisible.

Sam liked to hang out with these friends in bars with school chairs and mismatched tables whose legs, much to Grace's frustration, were wonky on the cement floors. Bars next to expensive barbers with old-fashioned chairs in, bars with bare brick walls and artistic photos on the walls of derelict buildings and names like 'Space Dog'. 'I'm just going down to the dog,' Sam would say and did not seem to find that funny. 'Want to come?' Er, thought Grace, um, well, no. 'OK,' she said, even though these places seemed to be permeated with the smell of pulled pork and only served something called 'craft beer'. What was wrong with a normal type of pub? She felt that these people looked down on her. She found Sam's friends cold and this confused her because Sam wasn't cold at all.

One night they went out with Ellie to a gay club in town. Ellie had been friends with Sam since Sam came to Leeds and Grace tried not to be jealous of that. She also tried not to think that awful thought that they had once had a thing. Grace didn't mind the club, she liked the feel of the bass coming up through her shoes, but she wasn't a great dancer.

'I'll just stay here,' she said to Sam.

'OK,' said Sam, not seeming bothered, and went to dance with Ellie in a close way that seemed much too familiar. Grace was left standing with her back to the wall holding her drink, smiling at nothing, trying not to stare at anybody in an unusual outfit. She felt horribly exposed; she was obviously not meant to be there. A girl with a short skirt who must have been all of twenty came over and stood next to Grace.

'Do you want to dance?' said the girl.

'What?' said Grace. The music was so loud she couldn't hear properly.

The girl put her mouth near Grace's ear and shouted into it, 'Do you want to dance?' and then to Grace's surprise licked her ear. Grace flinched away, and the girl grinned. 'I like older women,' said the girl. 'You're sexy.'

'What?' said Grace.

'I like you, you're sexy,' yelled the girl into her ear. The bass was building.

'Er,' said Grace, 'er, no.'

'Yes, you are,' said the girl.

'I can't dance with you. My girlfriend's over there,' said Grace to get herself out of this uncomfortable situation.

'Where?'

Grace pointed to Sam, who was dancing in a group of men with very few clothes on.

'She's sexy too,' said the girl. 'Come on, let's dance.'

Grace had always been very poor at saying no to the insistent.

'I'm too old,' she said. 'To dance,' although she meant 'for you to be chatting me up, dear'.

'No, you're not!'

'I think I am.'

'Oh OK, I get it, you don't like me.'

'I've got a girlfriend,' said Grace weakly.

'Right then,' and the girl moved off. Grace felt bad for having offended her. She considered going after her to explain things more clearly but the girl was no longer to be seen.

'Who was that girl?' Sam shouted into Grace's ear when she came back.

'I don't know, she asked me to dance,' Grace yelled back.

'Why didn't you go?'

'I didn't want to. Anyway, wouldn't you mind?'

'Why should I mind? Don't you want to dance?'

'I'm all right here.'

Ellie came up and pushed something into Grace's hand.

'Take this,' she shouted, grinning. Grace looked at her palm with the little white pill on top of it.

'I don't want to,' shouted Grace.

'What? I can't hear you,' Ellie shouted.

'I'm not going to take this.'

'Haven't you ever taken one before?' shouted Sam.

'No, and I don't want to start.'

'Fair enough,' Sam mouthed, and she went away with Ellie again, and they disappeared into the crowd and Grace was left against the wall, not knowing what to do with the pill or with herself for that matter. In the end, she dropped the pill on the floor and crushed it under her boot and left without saying goodbye to teach Sam a lesson. What lesson? That she shouldn't be abandoned? That Sam should mind her getting chatted up? That Ellie was a bad influence? Grace had a headache. As she walked back to her car she thought, I would much rather have been with my sisters in the palm house having a nice scone and a good cup of tea. She went home, expecting Sam to ring her soon, but then Grace fell asleep and when she woke up in the morning Sam still hadn't rung and Grace felt a surge of panic and rang her. It took a while for Sam to reach the phone.

'Are you all right?' asked Grace.

'Sure, why wouldn't I be? Where did you go?' Sam asked, sounding sleepy but not especially interested.

'Home,' Grace said to underline a point. Home alone. You let me go home alone.

'Didn't you have a good time?' said Sam.

'No. No, I didn't.'

'Then I won't take you again.'

Sam didn't seem bothered and Grace resented this although she was moderately pleased with herself for showing that she had boundaries. They never went to another club and Sam stopped asking her to go out with her friends. I don't want to go anyway, thought Grace, but it would still be nice to be asked. She invited Sam out with her friends but Sam always seemed to be too busy. This disconcerted Grace no end – this inability to mix their social circles, but what could she do? Nothing, it seemed.

'I've got to meet Ned, he's DJ-ing.'

'I didn't know he did that too. I could come there later,' said Grace.

'Don't worry, I know you've got an early start,' said Sam.

'I could bring Dolores. Or my friend Marcia, she's into music. Or Andy, you'll like Andy, he's funny. I'll get a couple of people together, I haven't gone out with any of them for ages. What time?'

'Are you sure that's their sort of thing? It's very experimental.'

'Sounds interesting.'

'Might not be their cup of tea.'

'What sort of music?'

'It's a fusion.'

'Of what?'

'This and that.'

Why don't you just say that you don't want us to come, thought Grace. That my friends aren't cool enough for you. That the three-year age gap between us is apparently some kind of unjumpable gulf. They're so young and hip and we, the over-thirties, would be better off with an evening in our slippers listening to something classical. Why don't you just say that?

Every time Grace mentioned the possibility of them visiting Eustacia or going to Tess's farm, Sam came up with an excuse. It got so that Grace was embarrassed to ask but she persisted. Her family were important to her; how could Sam know her properly if she didn't know them? Unless Sam didn't want to know her properly. And Grace felt a lurch of something she couldn't name. No, that couldn't be it. Sam didn't do family, she'd said that, it wasn't just Grace's family, it was a general rule and Grace would have to accept that. Maybe though they could try something more casual than a full-on visit. They could go to Bettys in York with Bella and Augusta for tea and cake. That wasn't too much to ask, surely. Sam said no. It was as if Grace was banging her head against a brick wall while denying that the wall was there.

This is Annie in therapy

'So that's what I said to him,' said Annie to Grace.

'And how do you feel about that?'

'It's not that I don't care about him, I do. I like him a lot. I just don't do love.'

'Would you say that you don't feel love or that you don't express love?'

'I love people but I just don't feel the need to tell them I do all the time.'

'Have you ever told someone you love them?'

'No, never. And I don't see why I should bloody start now.'

'You seem upset, Annie.'

'It was like he was expecting something from me that I couldn't give him. Like a baby bird expecting food from its mother.'

'That's a very interesting analogy.'

'Because we were talking about children?'

'Do you find it difficult when someone expects a lot from you?'

'I do enough of that at work. Living up to people's expectations. I did enough of it in my childhood too. My mother always expected so much of us.'

To Annie's chagrin she seemed to spend most of her time in therapy complaining about her mother.

'And your father?' asked Grace.

Annie had come to like her. She seemed calm, never surprised by anything and never looked at you as if to say, 'Why the hell did you say that?'

'He's a good person. He adores my mother. Does everything she wants. My biggest memory of him from when I was a kid, though, was him having to drop his work clothes, including his socks, at the back door and go upstairs in his underpants as soon as he came in so as not to get dirt anywhere. She couldn't abide dirt. I mean the sofa was wrapped in plastic, for God's sake! I'm talking about her again, aren't I? I like my dad, I do, it's . . .'

'Yes?'

'I think he's weak. Easily pushed around. He should stand up to my mum more. Do more stuff because he wants to do it. Not because she does.'

'Is there an example you could give me?'

'Well, there's this thing that's weird, well, I think it's weird knowing them: he was in this band with her when they were young. Twenties, before they had me. They did well round our way. Working men's clubs, that kind of thing. But they stopped it. I only know this because he told me once when he was the worse for wear. Lady V and the Dreamers. I can't work out if I like it or not. My mum – she's amazingly beautiful. Like a film star. And apparently, she could sing, though I've never heard her in my life. She's always been more interested in telling us off than singing.'

'And so then what happened?'

'She got pregnant. And after that maybe she didn't think it was a suitable thing. I mean, they didn't make any money, as far as I know. It was a laugh, my dad said. I don't think, don't get me wrong, I admire my mum, that his life has had a lot of fun in it.

Nailbrushes and the application of perfectly straight wallpaper to suit my mum's demands yes. Fun no. And I reckon he'd have liked to get back to the band but it was always my mum's decisions about everything. I don't want to be like her, that's part of it, the reason I don't want to have kids. I don't want to have to give up my life in the way she did. I might want to one day, but not right now. And she's on at me all the time. Even about living with Violet, I told you about Violet, didn't I? We have a good time together even if we aren't speaking that much.'

'Is there a reason for that?'

'She's got this girlfriend and I don't like her. I don't trust her. She's using Violet. She's that type. But Violet, how can I explain about her? She's easily led, that's the thing. She hasn't been very happy recently and then this woman came along, and I suppose swept her off her feet is the way to say it although that does sound dead old-fashioned. She's not even a lesbian, I think. Violet, that is. She's just got taken over by someone with a stronger personality than her. And there's nothing I can do although I've got a bad feeling about this woman, I'm worried that Violet is going to end up getting hurt.'

'And how do you feel about that?'

'Fucking frustrated.' There was a silence. 'Sorry for swearing,' said Annie.

'It's not a problem, Annie. It sounds like there're a lot of stressful events going on in your life right now.'

'And I haven't even told you about Dubai.'

'Yes?'

'I got headhunted. About four months ago. It's a big firm and the money's amazing.'

'That sounds good.'

'But it would mean travelling. They've got a lot of offices. Shanghai. Dubai. New York. All over the place. I'd have to move to one of them.'

'Is that a problem?'

'Well, I don't think I'm a great flyer but that's not really it.'

'Then . . .'

'I said no.'

'Could you tell me why?'

'How am I going to tell my mum? By the way, not interested in families at all, I'm going off jetting around the world.'

'She might not have the reaction that you're expecting.'

'You don't know my mum. She may well be proud of me and my job but she'd never say it. And she wants me to have kids so much she's blind to anything else. That's one thing. And then there's Violet. I don't know what to do about Violet. I couldn't leave her on her own. She'd . . . well, God only knows what she'd do.'

'But you would like this job?'

'I'd love it. I'd really love it. But there's no way.'

'And Laurence?'

'He may be the best chance I'll ever have. I should know better than to walk away from that. And I do like him, I like him a lot.'

This is Grace asking the wrong thing

They went fishing. Sam loved fishing. Grace didn't know what she felt about it until she tried it. That was Sam's advice to her as though it was truffles she was about to eat or tripe. Grace had already tried various things with Sam that she hadn't tried before and none of them had worked out well. The climbing wall had been a horrible experience for a woman with little upper body strength. She found herself halfway up it being shouted at by an instructor and Sam. 'Put your leg there! No, there!' and she looked at where she was supposed to put her leg and thought that they must be joking. By the time she got back down she was shaking all over. Sam patted her on the back and said, 'It'll be better next time, I promise.' The weed that they smoked together one evening was so strong that Grace was sick in Sam's loo. She had no interest whatsoever in looking at pictures of naked women as Sam had once suggested. And fishing, she found, was sitting for hours by the side of a river staring at the water in complete silence. Grace thought that if she had liked complete silence then she'd have been a Quaker. She hoped Sam wasn't going to take her there too. They caught a fish in the end, or rather Sam did but she took the hook out of the fish's mouth and threw it back. Why? Because she was semi-vegetarian and because she didn't like killing fish. It baffled Grace. She thought it was stupid but of course she didn't tell Sam that. She didn't tell her about the fox-hunting she'd done as a child either or how she had once shot a rabbit. That's not a good thing, she thought – when you start to edit yourself to fit. What was she afraid of? It was an easy question to answer. She was always afraid that Sam would find her boring and unadventurous, the kind of person who didn't enjoy new things. This thought depressed her. She was too set in her ways, she was too conventional.

And yet, and yet, in spite of the things that were difficult and that she didn't like, there were so many that she did. The shape of her hands, the smell of her shampoo, the way she bit her toothbrush into nothing, the dip of her back, these were the things that made her love Sam so why should it matter that there were things they didn't agree on? Sam sometimes farted very quietly in her sleep – you could find it funny or you could find it disgusting. Grace found it endearing. Wasn't there ultimately a level of choice involved in being with someone? This was what love was like for real, not the fairytale love, but the real, deep love that she had longed for; it was a weighing up of the good and the bad and deciding that the good won hands down. You chose to be with somebody because you accepted them as they were, faults and all, just as they accepted your foibles. And she knew that despite the things that didn't work, she loved Sam, and that now it would be impossible to be without her. And so she asked Sam about living together. Not marriage like Manfred had suggested, just living together. It was surely best to take things one step at a time. It took days to find the right words. They were sitting on Grace's sofa after a weekend that had involved so much sex it had left Grace worn out and longing only for a box set and a cup of tea.

'I was wondering if you might consider us living together?'

'Not my thing,' Sam said, and started to bounce her mug on her knee.

'Why not?' Grace asked.

'I like my own space,' Sam said and bit at the side of her thumbnail as though that was more interesting than the place this conversation might be going.

'You could move in here? You like this house, don't you?'

'I don't want to move in here,' said Sam.

'Or I could move to yours if you'd prefer that, sell this,' said Grace.

'No,' said Sam, looking at the bookshelf in front of her. 'I didn't know you had *Great Expectations*.'

'It's your copy. You left it here. Or we could buy somewhere else. We could have a garden perhaps and you could grow flowers. Or vegetables. You'd like that, wouldn't you? You could even have a room of your own if you wanted to put all your stuff in. A retreat from me.'

'No,' said Sam, and she got up and went over and picked her book off the shelf.

'Could you tell me why not?' Grace bit her bottom lip.

'I just told you,' said Sam, flicking through her book, 'I like my own space and doing my own thing. It's not a criticism of you, Grace, it's just the way I am.'

'Don't fence me in?' asked Grace.

And Grace laughed but it was a nervous laugh. And then Sam laughed too and came back over and sat on the sofa and pulled Grace down on to her so that they touched in as many places as possible. Which was her inoffensive way of shutting Grace up. It worked well. Grace didn't mention it again, but in her head she was in for the long haul and hoped that at a point in the indeterminate future Sam might change her mind. After all, Sam always liked her little house and the fact that it was a house and not a flat. She used to sit on the stairs to read and Grace would bring her up a cup of her grim tea and set it down on the step next to her feet, which Grace badly wanted to lay her head down on as though she too was an offering. The Catholicism must have stuck after all.

It was only a week later, and they had gone into the Co-op on the way back from the cinema when Grace saw that a furniture shop had opened next door. She looked in the window. There was one of those big kitchen clocks that imitate the old-fashioned ones in railway stations. She had always wanted one of those.

'Do you like this clock?' asked Grace.

'Sure,' said Sam.

'I might get it,' said Grace.

She went into the shop and Sam followed her and by the time she left she had the clock, a blue lamp, and two plaited rugs. Grace loved those things with a love disproportionate to their real value because she thought of them as 'ours'. Every time she stood on a rug or looked for the time she felt a glow of satisfaction and yes, hope. Maybe she will come and live with me. Maybe she will change her mind. Shadows of her early unrequited longings must have stuck with her and carried over so that she was once again grasping at someone out of her reach, except that this time the object of her affections was so near.

She had read once, she didn't know where, that in a relationship there is always one person who loves more than the other, there is a loving one and a beloved, an adoring and an adored, and she came to believe that this was true and at the time, she didn't care that she was on the losing side. She was glad to be allowed to adore Sam. She would have paid money to be able to do so.

This is Violet and gaiety

They never seemed to make it out of the house, but Violet didn't mind that, it always felt safer for her to be inside and she didn't know what the etiquette of being with a woman in public might be anyway.

'Have you always been a lesbian?' asked Violet as she stood swinging the kitchen door back and forth watching Sam make tea.

'Yes.'

'How did you know what you were?'

'I always did,' said Sam and shrugged.

'You're lucky, I think.'

'You don't have to define yourself if you don't want to, you know,' and Sam put her arm around Violet's shoulder. 'It's not necessary.'

'Isn't it? I don't really know what I am.'

'And does it matter?'

This conversation was making Violet uncomfortable and so she changed the subject.

'What do you like about your job?'

'It's good for my body and my mind.' Sam took her arm away and put some glasses in a cupboard. 'I like being outside. I like being knackered at the end of the day. I like plants and mowing the grass. I like all of it. What do you like about yours?'

'The shop's warm I suppose. And most of the time I can sit down on a stool behind the counter. And it smells of lavender essential oil which I don't mind.'

As Violet heard herself speak she realized how pathetic this sounded. She was supposed to have found something she wanted to do by now, wasn't that what people did? Found a career, whatever it might be. Stick to it. Like Sam, like Annie. God knows what Annie would have said to that list but Sam didn't ridicule it.

'Fair enough,' she said and went back to the kettle.

Violet liked sex with Sam, much more than she had expected. Which led her to believe that either she must be a lesbian, or bisexual, or that Sam must be really good in bed or that they were especially compatible. Or all of these things. Who was to figure that out without Annie's help? Sam didn't suggest things to her like men did, or worse still, produce stuff from under the bed; there were no requests to wear nurse's outfits or lingerie, there were no rough words during sex, she was not made uncomfortable by being ogled, it was no longer a matter of what fitted where. Sam's cheeks did not abrade Violet's or her fingers scrape. Sam was careful with her, there was nothing rough about it. For the first time in her life Violet felt caressed. Not as if, because of her size, she was so tiny as to be easily breakable, which is how some men had behaved with her, but carefully, because that was how Sam seemed to do everything, carefully and with focus. Violet watched Sam care for her plants with tenderness and felt like she was being treated the same way. She reviewed her past experiences and realized how much she had had to tolerate being touched by men before. How they had always been too big or too heavy and how she had often felt her pulse race when she was with them, not out of desire, but out of fear. You are going to squash me, she often thought, and sometimes even, I am going to suffocate. It was

such a basic thing to be afraid of. She was shocked by this realization. Even though Sam was tall she was not heavy, she was
what Violet's mother would have described as 'willowy', and it
never felt as if she was pressing Violet down, instead Violet felt
like she was being held and yes, it felt like she was being appreciated and wanted and even perhaps loved. If only there was
someone to tell this to apart from Annie, because Annie still
wasn't talking to her apart from basic instructions such as 'Take
the bin out. It's your turn.' This had never happened between
them before and Violet was shocked. If Annie was upset, she
would normally be forthright about it in a way that could be
wounding. She had thrown things before, if not directly at
Violet, then in the vicinity. She had no British reserve. She
liked to say that even though she came from Lancashire there
was Italian in there somewhere, and to look at her olive skin
this might be true. Violet couldn't think of what to do apart
from start a direct confrontation and she was incapable of that.
Who was she going to tell about Sam though if not Annie? She
thought about ringing her mother but couldn't face it. She had
always protected her from her encounters. Her mother might
be embarrassed or not know what to say and that would be
awkward. Plus how could she describe it to her? The mere
thought made the sex talk she had had with her last time look
easy. She thought about trying to bring it up in an average conversation, in the shop for example, she could drop it in while
talking to Starchild, 'Oh yeah, my girlfriend and me,' but felt
too uncomfortable about that. It didn't seem a suitable subject
for those of her friends who were of older years, even if they
might well be more liberal than she imagined. Is she my girlfriend? Is that even the correct word? She had no one else to ask
then but Sam and that seemed stupidly circular.

Violet was standing in the art gallery looking at a painting
by Paula Rego and marvelling at the stance of the artist that

was portrayed. She sat with her back against a table and with one elbow on it, and she was smoking a pipe, but it was her legs that amazed Violet, which were wide open in a masculine way and completely covered in a long bright red skirt on one side. On the other side, you could see her leg encased in a knee-length black boot. She had always liked Paula Rego, her scary fairytale fantasies, but there was something about this woman that she loved. Maybe because women are never painted like that. The woman was confident and relaxed at the same time; she was the opposite of many of the women in paintings by men who reclined erotically before the male gaze. Violet remembered how she had made Sam lie on her side the first time they had had sex and she blushed to remember it. This woman wasn't reclining because she wanted to be looked at, she was lying back because she owned her world and everything in it.

Violet loved the art gallery and always came by herself. Annie wasn't much into art and so had never come with her; Sam liked the Impressionists but she hadn't asked her to come yet. Going there had become a private thing, just for her. She could stand in front of one painting for an hour or two if she wanted. She could spend all day. Often she brought one of her sketchbooks and copied something. It was always a part of the body or clothing. An elbow. A neck. A shoe. It was a calm, contemplative place where no one bothered you, hushed and low-lit, safe from the world. It was where she came to think.

She thought about the letter she had received this morning, together with a note from her mother. 'Got this yesterday,' said her mother's note, 'and thought you should have it straight away. I'm sorry for not having phoned about it but I'm so busy,' and this seemed, after Violet had read it and the letter, even more extraordinary than the letter itself which was extraordinary enough on its own.

Dear Violet

I hope this letter reaches you, I have only your grandmother's
address. I am writing to you but I do not know if you are aware
that I am your biological father. I hope your mother told you so
that this will be less of a shock to you. I do not want to interrupt your life but I have things I need to say to you. I am dying,
I have cancer, and I don't want to be dead before seeing you. I
live in St Malo and it is not so hard to reach from England.
Please ring this number and you can speak to my wife. She will
arrange things for you. I'm sorry I cannot speak on the phone,
I am not having very good days at the moment. Please phone.
I would like so much to see you.

Jean Claude

She thought about her dad. The letter included a photo, as
though for evidence; she had never seen one before, always
assumed that none existed. In it he was holding a baby-shaped
bundle which must have been her and he seemed small, which
would explain a lot, and was skinny and wore a tight T-shirt
and tight jeans and a leather hat. He looked like a hippy. She
knew next to nothing about him, only the bare details she
had wheedled out of her mother when she was younger. Her
mother had said that he had been an antiques dealer but she
obviously didn't know if he still was. She had met him on a
French exchange trip. She wasn't happy in France and she
had come back to England for a visit when Violet was four
months old and that was that. It was easy to lose touch then,
before the internet, her mother had said, and I was too worn
out to protest when I got back home, and I was only nineteen
and anyway your grandmother didn't want me to stay in contact and so I gave in and I never saw him again. He stopped
writing and phoning and that was that. But then a neighbour

from next to Violet's grandmother's old home had passed on this letter.

He might be dead by now of course. 'I'm so busy,' her mother had said, she hadn't even phoned to warn her the letter was coming. Violet couldn't understand that, and she couldn't work out what she was supposed to feel or do, and she couldn't work out either why she couldn't talk about this with Annie, with whom she always talked about everything. Should I think about going to France? Shouldn't I? Should I? Shouldn't I? She looked at the artist in the painting and wished that was her, she didn't look like a woman who had any problems deciding anything. She felt a wave of anxiety that she normally was cushioned from by the paintings. 'The fear' had been only intermittent and therefore easier to cope with since she had met Sam. She had thought she was getting on top of it and was pleased about that because she hadn't needed help to do so, not even Annie's. She hadn't even needed to warn Sam about it. Perhaps, if she was lucky, it would go away completely. She sat down on a bench.

Annie. Annie. Annie. Come back to me, Violet thought, please, please come back. I really need to talk to you.

These are Sam's parents

It was a lovely thing about Grace's family, she believed, that no one had ever had the least bad thing to say about her being a lesbian, in fact no one had ever said anything at all. Eustacia has a low tolerance for dirt and enjoys needlepoint. Bella wants to grow up to be 'a muse' like Beatrice had once been and is the local area's best clay pigeon shooter. Tess is good at knitting ugly jumpers and has a crystal collection. Grace is gay. It was merely one more fact. She had had no closet to fall out of, no skeletons to reveal. Even her mother had never said anything offensive, which was probably a sign less of her openness and more of her complete disinterest in any other human being apart from herself. Grace had long taken this for granted, although she knew most people were not as lucky and she saw this first hand with Sam.

'I've got to go and visit my parents. Want to come?' she said to Grace, and Grace was shocked. Her next thought was, but why should I come? You don't want to see my family, I've asked and asked, and you've refused every time. She remembered the moment when she'd asked Sam to go with her to Ravel Corner and how callous Sam had seemed. 'Sure,' she said and took Sam's hand, deciding to be magnanimous and hoping that Sam would return the favour she was giving her. After all, she would meet Sam's family, it was exciting. She could find out all sorts of things about Sam that she didn't already know.

'It'd be better if you didn't touch me while we're there,' Sam said.

Grace let go of her hand. Good God, what would happen if they did? Would they be thrown out of the house? Tarred and feathered on the front lawn?

'It's a long way to go to Shrewsbury and back. Aren't we going to spend the night?'

'No,' said Sam, but didn't explain.

The house was a semi-detached at the end of a cul-de-sac, the tiny front lawn manicured, net curtains in the windows, and a Neighbourhood Watch sticker on the front door. Inside it was too hot and the décor was overwhelmingly chintzy; Grace felt as if she was in a greenhouse and sweat started to build under her arms. Sam's mother was a small woman with hair lacquered into a helmet; her father was tall and ex-army and had a ginger moustache. Sam looked like neither of them. They shook hands with Grace – Sam's dad's handshake was a tight grip, almost painful. Sam and her mother went into the kitchen to make tea, leaving Grace sunk into soft upholstery while marvelling at the number of porcelain dog ornaments. If you liked dogs that much, then how come you didn't have one? Grace realized that Sam's father was staring at her.

'Have you ever been up to Leeds?' she asked him.

'No,' he said.

Grace waited for a further comment but nothing was forthcoming. He continued to stare.

'This is a nice house. I've never been to Shrewsbury before. Have you lived here long?'

'Yes,' he said.

I know what's wrong, she thought, I'm asking closed questions.

'What was Sam like when she was little?'

Sam's dad stared at her.

'Little,' he said.

I can play rude too, thought Grace. I can play unfriendly if that's what you want. They sat in silence, Sam's father staring at Grace, Grace staring at the dogs, until Sam's mother bustled in with the tea things, Sam trailing her.

'Your cousin Helen's getting married, did I tell you?' she asked Sam as she handed round the cups of tea, without asking Grace if she took milk or sugar.

'No,' said Sam.

'They're having a marquee in the garden which I'm never sure is a good idea because if it rains you're all stuck inside, and I can't stand portaloos. And, of course, they'll be wanting to have children soon, won't they, Rupert?'

'At least they're doing things the right way round,' he said.

'Oh yes, it's awful isn't it when children have to go to their own parents' wedding. It's not right.'

'Not right at all.'

'And Lucy, you know Lucy, Susan's daughter from the end of the road, well, she's having a little one soon, isn't she, Rupert?'

'Must be about ready to pop by the look of her.'

'Susan's so excited. She's over the moon. She wants it to be called Rosemary after her mother, doesn't she, Rupert? You like that name, don't you?'

'Traditional.'

Grace ate the ginger cake as neatly as she could and drank the Earl Grey out of the bone china. Sam sat there fiddling with cake crumbs and didn't even look at Grace, while her mother asked about what to do with her borders and told her other bits of family news. Grace stuffed herself on the cake, the names of aunts, and the occupations of cousins. Sam's father continued to stare at Grace, Sam's mother to witter on. Grace felt the sweat running down her spine and her head starting to itch. She resisted the urge to scratch and wondered if there was any point her speaking at all. She decided not and nobody seemed to notice. It was as though she wasn't there until Sam's mother suddenly asked her, after not having asked her anything about herself, if she wanted to look at the photo albums. There were page upon page of Sams. A regular, labelled progression of them. Not like her own family's messy faded scrapbooks where children temporarily disappeared for months or years, as though fostered out for a while in a Dickensian poverty moment. For the first time, she understood that being an only child must be like being under a microscope. All that attention focused on you. This is Samantha on the beach in Dorset. This is Samantha playing in the garden. This is Samantha getting her A level results. She realized then why she was being shown them – this is what Samantha looked like before she took up with the likes of you. Sam's mother was subtler than she had thought. Those albums were a shrine to a daughter they used to have, before she went astray. Grace wanted to ask if she could take the albums home with her but she couldn't see any of them agreeing to that. To her disappointment, she couldn't even manage to pocket one photo. Sam said she had to get back for work tomorrow. Her parents didn't ask her how was work. It wasn't just Grace whose life was being brushed over. Grace half wanted to say something rude along the lines of, 'Your daughter likes pussy then?' and the thought nearly made her laugh. She smothered her smile and went to shake hands again when they left. Sam's father's grip was painful this time.

'It was so hot,' said Grace, as they drove back up the motorway. 'Is it always that hot?'

'Yes,' said Sam, and looked out of the window. She said nothing else for the whole journey until she indicated a layby and Grace pulled over.

'Are you OK?' Grace said. 'Do you feel sick?'

Sam said nothing, just put her hand on the top button of Grace's jeans and unbuttoned it.

'Here?' said Grace. 'But there are cars.'

Sam put her mouth on Grace's neck and bit hard enough to make Grace squeak. They did things to each other in the back seat that Sam's father would have turned grey at, but Sam never said a word. They drove the rest of the way home in silence until Sam said, 'Can you drop me off at mine?'

'Yes,' said Grace.

As Sam got out of the car Grace said, 'Can I ask you something?'

'OK,' said Sam, who looked very tired.

'Why did you take me there?'

Sam shrugged.

'Just thought you might like to come,' she said, and she shut the door and went into her house, leaving Grace with the engine still running. I hadn't finished my questions, thought Grace. I've just endured hours of driving plus hours of low-level aggression for nothing but some good ginger cake. You could at least say thank you. By the time she had got home though, Grace had made allowances for parental stress. No wonder Sam wasn't keen on families; who could blame her. She couldn't work out why Sam had taken her, though. As a buffer, to take some of the heat off her? Was that a very selfish thing to do or just a sensible one? Or was it to punish her parents? To shove it up their noses? That was a possibility too. Thank God I didn't have to grow up like that, she thought. Thank God for Cyril and Beatrice. Or perhaps Sam did it to hurt her? She ignored the last thought.

This is Annie listening to Laurence asking for more

This time he asked when they were in bed and Annie, thinking about it later, thought how clever this was. They were lying together in that companionable silence after sex, the silence that in the past had always made Annie want to get up and leave. She didn't mind though being cuddled like this, she didn't even object to Laurence stroking her hair when normally she would have told him in no uncertain terms to stop that at once before he ruined it. She could have done with a cigarette but Laurence didn't know she smoked and she had decided to leave him with this illusion. He stopped stroking her hair and laced his fingers through hers.

'Annie,' he said, 'you are wonderful. I think you are the most wonderful woman I have ever met. So beautiful. So intelligent. And above all so understanding.'

Am I? thought Annie, who was gratified to find a new positive character trait in herself.

'Such a kind woman.'

And the words, 'What do you want?' came into Annie's head but she managed not to say them. And then she felt something wet on the top of her head. She looked up and the wet fell on to her forehead. He was crying. She disentangled herself from him and sat up.

'Are you crying?' she asked, although it was a stupid question because he obviously was.

He wiped his eyes with the back of his hand and took a deep breath.

'I'm sorry, Annie,' he said.

'What for?'

'For everything,' he said and turned his face away from her.

'Look at me,' she said, and he turned his face back. She pulled up the sheet and wiped his eyes. 'Don't blow your nose on this though,' she said. 'It's Egyptian.'

He managed a small smile.

'What's going on then? You might as well tell me.'

'I don't know if I can.'

'You can,' she said.

'Right,' he said. 'I need a drink though first.'

'Come on then,' she said and got out of bed and put on her dressing gown. He got out the other side and put on his boxers and his shirt. They went into the kitchen where Annie got gin and tonic and lemons out of the fridge. She rinsed already clean glasses and found the ice and cracked the tray against the counter. Laurence caught a cube in his hand.

'Give me that,' said Annie. 'Don't go all dramatic and suffering on me. What's going on?'

She passed him a drink and he took a large swig and then put the glass down on the counter.

'I'm in a mess,' he said.

'What kind of mess?'

'A financial mess.'

'How big?' she asked.

'Enough,' he said, 'big enough.'

'How much do you need this time?'

He looked surprised.

'No, Annie, that's not what I'm asking. I regret asking for money last time, it was totally uncalled for, I should never have taken advantage of your generosity like that.'

'Drug habit?' she asked.

'No, nothing like that!' and he looked genuinely shocked.

'Sexual preferences I know nothing about. Dungeons. Whips?'

'God no, Annie! No, no,' and he almost laughed.

'What then?'

'Stupidity. Financial imprudence. I live way beyond my means, my portfolio has taken a bashing and so I can't rinse anything out of that, interest rates have gone up so the mortgage is taking a hike in the wrong direction, I have an old car that eats up petrol. It all adds up. And I'm not doing wonderfully at work, so there's no chance of a rise there. It's a mess as I said.'

'Sounds like it,' she said, and she crossed her arms.

'I'm sorry,' he said, 'that you should see me like this. I should never . . . I mean crying? I haven't cried since I was twelve and I got thrown off jumping a water obstacle.'

'There's nothing to be ashamed of. These things happen.'

'I'm sure they don't happen to you.'

'Maybe not. But you never know, do you? Right then. What can I do to help you? How much do you need?'

'But I can't pay you back. At least not right away.'

'I know you're not going to do a flit.'

'How do you know that?' he said.

'I just know,' and she went over to him and put her arms around him. 'And anyway, you paid me back before, didn't you? I know you'll pay me back again. How much do you need?'

'I'm so embarrassed.'

'You already said that, Laurence. You need to tell me.'

'A lot.'

'A lot a lot?'

'Enough.'

'How much?'

'I need twenty thousand,' he said.

She was surprised but she couldn't go back now.

'I'll get it sorted out in the morning,' she heard herself saying.

He held on to her tight. Her shoulder was damp with his tears. I am kind. I am understanding. I am generous. Who knew? Annie thought.

This is when it starts to go seriously downhill for Grace and Sam

And then, well, it went very wrong. Grace could pinpoint the day it became obvious that things were not as they should be. They were in Sam's bedroom and Sam was lying on the bed, arms up and hands behind her head. One knee up and one knee down. Wearing a pair of old green shorts dragged down low on her hips. Grace could see her hipbones sticking out over the top of them. The heating was at a ridiculous temperature like Sam liked it and Grace was too hot and hating the fact that she was in love with all of Sam. It was something she had never said to her and she wanted to be able to. She wanted to interrupt her with the most ordinary of sentences, to see if she could get a smile out of her, not a smile because anything was funny, a smile as a gift, a smile to show that she saw her, that her entry into the room did more than shift the sauna air around. Then it would have been easy. It would have been like a gate opening in a wall and Grace could have walked through it, gone over to her, and held her hand. She would have been able to get the words out and Grace needed them out of her like a bee sting. They were making her dizzy; she could feel them lining up behind her teeth like a marching band, the tall 'I' the leader. Holding them in was making her lips numb. I. Love. You. Not that hard to say surely? But she couldn't get them out. They were not words they had ever exchanged and Grace's greatest fear was to say her part and to be left hanging because 'I love you. I love you too' is a complete and perfect sentence and anything else would be a banishment to a world where Sam definitely didn't love her, a world that she couldn't bear to think about being in. The indentations of Sam's ribs. That hollow muscle that pulled vertically in between them. A muscle whose name Grace had never known. She moved into the doorway. Sam looked up. She didn't smile.

'Cup of tea?' asked Grace instead of saying what she needed to say.

'I'll make it,' Sam said, 'wasn't doing anything anyway,' and she got off the bed and put on the T-shirt that was lying on the chair.

'What were you thinking about?' Grace asked as Sam left the room.

'Nothing,' she said, and her voice came back from along the hall like a lingering smoke trail. Grace sat on the bed waiting and thinking, waiting and thinking, but Sam never returned. Eventually she got up and went into the living room where Sam was looking at a book.

'What are you doing now?' Grace asked.

'Nothing,' said Sam, not glancing up.

Grace chewed her lip.

'Walk?' asked Grace.

'OK.'

They went to the park and in the park, it was worse. Halfway round Grace realized that Sam hadn't brought her a cup of tea and she wanted to say this to her but she didn't because it would have come out as an accusation or a complaint and she wouldn't have meant it like that. They walked on, hands in pockets, their own separate pockets. Sam was wearing green and red striped gloves and Grace was wearing grey ones and she didn't ask Sam to hold her hand because she knew that she wouldn't want to and now love and tea and the containment of the words were all mixed up in her head and the tears started coming up the back of her throat and she was tired and she wanted to sit down on a bench and cry into the wool of her gloves. But she didn't sit down in case Sam walked away, kept on going, and she was faced with the humiliating choice of running after her or of staying put and watching the dusk come in on her own. To the imaginary tea question was added an imaginary 'Why didn't you wait for me' as they walked on. I love you Sam, Grace wanted to say, love love love Sam Sam Sam like an echo, but she couldn't reach her, she was gagging on her own sentences, there were pains in her chest where her heart was drowning, she could hardly breathe. She stopped.

'I need to catch my breath,' said Grace and stood lightly panting in the frosty air.

'It's cold,' Sam said, and hunched her shoulders and tapped her feet on the path.

'Yes. Very.' Grace couldn't think of anything else to say.

'I think I want to be on my own tonight, got stuff to do,' Sam said.

No! thought Grace. No! No!

'Right, yeah, fine,' she said. 'Me too. See you tomorrow?'

'I've got stuff on this week,' said Sam, stamping her feet now to keep warm.

'Yeah, me too.'

Where were these crappy lies coming from? Why didn't Grace tell her the truth? I want you to come and live with me and be mine for evermore. No, it didn't sound too good in her head either. She managed not to shout it out though.

'I'll go back to mine then,' Grace said.

'OK,' said Sam and shrugged her shoulders.

You are nothing to me, Grace interpreted the shrug as. She was the body language expert on Sam, or so she liked to believe.

She liked to think that she now knew more about Sam than anybody. But what if she didn't know anything about her at all.

They faced each other at the end of the park like duellists. But Sam would always win.

'Bye then,' she said, and walked off. Grace stood there and stuffed her gloved hand into her mouth to stop herself from shouting out to her. A woman hand in hand with a small child passed by.

'Why's that lady got her glove in her mouth?' asked the child.

'Because this is not good,' Grace would have said but the mother had already picked the child up and hurried off.

This is Violet and her bedroom wall (I)

Annie had been brought up to speak her mind. Violet had been raised to do the exact opposite, not to lie exactly, but to spare people's feelings. So that Annie, given something too small as a present, would say, 'Thank you. I'll have to take it back though because it's not my size and doesn't go with anything,' whereas Violet would say, 'It's lovely. What a beautiful colour!' and hide it at the back of a drawer. This had led to many ructions in the past and to Annie shouting, 'Would you say what you bloody well mean for once! I want to sort this out. Don't you?'

'I do. I do. But I can't cope with the shouting.'

'But the shouting adds to the fun!'

'Arguments aren't fun!' Violet said as quietly as she could.

'You wait till we get to the plate throwing!' shouted Annie.

But now the drama had turned to apparent indifference. They hardly saw each other and when they passed in the hall Annie looked right through her. It should have been that a toned-down Annie would make life a smoother place to skate along but it didn't. It just made it lonely. Violet didn't know what to do about it. Should she throw things at Annie? Should she do something heinous like mix up the food on their shelves or hide Annie's hairbrush or leave toothpaste smeared all over the bathroom sink? Maybe the best thing to do would be to bring Sam home with her and see what happened? But then Annie might have a go at Sam and that wasn't fair and anyway that might put Sam off her and she didn't want that.

She went to Sam's not only because she enjoyed the sex but for the company she couldn't get anywhere else. They still hardly ever went out and Sam seemed to be a creature of habit, they almost always saw each other on weekdays and Violet liked that; she admired people who had proper timetables and habits. She liked Sam's flat too and appreciated the fact that nothing much seemed to be expected of her when she was there. Unlike home, there weren't a lot of rules to be complied with, which felt strange at first but then relaxing. The tea towels were sometimes even unchanged for days. There was shower mould. Sam paid more attention to her jungle of plants than to the sponging of surfaces. They didn't always have sex either, it didn't seem to be a condition of Violet being there. Sometimes they did, sometimes they didn't. Sometimes instead of sex or before or after they did other things. They read books in companionable silence; Sam had lots of bookshelves and it was fun for Violet to sit and pull books out of them. She could leave them on the floor as well. She was even allowed to not use a bookmark. They listened to Bob Dylan on Sam's record player and they played Old Maid, which Sam had taught her. Often Violet sat by the coffee table and drew with a packet of pencils and a pad of watercolour paper that Sam had thoughtfully provided in case Violet had forgotten her sketchbook, and Sam gave her food that was easy to eat, like breadsticks and cream cheese, so that she didn't have to stop. Sometimes drawings came upon her like that – with an urgency that couldn't be denied. When she couldn't find paper, she'd do them on napkins or the blankest page of a magazine.

If Laurence was there when she got back from Sam's or from work, she wanted to go straight back out again; she didn't like him at all. She had never known Annie to have a boyfriend for more than a few months before. What's more she was annoyed with herself because she recognized that her aversion might partly be because she felt jealous, an emotion strange to her that seemed to involve constant irritation with Annie. Why are you talking to him and not to me? Why are you doing things with him and not me? Why won't you even feed me any more or tell me to tidy up or do anything at all apart from barely notice my existence? I am being ignored and it is horrible. I am a child rejected in the playground, she thought, I am a lowly worm not even worth treading on. It felt like the loneliness she had felt at school and might well have gone on feeling for ever if she hadn't met Annie who needed a flatmate in their first year of university. Violet still remembered Annie's reaction to her saying that she was studying English. She looked away and Violet thought, I've blown it, I've blown it.

'You're studying English which is a dosser subject for people who can't make up their minds. And you look like a flake.'

'I'm not a flake. I'm a cream egg,' she had said in an unusually assertive way.

'They're too sweet,' said Annie.

'They are, yes.' And Violet decided, you're not going to dismiss me that easily and put her case. 'I'll wear heels if you want. If I could find any to fit me. I am very wishy-washy. I can't normally make up my mind about anything apart from *Wuthering Heights*, which is a book about windows mostly I think. I like Chocolate Buttons and Milky Bars. I'm pretty good at washing up. My room will be a complete tip but I'll keep it in my room. Or you can put me in a cupboard. I don't smoke. I'll mostly be in the library. What do you like then? In chocolate terms, I mean. I think it's an important question.'

'Fruit and nut,' said Annie putting her hand out to shake. 'Am I going to regret this?' she asked.

'Most probably,' said Violet.

She remembered herself wincing at Annie's titan-like hand-shake. Thinking about this conversation made her extremely sad. I'm losing Annie, she thought, she's going away. One of these days she's going to kick me out and that'll be that. And 'the fear' seemed to have increased again. She still hadn't told Sam anything about it. What if it made Sam go off her? People were funny with things like that. There were days she still woke up and felt so drained that she couldn't get out of bed. She threw herself out instead and knelt on the floor with a tightness in her chest. The bathroom seemed many miles away. When she knew Annie would be out she crawled towards it and sat on the floor in there brushing her teeth so hard she made her gums bleed. Sort yourself out, she thought. Sort yourself out. And she thought about her father, she thought about him every day.

The only thing she could do to cope with all this uncertainty was to draw. Once, and just once, while drunk, she had done a drawing on her wall at Annie's. It was of a heron she'd seen in the park and the old man with his dog that was looking at it. It wouldn't rub off after and so she had put a poster of a painting by Matisse over it and hoped to God that Annie never found out. She had taken to looking at it now and then. It was, she was surprised to think, quite good. But I didn't get the hands right and the heron's feathers were too flat. Annie wasn't home. Violet took down the poster and started to draw with a 2B. By the time she had finished the picture had expanded and could no longer be covered by the poster. There were reeds now and some trees. Shit, she thought, shit. At least Annie, as far as she knew, never came into her bedroom any more. She needed to cover it with something, though, and didn't have another poster big enough. As she stood wondering what to do she realized what the drawing lacked. She wanted to put colour on it. She wanted it badly. When was the last time she really, really wanted anything? She got out her pastels and began to shade it. When she looked at the time, an hour had passed. She remembered that Annie had hairspray and went to the bathroom to find it but when she sprayed it on the wall to fix the pastels, colour ran on to the carpet. She scrubbed at it with a T-shirt and got most of it off. She waited until the wall dried and then put the poster back and where the drawing had expanded put her own sketches up to cover it. They looked nice next to the Matisse. She should have felt guilty and possibly afraid of Annie's reaction but she didn't, she felt better. That's what she needed to do. Draw more.

This is Grace and why her job was pointless

Grace no longer loved her job. She had begun to think of herself as not very helpful at all. It was just shelling out money for nothing when what her clients needed was a priest. Absolution. They needed to sit in a confessional and then walk out of there with a list of their sins and their required acts of contrition, but all Grace could do was to make sure the session ran to its allotted time and pass the tissue box if needed. She sat looking at their twisting hands, their tapping feet. At the way they pulled at their rings or fidgeted or coughed. And she listened, all she could do when it came down to it was listen and she wasn't even great at that any more. She had thought that she had a talent for it but all this time she had been kidding herself. Here we go again, she thought, here we go again.

Her husband said that she was jealous. Her mother said that she was daft to listen to him. Her dad never spoke to her but then again, he never spoke to anyone. She suspected that her son did drugs but she was too afraid to ask him. Her daughter had a horrible boyfriend with metal decorations on his face and probably also in unspeakable places and she had found a condom packet underneath her bed when she was tidying. And the packet was empty. She was only tidying but her daughter had accused her of spying on her and now she wasn't speaking to her. And the thing is she thought it was her fault. Grace watched her cry and she did feel sorry for the woman but she had come to disbelieve in therapy; she had come to believe that it was all a waste of time. She would have been better off spending the money on going to Majorca or Tuscany or Rotherham. She would have been better off with an over-enthusiastic trip to a retail park or to Lourdes. Grace had started to think that what she should be doing was giving clients a big slap. She could have started with the slap, worked up to a hug, made them a cup of tea and then given them a cream slice and the Argos catalogue or the Next catalogue depending on personality type. This should have been part of her training: which catalogue to give. She could have got sponsored. Of course, it wasn't all her fault. Who did she think she was? The President of the United States? She was deluded in the assumption of the grandiose nature of her culpability complex. This stuff happens. Nobody talks to anybody and all of it is shit. Stop thinking about it all and go and eat ice cream.

Grace had, she came to believe, been watching people cry for far too long. The big grown men. The girls who hid their hands with their sleeves so that you couldn't see the razor scars. The middle-aged women with the stretch marks underneath their clothes from years of binge and starve. Her store of kindness had run out and her heart was now packed, she had discovered, after years of listening to the repetitive nature of anxiety and pain, in ice. She had buried it at the bottom of a large chest freezer beneath layers of out-of-date steaks and strata of soft fruit that no one ever got around to eating. Her professionalism had got to her finally. She had stopped being able to empathize, stopped being able to feel. She was watching but she wasn't there. She tested herself at home. She watched *Steel Magnolias* but when Shelby died she didn't cry. Death no longer moved her. She watched *ET* and Elliott's screaming only got on her nerves. She was in the wrong job and why was that? Possibly, she was scared to say to herself, it was because of Sam. She was so preoccupied with the way their relationship was deteriorating that she couldn't think straight. It was wrong to blame Sam, though, it was her fault. She could see the person she was becoming but couldn't stop the development. I am shrill, she thought, I am shrewish and a nag and difficult to be with and I don't like myself any more. And I don't know how to stop myself being these things.

And then something happened that Grace hadn't been expecting.

It was a Saturday morning and she was sitting on her sofa with Sam watching a TV programme about cooking that Sam enjoyed but that she wasn't at all interested in and so she was gazing at the wall instead while she ate Shreddies. Sam had turned up the night before and they had had sex and things had seemed better again. Maybe we just had a hiccup, thought Grace. That's all it was. And as for my obsession with wanting to tell her I love her, that's just my neediness showing. She had decided to do her best to make her expectations more realistic. The doorbell rang. Grace went to answer it. Eustacia was on the doorstep.

'What is it?' said Grace. 'Has someone died? Is it Cyril?'

'No,' said Eustacia, 'I just popped over. I finished the commission I was working on and didn't want to start anything else and I woke up early and thought, I know, I'll just pop over to see Grace.'

'You'd better come in then,' said Grace, knowing full well that Eustacia never 'popped' anywhere, she was timetabled up to the hilt.

'Sam, this is my sister Eustacia,' said Grace as they stood in the sitting room. Sam remained sitting on the sofa.

'Hi,' she said.

'How do you do. It's very nice to meet you,' said Eustacia, 'I've heard a lot about you.' And she moved forward to shake Sam's hand. Sam put her hand out listlessly and Eustacia shook it. Sam returned her eyes to her TV programme and put her feet up on the coffee table.

'Are you two going out somewhere?' said Sam, not looking at them.

'No,' said Grace. 'Would you like a cup of tea, Eustacia?'

'Yes please,' she said.

'Going to change,' said Sam and left the room.

'She's just shy,' said Grace and went to boil the kettle.

Five minutes later they heard the front door slam and when Grace went and opened it, Sam was nowhere to be seen.

'I shouldn't have come unannounced,' said Eustacia. 'I'm sorry. I frightened her off. I should have phoned but I didn't want you to say no again. That was wrong of me. I just wanted to meet her very much.'

'It's not your fault,' said Grace. 'She has a thing about family. I told you about her awful parents.'

'I wanted her to see that I wasn't like them,' said Eustacia and looked as if she might cry.

'Don't worry,' said Grace and put her arm around her. 'It's not your fault.'

She couldn't remember the last time she had felt so furious. She felt ashamed of Sam's poor behaviour but at least it made her finally understand that Sam would never fit into her family. She just didn't want to. Why had it taken Grace so long to get this? And did it matter that much? She looked at Eustacia's sad and disappointed face when she saw her off at the doorstep. Yes, it mattered, it mattered a great deal. Sam didn't want to belong to Grace's world and she wasn't bothered, it seemed, at integrating Grace into hers. She would never come and live with Grace either; Grace saw that she had been kidding herself about that too. Perhaps to her then it would always be a casual thing, something that could be let go of at any moment. So where did that leave them? I could stop this, Grace thought, I could stop this now if I wanted to. But that was so much easier said than done. How do you stop loving someone? How do you stop wanting them? By an effort of will? Do you just wake up one day and weigh the thing up and say, no, I don't want to do this any more; Sam doesn't love me but I love Sam, Grace realized fully for the first time. What on earth am I going to do now?

This is Annie and what was missing

The money was bothering her. It shouldn't have been but it was. She thought about it in the morning when she woke up and she thought about it at night before she went to bed. It wasn't that she wanted him to grovel. Or was it? Maybe she did, even though this didn't fit with her new kind persona. Perhaps she wanted him to say how grateful he was every time he spoke to her, perhaps she wanted him to fall on to the floor and grab her legs and expound over and over on her massive generosity. She needed at least one more thank you but that thank you was not forthcoming and so, every time she saw him, she felt under-appreciated, and that did not sit well with her. In fact, she realized now, she was annoyed, very annoyed, and not just with him but with herself for lending him the money and getting herself into this situation. At the very least she should tell the therapist and try and 'work through it' or whatever you did. What else was she paying her for? And above all she was annoyed by her lack of honesty with everyone. She had always prided herself on her directness. No matter if other people might find it abrasive, that was their lookout, it was important to be honest, but now she wasn't even being that. What was happening to her? And she had always thought it was her mother who was the one who was the control freak but this morning she had found herself repacking her handbag again and again into ever more organized sections. She hadn't hired a cleaner but the flat was cleaner than ever. She had even scrubbed the inside of all the kitchen drawers and cupboards, on a Saturday, on her hands and knees with rubber gloves on trying to get into a very difficult to reach corner while she looked forward to bleaching her moustache. What had happened to fun?

She stood outside Violet's bedroom listening to her faint snores and wanted to go in there and tell her about Laurence and ask her what to do but she couldn't make herself. Annie never backed down. This bloody Sam woman, getting in the way. She went to Manfred's in search of sugar.

'Good to see you, Annie. Today you look especially radiant. Let me give you the Turkish Delight I've had tucked away for you.' He started rooting under his counter and then came up for air with the box in his hand. 'There you go. I meant to ask you when I saw you, did you get Violet to the therapist?'

'No. I've been going instead.'

'That's good.'

'Is it?'

'Yeah, I'd probably go if I had the . . . I was going to say something there . . . let me stick with "nerve".'

'Part of me thinks it's weak.'

'I think it's the opposite. You're trying to deal with stuff. Good on you. Now, this is not your ordinary Turkish Delight,

I'll have you know. This is the one my family favours. It's a cut above the rest.'

She came out of the shop feeling better. She rang Laurence.

'I'm coming round later,' she said.

'Are you?' said Laurence, and she didn't like his offhand tone.

'Yes, I am. Eight o'clock suit you?'

'Could you perhaps bring some wine with you? I'm low.'

She wanted to say, no, I bloody well can't, I'm the woman, women don't bring the wine, but she didn't.

'I'll pick something up,' she said.

It was seven o'clock and Annie was still ironing, she found it soothing after a long day, ironed sheets, tea towels, socks, knickers even. Her drawers were a marvel of folded beauty, or an anal nightmare depending on how you thought about these things.

She heard Violet tiptoe into the room. She had known full well that she was there, but, as normal now, had ignored knowing this fact. They were like magnets that repelled each other. Now she didn't turn around.

'What are you doing on Tuesday evening?' asked Violet.

'Why?' said Annie, still not turning around.

'I wanted, I mean, if you would like it, I mean . . .'

'What?' asked Annie, who now took out aggression on the iron, which was squirting steam into her face.

'Would you like to come out to dinner with me?' said Violet, sounding nervous. 'And with Sam too? It would be nice for you to get to know her, she's . . . she's . . .'

'Fine.'

'Great,' said Violet.

Annie wrestled the iron back under control and continued ironing.

'Anything else?'

'No,' said Violet and Annie heard her go back to her room.

Annie looked at her watch. She was going to be late getting

to Laurence's but so what? Nothing wrong with making a man wait. Should she just have agreed to that? Probably not. It would be an awful evening, she would guarantee it, but she supposed it might help mend things with Violet and that could only be a good thing. Or maybe it would be easier to follow Violet into her room now and ask her what the hell was going wrong between them? But that seemed too much of a capitulation.

'Thanks for the wine,' said Laurence when she got to his and handed it to him. He looked at the label. She had deliberately gone for cheaper than she would normally buy just to teach him a lesson, but he made no comment, only slipped it into the freezer to chill quickly. He sat down at the piano and started to play something quiet. She was waiting to be told that she looked beautiful, although she had made only minimal effort on purpose, but he continued playing without looking at her.

'You wanted to see me, Annie?' he said. 'Anything I should be worried about?'

Again, that offhand voice he'd used on the phone. Annie was fed up with this.

'Have you sorted things out now? Financially I mean.'

'Oh yes,' he said, still playing and without looking at her. 'All sorted.'

Thank you, thank you, thank you, you are wonderful, thank you, thought Annie.

'Would you like to go and have a peek at the wine?'

'No,' said Annie.

He looked up.

'Everything all right at work?'

'Fine.'

'Good. Good. The glasses are in the cupboard over the sink.'

'Did you not hear me?'

'I beg your pardon?'

'I'm not getting your wine. Well, my wine. I'm not setting one foot in your kitchen. It's your house.'

'Are you sure you are OK, Annie?'

'Fine,' said Annie and crossed her arms.

He stood up and came round the piano to her and kissed her lightly on the cheek.

'I'll get the wine then,' he said. 'Bed?' And he went to the kitchen. She looked round the room. The horse pictures were still there, the collection of Dickens, the bottles of spirits. In one of the games she had played with her brothers as a kid you got a tray and filled it with objects and then took one away and the others had to guess what was missing. She'd always won. There was something in the room that should have been there but wasn't. She looked at the mantelpiece which had never fitted in this room, too big and not a real fire, one of those artificial flame jobs. She had always thought it looked naff. There were two china dogs at either end, two candlesticks, and then some horse pictures but a gap in the middle. Had it been there when she had last come, or had she never noticed the gap before? No, now she thought about it, nothing ever had been in the middle and it looked uneven. She was compelled to go and straighten things up. Tucked just behind one of the horse pictures was a card for a drinks party for an address in Harrogate. It was from 'Rex and family'. She had only met Rex twice and not liked him either time, something to do with the way froth collected on his rubbery lower lip when he talked. She hadn't got the impression he liked her much either, so perhaps this was why Laurence hadn't invited her to go to the party with him. She hadn't met any other of his friends or members of his family but had presumed it was because he wasn't close to many people. For the first time it occurred to her that he might be ashamed of her. She was instantly angry. What right did he have to be ashamed of her? Just because they were from different backgrounds. Her mother came into her head saying, 'We're just as good as anybody in this street, Annie Barnes, and don't ever let anyone tell you otherwise.'

Laurence called through, 'Are you coming, Annie?'

She hesitated. Perhaps it was all in her head. She mentally reviewed her underwear. Grey silk. She looked very good in it. It seemed a waste to not show it off. So what he hadn't said thank you again? And she didn't want to go to Rex's party anyway. She was just being over-demanding and like her mother and that was the last thing she wanted. She went into the bedroom and took off her dress.

'You look beautiful, Annie,' he said and reached for her and she let him.

This, Grace thinks, is because it's all bollocks

Grace hadn't spoken to Sam for three days, not since Sam had snubbed Eustacia. She was seething still, and finally she phoned Sam's flat but Sam didn't answer. This angered Grace even more, although she managed to leave a reasonable message. All right, she left three and they were identical.

'Hi, this is Grace, could you ring me?'

Sam didn't ring back. What sort of person didn't have a mobile phone? It was beyond annoying. It was 9 p.m. Grace saw by her kitchen clock. 'Our' clock. She watched the minute hands move. She put on her coat and her boots and went out of the flat. She knew it wasn't a good idea to do this but she did it anyway. She drove to Sam's but Sam didn't answer when she rang the bell. There were no lights on in the flat upstairs. Grace sat all night on the doorstep. She knew that it was a ridiculous thing to do, she knew this as she was doing it, and there was a part of her brain, even if it was only a small part, trying to persuade her to go home. The trouble was that she was stubborn, and her brain wasn't using the right language. She didn't respond well to commands so there was no way it was going to win. 'Go home, you're an idiot, what are you doing? This is obsessive and pathetic. I'm sure there's a good reason she isn't home yet. Go home.' Grace ignored all of this. She had forgotten her gloves and her scarf and so she stuffed a hand into either sleeve and burrowed her neck down into her coat, using her breath to keep her face warm, but she got colder and colder, her bum on the cold stone step absorbing the night chill. She felt an increasing sense of panic. 'Where is she? Where is she?' And it was frightening, being out there, never knowing who was going to come by. There was a streetlight a house or two down and people came along the street and she heard them approaching and was relieved every time it was a woman. Nobody approached her and mostly she was in the company of the bins and an abandoned armchair. She tried not to think about rats. She did the calculations, willing time to pass and yet willing it to stay put at the same time so she didn't have to lose faith in the fact that Sam hadn't yet come home. It was past pub hours. Now it was past most bars too. Clubs would be shutting now. Maybe she'd stayed at Ellie's but Grace knew that Ellie was on holiday. She must be with another of her friends then. Yes, that was it, she was sleeping the night on somebody's sofa. She wouldn't be home at all, so what was the point of Grace staying. Grace wanted to go home where it was warm and clean and there were no sudden noises, no taxis or car alarms. She wanted a cup of tea and her own bed, she wanted to go but she couldn't make herself, as if, if she went now, all her efforts would have been wasted. She didn't move, and she got colder and colder, and dawn crept in wan and grey and then it got light at last and the birds started. It was 8 a.m. It was morning and Grace had spent a whole night on a cold step and would never tell anyone she had done so because all she felt was shame. And then Sam rounded the corner and she was swinging her keys and when she saw Grace she didn't stop. Instead she walked up the steps and stood on the one Grace was sitting on and she looked down at her without anything registering in her face. It was as though she had expected Grace to be there. And she didn't look tired, she looked like a woman who had been for a bracing walk in the early morning. She was wearing her favourite earrings – peacock feathers, the tips of which touched her shoulders. Grace wanted to speak but she couldn't.

'Do you want to come in then?' Sam asked and there was something of a smile there as she looked down at Grace, a small smile, the one you might use for a child when you're tired and have had enough of them for the day.

'If you don't mind,' Grace said.

Grace was stiff when she got up, it took a moment for her to unbend while Sam held the door open for her. Up the stairs but without accident this time.

'Can I use your loo?' Grace asked. She went in and locked the door. She weed the longest wee she remembered ever having weed. Then she flushed and put the seat down and sat on it. She felt numb. There was a knock at the door.

'You OK?' Sam asked through the door.

Grace was in no fit state to say anything.

'I'm going to bed.'

Grace put her hands over her mouth. I won't ask. I won't ask. She got up and went into the bedroom where Sam was already in bed, facing the wall, and she took off her coat and jeans with shaking hands and got into bed. The covers on the bed were cold and she was shivering. She lay there not touching Sam and after a while she felt Sam caressing her back with long strokes and she wanted to turn into that hand and she also wanted to stay as far away in the bed as possible. Sam moved towards her so that the length of her was against Grace's back, and she put her hand around Grace's waist and hugged her. She pressed her lips on the back of Grace's neck and yet she said nothing, no explanation, no apology, no questions. She moved her hand down Grace's belly and pushed them into her knickers and stroked Grace. Then Sam rolled over on top of her, took her head in her hands, and kissed her long and slow and Grace spread her legs and Sam lay between them. She never said a thing, instead she did sweet things to Grace, touched her just so. Afterwards Sam moved away to the side of the bed, her back to Grace, and went to sleep, and Grace stayed awake and watched the light move across the ceiling.

This is Violet's ill-starred evening

When Violet came out of her room Annie was standing in the kitchen with a gin and tonic, staring into space. She didn't offer one to Violet like she always did. She didn't comment on Violet's appearance either, which she should have done. Annie was wearing a knee-length black dress with a wide skirt and a string of big pearls around her neck. Her hair was down. She looked beautiful and Violet wanted to tell her that but didn't.

'Are we off then?' asked Annie, as though she didn't care one way or the other, as though she wasn't normally a person who harangued Violet to hurry up, who actually tapped her foot.

'Yes,' said Violet. And knew then it was all going to go wrong.

'You're not living in this century,' said Annie, after she had understood that not only did Sam not have a car but she had no mobile either.

They were sitting in a Lebanese restaurant which didn't serve alcohol, it was bring your own, and Annie, as a gesture of friendliness, had bought three decent bottles, two of white which is what she and Violet drank at home, and one of red, in case Sam preferred that. Violet had forgotten to tell her that Sam didn't drink.

'Why not?' asked Annie, who was looking down her nose at Sam's jeans and T-shirt.

'I just don't,' said Sam.

'Are you an alcoholic?' asked Annie, twirling a lock of her lovely hair around her fingers. Violet felt sick. That was one of Annie's tells for dissatisfaction.

'No, I'm not,' said Sam.

'You don't like the taste?'

'It's not that.'

'Then why?'

Sam shrugged.

'It holds no interest for me.'

'Why?'

'Because I find being drunk dull.'

'Fine.'

And Annie went to pour for Violet but Violet put her hand on top of her glass and Annie poured a little wine over her hand and didn't apologize.

'Don't you want any?' she asked.

'I don't feel like drinking,' said Violet as lightly as she could, wiping her hand with a napkin.

'Since when did you join the sober club?'

'I don't feel like drinking tonight really.'

'Right. More for me then.'

Sam chose veggie food.

'Are you a vegetarian?' asked Annie.

'I feel like eating this today,' said Sam and she smiled in what Violet chose to believe was a conciliatory manner. Annie didn't smile back. Violet's own fake smile was as nervous as it could get and was making her mouth ache. Annie chose lamb and a great hunk of it arrived on the bone, semi-rare. Annie attacked it with gusto and then proceeded to wade her way through the entire three bottles which was, despite Annie's prodigious head for drink, enough to get her drunk and since a non-drunk Annie was a force to be reckoned with, a drunken Annie was a bulldog.

'Why are you fucking Violet?' asked Annie, admittedly in a light conversational tone as though commenting on the ambience. This enlivened the sweet.

'Because I like her,' said Sam, as though she was used to being asked this question in public by a person she didn't know. Violet had to admire her composure. Annie, unusually, seemed to be losing hers. Perhaps she should have had a drink herself. Or many.

'But she doesn't even know if she's gay or not! Don't you care?' asked Annie.

'No,' said Sam.

'Are you in love with her?'

'Annie!' said Violet.

'It's a relevant question.'

'I don't feel that it's anything to do with you, Annie,' said Sam.

'I'm her best friend. I'm the one who looks out for her when she goes off on one of her idiotic man benders and so I have every right to do so when she gets in a mess with someone like you.'

'Like me how?'

And Violet sat there, wishing she was in the coat cupboard at the nightclub she had sometimes worked at. She would be safe there, hidden under a pile of smelly coats.

'You're messing with her head because you feel like it. You don't give a shit about her.'

'I do care about her, yes. But I don't think the fact that she is undecided about her sexuality is a problem and I think that you are way over-involved in the relationship between Violet and me, which has absolutely nothing to do with you.'

'You can fuck right off, you self-righteous up-yourself bitch!'

'I think you might have had too much to drink, Annie,' said Sam.

'I don't want you in my house,' said Annie.

'That's fine by me.'

'Please stop,' said Violet in the smallest of her voices.

'Well, I don't want you there. Not ever. I'm off now. You can fucking pay.'

'That will be fine,' said Sam smiling.

'Violet?' asked Annie, standing up unsteadily. 'You coming or are you staying with Ms too good to be true here?'

'Here,' whispered Violet.

'Right then.'

And Annie got her coat from the coat stand, knocking it over in the process, and stamped out on her high heels. 'The lesbians are paying,' Violet heard her say to the waiter on passing. He didn't seem to know what to say and settled on, 'Thank you.'

'I hope she's not going to try to drive home,' said Sam, putting her hand gently on Violet's arm. Violet put her hand on top of Sam's to steady herself. It didn't work. 'Are you all right, Violet? Come home with me.'

And she did. She wasn't sure if she wanted to, but she did.

This is Grace's disintegration

It was falling apart and there was no way to put it back together again.

'I told you – I don't do family,' said Sam.

'I'm not surprised with a family like yours!'

'What do you mean by that?'

'They were awful,' Grace said or rather almost shouted. 'They weren't interested at all in your life and they obviously have a big problem with you being gay.'

'That's their issue, not mine.'

'Doesn't it make you angry?'

'No.'

'My sister only wanted to meet you! Why did you walk out? You could at least say you're sorry.'

'I'm sorry if it upset you but I did tell you.'

'Why did you take me to Shrewsbury?'

Sam sighed.

'I thought they might like you.'

'Or you wanted to shove it in their faces?'

'No, I thought they might like you. I wanted them to see that I'm with someone nice and that my life is good and then they might leave me alone.'

'What do you mean leave you alone?'

'They email me a lot.'

'Saying what?'

'Oh, you know, just stuff.'

'Like what?'

'I don't want to go into it.'

'This is what every conversation is like with you! You won't talk about anything! I don't even know why I bother speaking to you!'

Every time they spoke or saw each other now it didn't work. There was a lot of slamming the phone down on Grace's side. There was a lot of not answering the phone on Sam's. There was sex used as a cross between a truce and a continuation of the war. Sex in no-man's-land. She could no longer get from Sam what she needed and it made her feel as if all this time she had been a drug addict without knowing it and now the drug was getting withdrawn and what she had left were the symptoms of withdrawal – the low self-esteem, the tendency to either shout or beg, and most of all the panic that gripped her so hard that she could hardly eat. She wanted to be able to leave Sam but she couldn't seem to detach herself. She wanted to get up and walk away but she couldn't even get as far as the door.

'I'm not dealing with this,' Sam said on the phone in her most reasonable voice, the voice of a calm and logical person forced to cope with someone who was neither of these things. 'I don't like to be answerable to others. I need to do my own thing. I thought you knew that.'

'Can I come round? Tomorrow?'

'I've got stuff to do,' she said, and Grace wondered if that was true or not.

'You're so far away.'

'I'm only down the road.'

'I mean I can't get to you. I don't know where you are any more.'

'I've got to go. I'll phone you tomorrow.'

Sam put the phone down and Grace stood there with her phone still in her hand listening to the silence. The silence was a great big place like a desert, full of cutting winds. Grace sat down on the floor and stopped herself phoning back by digging her nails into her arms until she made marks. Apparently, this was called self-harm. She called it damage-minimalization herself. She felt like the ice on the puddle Sam had put her foot through and was stamping down on again and again. All this time, all this attention and time she had focused on Sam, and for what? She had neglected her friends terribly, never mind the way she had ignored her sisters and done her job poorly to maintain a relationship with someone who was almost indifferent to her. Someone cold and unfeeling, which perhaps was partly her parents' fault. But she was always making excuses for her. How much of this was Sam's fault anyway? It was hers for getting into this mess. This is nothing more than an obsession that I need to stop. I'm the one with something wrong with me, she thought.

In the end, it was all repetition. One tune over and over. Until suddenly that was it, it had stopped, and Grace was left standing there, shell-shocked, thinking what, it's stopped, and she couldn't bring herself to believe it and she would have done anything, anything to crawl her way back to the pain but it was all too late.

This is Annie and the spot check

Annie was normally always prepared for a spot check. She had easily de-frostable food in the freezer, spare coffee in the cupboard, didn't run out of milk, cleaned up after herself as she went along, cleaned up after Violet in her wake, made sure her sink was bits of food free when she went to bed at night, had drawers with those plastic things in them for segmenting your underwear, hoovered under the furniture, had an updated file for her accountant, and never ever failed to delete unwanted email. What she was not ready for was her mother. Her mother did not do the unexpected visit, her mother hardly drove herself anywhere, but here she was, at 11 a.m. on a Saturday morning, standing in Annie's kitchen taking off her driving loafers and putting her heels back on.

'I'll give myself a quick touch up,' she said to Annie and tic-tacked off to the bathroom. Annie recognized this sound both as one from her childhood and therefore her mum's authority, and also as the sound of nights out when she could have had her way with any man in the room. It was the sound of confidence and power. Annie began to pray to an unknown god, the god of order perhaps, that she had not left her contraceptive pills by the sink, or even in the cabinet, because the likelihood of her mother looking in there was high.

'You should get dressed, Annie,' shouted her mother from the bathroom and Annie looked down to see that she was wearing, of all things, a grubby T-shirt, a sports bra, and the tracksuit bottoms she used to clean in, because she had been about to do her annual clothes audit and every item she owned from knickers outwards was piled high on her bed. No, I will not, she thought, it's my bloody flat, I'll wear what I want, even if what I have on are these disgusting things. She put her thumbnail in her mouth and chewed off the end deliberately. It's my bloody flat. It was probably good that her mother was here, perhaps this was the time she could finally tell her about not wanting children right now. Grace had encouraged her to address it when she felt able to. It was better that she was on her own turf. Yes, she would do it even though the prospect terrified her. Grace had said they should aim for 'a dialogue', after all. She'd had enough of her mother telling her what to do. It was her life. When she came out of her room her mother was standing with the fridge door open.

'You shouldn't have raw meat at the top, Annie, that should go on the bottom shelf. Have I never told you that? I'm sure I have. And I'll have a coffee but not if it's out of that contraption. What's wrong with Nescafé, I ask you?'

'There's a jar in the cupboard above the kettle.'

Her mother turned to stare at her and waited for a beat which meant, you are the hostess, I am the cherished guest. Annie didn't move.

'I suppose you're wondering why I'm here? How's that Laurence?'

'He's OK.'

'That's not very forthcoming, is it?'

'He's fine.'

'Quite a nice lad, that one. Clean. Good manners. I hope he's never seen you in those awful trousers you're wearing. What are they – jogging bottoms? Really, Annie, could you not find anything else clean? Have you no laundry system to speak of? And that Violet? Where is she?'

'Out.'

'With one of her young men, is she?'

'Not exactly.'

'I can see when I'm not wanted.'

Annie couldn't imagine a more irritating phrase than the last apart from, 'You've put on weight since I last saw you.'

'I'm surprised that you're here, that's all,' Annie said. 'You never come on your own.'

'I've got better driving shoes now. And I've got news to tell you and so I thought I'd come to visit.'

'You're moving again. You're getting divorced. I'm adopted. Grandad Arnold has popped his clogs. They've run out of your favourite Chardonnay in the M&S food hall and despite your protestations they won't restock. Any of those do you?'

'Annie, I don't know what has got into you this morning! Is it your time of the month?'

And that is the other phrase, thought Annie. How had I forgotten?

'If a man was to say that I'd punch him,' she said.

'Why does that not surprise me?' asked her mother. 'And I wonder why you're not married yet. Sit down.'

'I'll stand, thanks.'

'Fine. I'll sit down.'

Annie's mother took over the sofa as though it was centre of her queendom, carefully spreading her linen skirt to minimize the creases. She plucked at her blouse which was of course pristine despite the journey and then patted her chignon to check if she had any hair out of place, which she didn't. Annie hovered, a pretender in her own home. She always felt like her mother's doppelgänger, but the inferior version and not just the younger.

'Your father and I are going on the road,' said her mother casually.

'What, like Jack Kerouac? You're going to bum rides and

hop trains? Or are you going to get one of those big caravan things?'

'You don't listen. We're going on the road. We're going on tour. Amsterdam. That's the first one. Then we're going to, I think, Hamburg. Then Bremen, even though I don't know where that is. Then back to Holland.'

'I am finding it hard to follow this conversation.'

'Well, you know that your father and I had ourselves a little band when we were young? Lady V and the Dreamers? Don't ask me, the name was all your father's idea. Well, it turns out someone, all those years back, took a video of us and they found it again and went and put it up on that there YouTube and before I know it we've got 250 likes and then 1,000 and then Michael Wrigley of all people rang up . . .'

'Michael Wrigley?'

Her mother looked vaguely sheepish.

'Now Annie, don't get aerated about that. Turns out that now the lad is very entrepreneurial and knows all sorts of people who put on gigs . . .'

'And you didn't think to tell me this at an earlier stage? That it might have been a good idea? Because now the story has jumped on and you're off to Holland?'

Her mother eyed her speculatively.

'I'm sure I don't know why you're getting into a right tizzy about this.'

'What, like you, you mean? You the queen of all spectacular rages, you who once threw a cut-glass decanter at our Eddie's head? A full decanter, mind you.'

'Annie, would you please sit down and hear me out. I thought you'd like this. I know you've always wanted me to be more independent, more like you. You know, off doing your own thing. I look back on my life and I think have I wasted it? But now it's expanding. It's wonderful.'

'I'm glad to hear that bringing up me and my brothers was a waste of your precious time!'

'That's not what I said. Can't you see? I'm free now, we're free, your dad and me, to do anything we want to do. The world is our oyster. This has come just at the right time. Maybe you want me to be your poor old mum, stuck at home dusting for the rest of my days, but I don't. There's so much more for me. I thought you'd love this. I really did. I'm disappointed in you, Annie.'

'Michael Wrigley cheated on me. Not that I've ever told you that. With Tiffany Jones. That's why I broke up with him. And I don't want children. Not right now. And I don't want to get married. Not right now. I'm not saying not ever but I've got other stuff I want to do. I got offered this job.'

There, it was out, all in one breath. She had thought it would be cathartic. It wasn't. Her mother stood up.

'And why exactly did you choose to tell me all this now?'

'Because Michael Wrigley is not who you think he is. And because you think you can go and do whatever you damn well please but you object if I try to do what I want to do and not what you've decided is best for me.'

'And not wanting children. You couldn't have told me before?' her mother said.

'I tried.'

'When did you try?'

'I wanted to.'

'I'll have no grandchildren.'

'Well, maybe my brothers . . .'

'Chance would be a fine thing. Now you listen to me, young lady. That Laurence is a catch. You won't get any better, not at your age. You'll be over the hill before you know it and then what? Then what?'

'You're like something out of the dark ages.'

'How dare you! You haven't got your priorities right, not at all.'

'You're being stupid.'

'Don't speak to me like that.'

'I'm a grown-up. I have a life. I have a job. I can speak to you however I want.'

'If your father was here right now . . .'

'He wouldn't do anything. He never does anything. You tell him what to do all the time. And you've been telling me what to do all my life too. Study this. Go there. Be that. Get married to some suitable character who doesn't exist. Have children because you want them. Not because it's the right time for me. Oh no. Well, you can shove it, Mum, you really can.'

Annie was so angry she was shaking. She looked down at her feet, which were bare. She had forgotten to put her mules on, and then she looked up to see her mother stand up and wedge her feet firmly back into her shoes, pick up her handbag, and leave the room and Annie listened for the slam of the door that had punctuated her childhood when her mother took umbrage at a minor infraction of her many rules. But it didn't come and instead there was a soft closing of the flat door so as not to inconvenience.

Annie sat down on the sofa. Well, that went well then. I expressed myself very coherently. I must make such a good lawyer. Fuck, she thought, fuck.

This is Violet and her bedroom wall (II)

Violet hadn't appreciated before what a strong personality Sam had, being used to, as she was, the strength in Annie. She had a quiet firmness, had Sam, that brokered no argument, a calm parental authority. And the truth is that Violet liked this of course, she liked being told what to do, where to go, how to do things. It cancelled the whirling indecisions of her wandering brain and meant she never, ever, had to grow up; she could always be the little girl in the fairy story. She spent more and more time with Sam now and less and less at home; Annie and her had stopped speaking completely. Even if Annie wasn't there she moved around the flat quietly trying not to displace the air. Sam seemed to like her being at her flat, but Violet noticed that she never let her leave anything behind her as was Violet's scattering wont. So where was her home now? Where did she belong? And to whom? She would like to belong to somebody; it would make her feel safer. Everything was temporary and nothing was fixed and so she asked Sam if she could come and live with her. Sam didn't say anything for a while. Was this a row, Violet wondered. The lack of an immediate answer meant she ended up in a panic attack, with Sam sitting on the edge of the bed with her making her blow into a paper bag that had once held organic apples. She inhaled the crisp smell. In and out. In and out.

'I'm sorry,' Sam said, 'I didn't know that would upset you that much.'

Violet couldn't say anything.

'I don't know what to do now,' said Sam. 'How can I help you?'

'Please don't make me go,' said Violet when she could breathe, although her voice sounded more like a croak.

'I'm not trying to do that,' said Sam, still as gentle as she always was.

'I know I'm being . . .' said Violet. 'Clingy. If that's the right word. Maybe it's a bit to do with Annie. She's gone all . . . far away. And now you seem far away too and I don't know what to do.'

'Getting like this doesn't seem to be a great option. I'm sorry but I don't do living together,' said Sam, and Violet waited to be hugged but she wasn't and couldn't instigate the movement herself.

'Never?' she asked.

'Never.'

'But perhaps you could . . .'

'No, I don't want to. But I do like you, Violet, and I'd like to keep seeing you.'

And she nuzzled Violet's ear.

'Tickles,' Violet whispered.

'I know,' Sam said. And did it again.

One part of Violet was used to this kind of sex now and one part was still surprised every time. She normally spent the first few minutes in a mild state of disorientation – I am in bed with a woman, what do I do? But each time they did it this early stage got shorter and shorter and Violet imagined a day would come when it would all seem so normal that it would disappear entirely. She was more assertive with Sam than she had ever been with a man; she sometimes even instigated the sex, which she had never done before. Tonight, she wanted to see if she could make Sam come more than once. She ignored her own arousal and put her mouth on Sam until Sam whispered to her, 'Please don't stop.'

After Sam had gone to sleep, Violet lay awake and thought about the day when she had gone to the birthday party of a child in her class and one of the children had locked her in a cupboard and left her there and although Violet had screamed and banged on the door no one came for what seemed like a very long time indeed. Looking back on it, it could have been only minutes but at the time she was terrified that she would have to remain there for ever. Eventually the child's mother let her out and called her silly for getting herself locked in. The other children sniggered and turned their backs on her and Violet realized that she had wet herself, that there was a large damp stain all over the skirt of her white party dress. Despite the sex, despite the things she had made Sam feel, she felt like that tonight.

The next morning, after she got home from Sam's, the flat was quiet. Annie might be in or she might be out. Violet tiptoed to her bedroom door to see if she could hear anything. She couldn't. Well, she'd just go to bed. That was her plan. 'The fear' had trailed her all the way home and was about to become overwhelming. But instead, six hours later, on half of the walls of her room was something resembling a mural. She stood, exhausted, her clothes and hands covered in a layer of pastels. At least she had put down a sheet so that it wasn't on the floor. That was something. It should have depressed her, Sam's refusal, but it hadn't after all, it had energized her. And she should be feeling enormously guilty because of the mess she had made in what was, after all, very definitely, Annie's flat, but she didn't feel bad about that either. She felt satisfied and calm. She had made something. She had made something bigger than anything she had ever made before. Drawing for her had always been such a private thing that she was unwilling to share them with anyone. Only Annie had ever seen them and Annie wasn't given to praise. But the fact that Sam had liked them and that she had been brave enough to share them with her had helped Violet, she realized now. And yes, it was embarrassing that she had asked Sam that, but it was more that she had been feeling insecure than that she really wanted to live with her. She was glad, on consideration, that Sam had said no. She didn't want to live with her. She wanted to stay living with Annie. Even though, if Annie was to see the world of old ladies and dachshunds and trees and flowers she had created on her walls, she might well throw her out. Well, she thought, I'll just have to keep the door closed, won't I? She was proud of what she had made, she didn't want it covered up. It was good. She could recognize it was good. She took some photos of it with her mobile and then she changed her clothes. She remembered that in her knicker drawer, tucked up with her vintage gloves, was her father's letter. She took it out and looked at it and made a list about why not to go.

1. I know next to nothing about my father and he might well be a complete bastard.
2. I will have to go all the way to France.
3. I have no money to go all the way to France.
4. What if 'the fear' overwhelms me while I am there and I get stuck?
5. I am scared of all forms of transport including escalators.
6. But she couldn't think of a 6.

This is what Annie had to say that Grace didn't want to hear

Annie sat staring out the window. Grace stared at Annie but her mind was on Sam. It was always on Sam now and she had forgotten what they had been talking about.

'I was horrible to my mother, I said some horrible things,' said Annie, and Grace was glad that Annie had spoken first. 'But I don't want to talk about it any more.'

'That's fine. We don't have to. Is there anything else you want to talk about?'

Annie turned her face back to Grace.

'It's Violet. I didn't tell you but we're not talking at all. It's that girlfriend she's got. I mentioned her, didn't I?'

'Yes, you did.'

'She's a bitch. I can't stand her. She's completely up herself but Violet, she just can't let it go. I don't know what's going on.'

'What is it about her you don't like?'

'She's a gardener in the park, and it's not that I think there's anything wrong with that . . .'

Annie looked at Grace.

'Are you all right? You're looking pale. Are you getting ill?'

'Could I ask? The woman's name. I mean the woman that Violet is seeing. Her girlfriend.'

'Sam. Her name's Sam. Anyway . . .'

Everything she said was going to sound like an accusation. But this was an accusation. Because this was happening. Sam was seeing someone else. Grace needed to get her head around it. But she couldn't.

She sat in her car outside Sam's house for twenty minutes. It felt like flu, like she was getting the flu, shivery and sick. She got out of the car and locked it. She went towards Sam's house as if it was the last place on earth she wanted to go, and then she remembered the night on the doorstep. She didn't want to say anything. Maybe she wouldn't say anything? Perhaps she could ignore it. Pretend it wasn't happening. After all, people did denial all the time, how many people had she seen over the years who were experts in it? Couldn't she adapt? It was going to sound like an accusation, and what if Sam denied it, then where would she be? What if Sam said that she was jealous and paranoid? Perhaps she was jealous and paranoid, like she had been when she'd sat outside Sam's all night. But she had been right, hadn't she, she'd been right. When Eustacia had said, 'When you know you know,' had she been talking about something else? Perhaps she should have rung her first. She was sensible, she would know what to say. Shit. Shit. Shit. Grace rang the bell. Sam answered the intercom.

'Oh, it's you, you should have called first,' she said, 'I'll get the door.'

Grace heard Sam come down the hall. She opened the door.

'There's someone else, isn't there?' Grace said.

'You'd better come in then,' said Sam.

Inside Sam didn't offer her a cup of tea like she always did, she didn't suggest that Grace sit down. She stood by the door calmly.

'What do we do now then?' asked Grace.

'What do you mean?'

'Aren't you at least going to deny it? That's what people do, isn't it?' Grace heard herself use a voice she hadn't heard before. It was a roller derby voice.

'I am seeing someone else,' said Sam.

'And that person's name is Violet,' said Grace.

'Yes, it is. How did you know that?' said Sam and she looked vaguely interested but not that much.

'I'm sorry,' said Grace, 'is this conversation boring you?'

'It's not very interesting,' said Sam.

Grace found her fists bunching.

'I can understand that you might be angry, Grace,' said Sam.

'Might be?'

'But I never had any commitment to you. I thought you'd accepted that. I haven't made any promises. I haven't broken any vows. We're not married. We don't even live together.'

'Which is your fault!' said Grace.

'What is?'

'That we don't live together! You said you didn't want to!'

'I'm sorry, Grace,' said Sam. 'That's all I can say.'

She didn't look ruffled at all, she looked as if she was apologizing for having run out of milk.

'Why? Why? If you wanted to be with this other woman, with this Violet, then why didn't you dump me?' asked Grace and she was aware that her voice was getting louder and louder.

'I didn't want to hurt you,' said Sam.

'And you thought this wouldn't hurt!' shouted Grace.

'I think we are going round in circles, Grace, I said I'm sorry,' said Sam, continuing in her reasonable tone. 'Maybe we should just leave it there. We've been in different places for ages, if you'd admit that.'

Grace moved towards her. She wanted to hit her. She wanted to put her elbow into Sam's face and knock her down to the ground. She wanted to kick her in the shins. Sam stood her ground.

'Grace,' she said, 'I'm sorry if I hurt you.'

'Too bloody late,' said Grace and stopped and started to cry. Sam stood looking at her, even though Grace was now crying so much that she had hiccups. What Grace felt was mostly shame, she felt like a child whose parent was ignoring it for a very good reason. She sobbed into her hands and Sam did nothing. After about five minutes Grace turned and walked out of the door, down the stairs and out into the street. She stood in front of her car, still with hiccups, and the feeling overtook her that if she drove away now she might never see Sam again. She turned back to Sam's house and walked back towards it but then she turned around again and went back to her car. All she wanted to do was go home and hide but she'd have to drive home first, and she didn't see how she could see to drive because tears were coming out of her eyes at an alarming rate. She rubbed her eyes with her sleeves and then she remembered the first time she had ever seen Sam. How she had had tears in her eyes. She should have known then and there that she would love Sam and that Sam would never love her back. She should have known that when Sam turned her back on her. Stupid. She knocked her head against her palm. She heard a person coming up behind her and tried to breathe deeply in order to pretend that she was a normal person and not a hysteric wailing in the street.

'I've called you a taxi, Grace,' said Sam. 'It'll be here in a minute. I don't think you should drive if you're like this, it's not safe.'

There was part of Grace that wanted to scream, 'Well, I'm

not safe, am I! And whose fault is that!' And there was a part of her that appreciated the thoughtfulness and wanted to say thank you.

'Have you got a tissue?' asked Sam.

Grace shook her head and mucus slipped out of her nose. She wiped it away with the back of her sleeve.

'Here,' said Sam, and she handed Grace not one tissue, but a whole box. They were value tissues, Grace saw, so at least she would be crying cheaply. She blew her nose.

'Do you want me to wait with you or not?' asked Sam.

Grace shook her head.

'OK,' said Sam, but didn't go. 'I'm going to ring you later to make sure you got home OK.' She leaned into Grace and said, 'I've never been good at saying goodbye.'

She walked away from Grace and Grace wanted to slump on to her knees and press her forehead on the ground but then a car approached, and it was the taxi. She took a deep breath and got in. The taxi driver was a woman. Was that good or bad? But she said nothing to Grace, just pulled away from the kerb, and Grace looked back towards Sam's house but Sam had already disappeared.

This is Annie breaking glass

'I'll ring you tomorrow,' he had said last night, but he hadn't. If there was one thing that Annie hated more than anything, more even than the sight of women whose underwear lines you could see under their too thin leggings, it was people who didn't do what they said they were going to do. Surely Laurence knew her well enough to know this. Even the most junior person in her law firm knew it. Well, she wasn't going to phone him, that's for sure. She would get on with paperwork. An hour went by, then two, and he still hadn't phoned. If her father had ever done that to her mother she would have gone plate-throwing level insane, but then her father never had done that to her mother in her recollection. Thinking about her mother put her teeth on edge. She wished that she had reacted better to her visit, been cooler about things. Or been in any way calm and collected. She looked back at that day with nothing but embarrassment. She hadn't spoken to her since. She wished that she had the kind of mother you could sit down and confide in, like a friend. But she did have someone to confide in, didn't she? She had Violet. She didn't even know if she was home, Violet was so quiet these days. Ignoring weeks and weeks of silence, she went and knocked on the door but there was no answer and so she didn't open it. I wish you were here, she thought, and then, pull your socks up, Annie, and she phoned Laurence but there was no reply. Now she was very annoyed. She found herself grinding her teeth. She went to the bathroom and put on a face mask. Even if he did ring now, she wouldn't answer the phone. But he didn't ring all evening and Violet didn't come home and Annie went to bed in a flat whose silence was oppressive.

When she woke up in the morning Annie felt enormously sad, and if Violet had been there she would have gone straight to her and, for the first time ever, asked for a hug.

Her phone rang. It was Laurence. She didn't pick up. Why should she? She steadied her hands on the kitchen counter until the ringing stopped and then she listened to his voicemail.

'Oh, hi Annie, been busy, forgot to call. I was wondering, could you lend me another few thou? Five maybe? If you can spare it, that is. Anyway, I'll try and get hold of you later.'

Annie found that the screen of her phone was cracked, and she found that she was the one who had cracked it against the marble. She dropped it on the floor and resisted the urge to grind it under the heel of her mule.

This is Violet and her father

She sat next to his bed in the hospice. Violet had only ever been to Paris before; she hadn't been expecting the sea and the way it made things feel bigger, including the sky which was today the colour of zinc to match the grey waves. The receptionist in the hotel had said it was better to come in the summer when everything was blue but then, she said, there were so many tourists. Violet was grateful that she didn't have to fight through hordes. The receptionist told her it was a two-mile walk or she could take a taxi and Violet decided to walk along next to the beach. The wind was so strong that her scarf blew sideways and nearly strangled her but she liked it, she felt like she might fly away. She fought her way along wondering why she was here and why she had been so impulsive. She had got up yesterday, and, because she didn't have the money, borrowed it off her mother.

'Do you want to come?' she had asked her mother on the phone.

'No, I don't think I need to. Anyway, he didn't ask to see me.'

Violet could hear a tone in her mother's voice. Did she feel rejected?

'Are you quite sure?'

'Yes.'

She didn't even tell Annie she was going. She didn't tell Sam either. Instead she had rung the woman who was her father's wife. Luckily, she spoke some, if stilted, English. She seemed pleased to speak to her and told her that Jean Claude was in a place that was not a hospital and not their home and that could Violet come quickly if she was going to come at all. Violet flew to Paris, a surprisingly calm journey that only involved her praying not to crash on take-off and landing, and then took a train to Brittany on which she discovered a better quality both of sandwich and of seat covers. She didn't speak any French but it turned out to be easier than she had expected, you could always communicate with gestures that seemed more abandoned than those in England. Part of her had wanted it to be hard, an epic adventure, a journey into the unknown, but it was only France after all, not the end of the world. Her anxiety level was no worse than it was at home, it was if anything better because the differentness of everything distracted her. She drew all the way and was very pleased with the fact that the extreme version of 'the fear' didn't seem to have accompanied her. Maybe it didn't speak French.

'It is going to rain,' said the man who was her father.

'It looks like it, yes,' said Violet.

His hands were on the top of his blanket. Was she expected to grasp one of them? She had no idea about the etiquette of this situation. Surely there was more to talk about than the weather?

'Have you ever been to Brittany before?'

'No, never.'

'And what do you think of St Malo?'

She had always liked the French accent. San Marlow. 'It's beautiful. I mean I like the idea of it too, it's like a hidden city. I like the walls around it.'

'Yes, a city of pirates,' he said. 'We are always either hiding from the law or being the law,' and he laughed, and it was a raw laugh that sounded like it hurt his throat. He coughed.

'Do you need a glass of water?' she asked.

'No, no,' he said, and he smiled faintly. 'Your mother and I,' he said, 'do you know how we met?'

'At a disco, at least that's what she told me.'

'And it is true. My sister was there, she was not allowed to go on her own. All the English girls, we thought, they were so, their jeans were too tight. Too much lipstick on girls that young. But not your mother, not with her lip,' and he gestured at his mouth. Violet had only seen her mother's hare lip in

223

photos, she had been operated on when Violet was two. Now her mother always wore pink lipstick the colour of the inside of a mouth. She had never considered that before. 'I liked her. Pretty but not knowing it. That is the best way to be. And then we, you know, it was the beach.'

Not another sex conversation, thought Violet.

'And then your mother she wrote me. I remember the paper, little hearts. I am pregnant. I was in a lot of shock. But you knew about this, yes?'

'We've never talked about it.'

'If you cannot talk about these things now, then when can you? We married so quick and we came back here and then . . . well, it didn't work.'

'Why not?'

Violet's throat was tight too. Her father gestured towards the water and she gave it to him. He took a long sip.

'She was nineteen, I was twenty-two. We did not know each other. And the baby, I mean you, you screamed. A lot. All the time. It was not easy. I was trying to make money, you know, buying old things and selling them, but then it was not so profit-able. And your mother, she was alone a lot, she was very lonely. Now I know that it was the depression after birth but then . . . I was not helpful, I know. I shouted. At her. At the baby. You. I did not have patience. I should have been a kinder man. A better man. And then your grandmother came and took you away, that quick, like the wedding, so quick, and your mother said maybe she would come back later, I mean your mother and you would come back, but she never did, you never did.'

Her father seemed exhausted by the effort of speaking. He closed his eyes and his eyelids had faint blue veins on them like deltas. Violet didn't know what to say. She tried to work out if she looked like him. He was certainly smallish but perhaps he had shrunk being ill. He had dark brown hair though and not black like hers. Something about his eyebrows? She had always had thin eyebrows that didn't need plucking. The colour of his face was too pale, as though he was afraid and had blanched. He opened his eyes again and looked at her.

'I am sorry. That is what I wanted to say to you. I am sorry not to be your father. I know you had another father and that is good, I am happy for your mother about that. For you. But I am sorry I did not try more.'

'You were very young,' said Violet, and realized that she did think this.

'No excuse,' he said and reached his hand out. She took his, it was icy. Before she knew what she was doing she put it up to her mouth and blew on it. Her mother had used to do that to her. Her father did not seem to think that was strange but smiled, even though it was the tiredest smile that she had ever seen.

'What do you do with your life?'

'I work in a shop.'

'Do you like it?'

'Not much.'

'Then what do you like?'

'I don't know.'

'Then this is my advice to you, Violet, and you should listen. Not because I am your father, your father is Steve, and not because I am dying, but because what I will say is true. You need to find something good. Something that you like and that you think is important. Me, you can say, what did he do, he sold antiques, pah, what is that. But to me they were beautiful things and I sold them to people who I thought would treat them well. I gave beauty and I think that is a good thing, to do that. I would recommend that, if you need my advice, I would like to give you that one thing. What is that? In all your life, what is beautiful?'

'I . . . I don't know.'

'Then find your most beautiful thing,' said her father, with his hand on her hand. 'And hold on to it tight.'

This is Grace when it's all over

Sam was sitting on the sofa and Grace was sitting in the chair. They were in Grace's house; Sam had rung and asked if she could come to get the coat that she had left behind last time she was there. Grace looked at the dying cyclamen on the window-sill, it needed watering, but she had not noticed her plants for weeks. Anyway, they were Sam's plants if you looked at things properly. All the fight had gone out of Grace in the last two days. She had taken the time off work and stayed in bed, eating only shortbread and drinking only water, like some medieval penitent. Alternately crying and wanting to shout and scream and bang on the walls. She rang Sam several times but always put the phone down after she had heard Sam's voice on the voicemail. And then she cried some more, until her face felt waterlogged in the way that your fingers do when they've been too long underwater. She hadn't washed. She hadn't even brushed her teeth. Eustacia had phoned and left a message asking if she wanted to come over. My sister is a good person, thought Grace, I don't know if I am. And is Sam? What is Sam? Am I supposed to hate her? Because I do and then I don't. And this Violet girl, Annie's friend, but then Grace felt her guts begin to twist up and she wanted to be sick. She wondered if it would have been better if she had learnt to meditate in the past and so would now be able to enter a zen state, but it was too late now. The only thing that kept her from complete despair was mini revenge fantasies. She would go round to Sam's and steal all her books and burn them in her yard. She would go to the park and cut down all of Sam's beloved trees with a chainsaw purchased specially for the occasion. Unfortunately, the sensible part of her kept coming up with objections to these ideas. There were a lot of books, how would she get them in and out of her car? She had never used a chainsaw and the thought of doing so scared her. She would need to buy those Kevlar trousers. And what if she changed her mind? Would B&Q take the chainsaw and the Kevlar trousers back? Would they give her a full refund or only an exchange note? She could do with a better drill. This is the way her brain went round and round.

'I like you a lot, Grace,' said Sam. 'I think you're a great person but I'm not the person you want me to be. You need somebody like you, somebody who wants to settle down and I'm not that person. I'm happy with my life as it is but you want more, and I can't blame you for that. Do you understand what I'm saying?'

'I'm not a child,' said Grace.

'Of course you're not,' said Sam. She sighed, and she crossed her legs, and Grace looked at her foot swinging and there were so many things to say that she said nothing. There was a script for this but she'd forgotten the lines. Grace didn't want to look at Sam's face because she was so beautiful that she couldn't believe, she didn't want to believe . . .

'Everything is shit,' Grace said, and was surprised that the words were said out loud since they echoed round her head most of the time.

'It'll get better,' Sam said, and crouched by Grace's chair, near enough that she could smell her hair and it hurt so much having her there, knowing she was going to go.

'Don't go,' Grace said.

'I have to. It's for the best. Otherwise this will get worse and worse and you'll end up hating me.'

'I already do.'

'I know.'

'But I don't really.'

'I know that too.'

'Will I see you again?' Grace asked.

'I expect so,' said Sam. 'Take care of yourself, Grace.'

'Please . . .'

'I can't.'

'Did you ever?' Grace asked.

'What?'

'Love me?'

'Not in the way that you want.'

And Sam kissed her head. Like you do to a child. She stood up. Grace grabbed her hand. She stroked it with her other one and then detached it. Gently. Like she planted marigolds.

'Bye,' she said and left the room. Grace heard the front door shut.

'Bye,' Grace said but no sound came out.

This is Annie and the alternative therapy

Annie was in the hairdresser's having her lowlights done; her stylist knew better than to butt in when she was as thunderous as this. She looked at her face in the mirror. One of these days the frown lines on her forehead would fix. She wondered how she would age – like her mum who had frown lines on her forehead and lines around her lips or like her dad whose lines were around his eyes. And did it even matter? Her stylist Mark pulled too tight on her hair. 'Don't do that again!' Annie growled, and Mark ducked his head. Laurence hadn't even said the word 'thousand', he'd said 'thou' like he couldn't be bothered to enunciate the rest. It wasn't that she despised him so much, she realized, but that she despised herself. He was taking her for a rube, a pushover, and she was one. It was nobody's fault but her own and she wished that she had told her mother, who at least would have put a stop to this months ago. She

wished she could have told anyone. She pictured Violet's raised
eyebrows. And how would Violet age? She didn't look a lot like
the daft cow who was her mother and who knew what her dad
was like? And what was the point of calling Violet's mother a
daft cow when it was she who was one. How stupid she was.
'Another five thou, Annie?' he'd said. 'If you could spare it.'
And worst of all there'd been a moment, albeit a very brief one,
when she had considered it. Part of the problem was an arro-
gance in her, she thought, of course I can bloody spare it, what
do you think I am? Broke? Think about what? Going to the
cash machine and taking out notes and throwing them to the
winds because that, it seemed, is what she had been doing.

When she left the hairdresser's, there was an old drunk with
a face like burnt piecrust and dirty hands sitting a couple of
doors down on the pavement with a Jack Russell at his feet. As
she passed him she could smell the drink wafting off him. And
Annie would have liked to go into the off-licence he was next
to, buy a bottle of gin, preferably Bombay Sapphire, and sit
down on the pavement and have a drink with him. She wondered what her mother would have to say to that. Five thou.
Five thou. She was so deep in thought that when someone
called out 'Annie' she didn't even hear them at first. 'Annie,' the
voice called again, and she looked up to see Manfred crossing
the road. It was strange, she had never seen him out of the shop
before, he looked taller, and when he reached her seemed to
have grown so much in stature that he was looking down at her
from a great height. Maybe she was so used to seeing him
behind a counter that she had lost all perspective.

'I need to sit down,' Annie said to him, 'I don't feel right.'

The café was warm and steamy, you couldn't see out of the windows. She had a cup of tea with two spoonfuls of sugar and he had
a black coffee. His fingernails, she noticed, were nicely trimmed.

'I don't know where to start,' she said.

'Start anywhere.'

'Violet isn't speaking to me. And she's turned into a lesbian, which is fine, but her girlfriend is horrible, and my boyfriend keeps borrowing money off me and I seem incapable of saying no. That do you?'

The waitress brought them a pile of warm white toast. There were individual pats of butter in little foil packets. Annie picked one up. It was squidgy. Manfred offered her the plate and she took two slices.

'Do nothing.'

'That's not very useful advice.'

'About Violet, I mean. Nobody likes being told what to do. My ex banned me from black coffee and now I drink five cups a day. Let her work it out for herself. She will, I reckon. If she has any sense, she'll figure out the girlfriend is a waste of time without needing you to tell her that.'

'You mean let her get out of her own mess?'

'Exactly. And about the other thing. How much are we talking?'

'I shouldn't be telling you this.'

'Possibly not. But you're here now, aren't you? Have some more toast. You need to keep your strength up. Shall I ask for some jam?'

'I'd prefer honey.'

'Then I'll ask for honey.'

He went over to the counter and Annie, while looking at his bum in his jeans absent-mindedly, decided that she would tell him the truth. Manfred sat down opposite her again.

'She's bringing it now,' he said.

'Twenty thousand. And he's asked for five more.'

'Bastard,' he said, 'the bastard. Sorry to be rude but there's no other word for someone like that. Well, there are other words but I won't be saying them in your company.'

'I couldn't have put it better myself,' said Annie.

'Sounds like he's taken you for a ride.'

The waitress put the honey on the table with a lingering look at Manfred. He didn't notice, he was concentrating on opening the jar. He passed it to Annie and gave her a teaspoon.

'I should be telling my therapist this, not you,' said Annie, and she took another slice of toast.

'I'm cheaper,' he said.

'You are that,' she said, ladling honey on to her toast. 'Honey?'

'Don't mind if I do,' he said. 'Have you said you want it back?'

'Not in so many words.'

Annie stirred her tea and poured in milk from the little metal jug. The tea was too strong and too hot but she drank it anyway. It almost made her gag.

'It might be best if you said yes or no,' he said.

Manfred was on his fifth slice of toast but Annie didn't disapprove. She was on her fourth herself now. He ate neatly while she dripped honey down her elbow.

'No,' she said.

Annie looked away at the waitress balancing dirty plates on her wrists.

'Why not, if you don't mind me asking?'

Annie didn't say anything for about thirty seconds. He kept on with his toast.

'I don't come from money,' she said.

Manfred wiped his mouth carefully.

'We had hardly anything when I was little but then, well, my dad made money and we moved up in the world, if you'd like to put it like that. Other people said we had "ideas above our station".'

'And did you?'

'My mum, yes. My dad, he wanted to make my mum happy.

231

But I'm like my mum, I like what money can buy you, I'm naturally high upkeep. I like the best. I thought if I lent him money it meant that I was like him. Like I didn't care about it. It proved something about me, that I was what my mum called "a better class of person", which means in her language that you're so rich you don't have to worry about money at all. But it didn't prove anything. I'm a fake. I do care. When it comes down to it, all I've done is stood back and let someone rob me blind. I'm disgusted with myself.'

'Hmm,' said Manfred. 'Shall I tell you something?'

'Go on then.'

'It's a pity you can't smoke in here these days.'

'Was that what you were going to tell me?'

'I was going to offer you one, that was all.'

'Do you smoke?'

'No,' he said, 'but I keep a packet in my pocket.'

'Why's that?'

'I used to smoke, I gave up ages ago, but I carry the packet around with me to prove to myself that I've got some will-power and that I can make good decisions if I want to. You must be one of the most intelligent people I know. You know what to do about the mess you've got yourself into. You don't have to put up with rubbish from bastards who should know better. You can make a better choice. You can make it right now. Or there is the other option of course.'

'What's that then?'

'I go round and sort him out.' He looked serious.

'Are you in the habit of sorting people out?'

'No. But I was a fighter when I was a kid. I'm sure I'll manage. Do you want me to?'

'No, but thank you,' said Annie.

'What for?' he asked.

'Just thank you.'

'You've nothing to thank me for. I should thank you. Buying me coffee. It's very nice of you. I hope to be able to repay the favour some time.'

'I'd better be going,' said Annie.

'Yeah, me too, the lad I've got on the till will be wondering where I've got to.'

'I didn't know you'd got someone with you now.'

'Yeah, training him up so I can have the odd day off. Was thinking about what you said. Thought I'd do some courses. Brush up my German and my French. Not to do anything special. Do my brain good.'

'That's great.'

'Yeah, well, I've got you to thank.'

'Was I being pushy? I'm sorry if I was.'

'I'm saying nowt.' He laughed.

'I've got to go to the ladies.'

'I'll see you later then.'

He wiped his mouth and his hands carefully and stood up. Annie stood up too. He put out his hand to her but instead of shaking it she leaned forward and kissed him on the cheek. He smelt of coffee and Imperial Leather. He coughed, stepping back.

'You're much too good for him,' he said, and left the café before she could respond.

This is Grace and the aftershock

So that was the end. At first, she was mostly numb. Everybody was very kind to her after she'd told them. After she'd told them and yet again started crying. One part of her thought that she was doing well. She didn't phone, write, email or text. There was no social media interaction. Not even while drunk.

She didn't stalk. She didn't even go to the park. Instead she went to Manfred's and bought a hammer because the handle had fallen off hers. 'Doing some DIY are you, Grace?' She didn't reply. She walked quickly home in case she saw Dolores or someone she knew in the street. She was, she found when she came through the door, wearing a coat over her dirty pyjamas and she hadn't even realized it. At least she wasn't wearing slippers. She looked in the mirror next to the front door. Her hair was sticking up on one side and she had eye bags like a basset hound. She went into the sitting room and put 'our' clock on the floor and smashed it into bits that went all over the place and that would probably lurk in corners and end up cutting her feet. She took 'our' lamp and 'our' rugs and left them on the front doorstep in the hope that someone would remove them.

Grace wanted to be doing the stuff other women seemed to do under these circumstances: going to the gym, buying new clothes, getting their hair done, taking up a stimulating hobby and meeting someone attractive in their macramé class. Or she wanted to be like a man: go down the pub, get legless and pull whatever stranger they can find. She was a failure even at break-up.

When her clients had gone she'd empty her rucksack on to the table and try divination from the contents. An empty cigarette packet (she'd taken up smoking) and a packet of those cotton buds that she liked to stick in her ears, although she knew you weren't supposed to. Tissues. A half empty packet of aspirin. A lidless biro that stained her hands blue.

She was once the jigsaw solver. She picked up the pieces of people's lives and tried to fix them back together. Except they were less of a jigsaw and more of a broken plate, she had often thought. With splinters and larger pieces and bits that had been lost so that you could never fit them completely back together again. Sometimes they made something better than before.

Sometimes they made something that looked so different from the original that she had no idea what would happen to that person, how they would fit back into the world. Sometimes the result seemed completely botched. But it wasn't her job to consider that. It was her job to try. And yet she couldn't seem to do it for herself.

'Denise, what do you think you've got out of today's session?' said Grace by rote. They were meaningless words for her now. How could anybody get anything out of anything?

'Not a lot,' said Denise.

'Perhaps we could discuss this next time.'

'I don't think I'm going to come another time.'

'Right,' said Grace. This had never happened to her before. There had been the occasional violent break of course – the clients who disappeared leaving no trace – but mostly, apart from the ones who seemed like they would never leave, it was a quiet tailing off carefully orchestrated by Grace. 'And is there any particular reason for that?'

'You don't listen to me.'

'I'm sorry you feel that way.'

'You used to. Or I thought you used to. But now you don't. I'm not coming any more. It's a waste of my time and money.'

'I'm sorry you feel that way.'

'You already said that. It's like a robot is here now, like you're not here.'

'Well, I'm sorry . . .'

'Stop saying sorry!'

'I'm . . .'

'I'm up to date on my payments.'

And she got up and walked out of the office and closed the door. Everybody rejects me, Grace thought. I can't do this job any more. It's beyond me. It was Annie coming in next, she hadn't been for a couple of weeks, and Grace didn't know how she would manage to sit there quietly in front of her and not say anything about Sam and about Violet. It would be a breach of confidentiality to do so, it would drag her personal life into a client's world and she had never done that before. No, she couldn't face it. She would say she was sick. She would go home immediately. She stood up and her mobile rang. It was Eustacia. Grace had stopped answering her calls along with everyone else's. But that's sisters for you. They're persistent. She knew that if she kept the hiding up much longer Eustacia would drive over and camp out on her doorstep until she let her in. To her own surprise, Grace answered the phone.

'Grace?'

'It'snogoodican'tcopeanymore!'

This is Violet and her bounce

Violet got home from France but Annie wasn't in. She dumped her bag in her bedroom and decided, looking at the mess around her, that's it, that's enough. All I do is cause Annie stress, it's not fair. If I'm going to keep living here I need to sort myself out. She threw away the bits of paper with random rubbish scribbles on them and the old bus tickets and the crumpled receipts that were strewn about everywhere. She put her dressing gown on the hook on the back of the door where it was supposed to go. All her clothes were pulled off the floor and the dirty ones put in the wicker laundry basket that Annie had bought for her and the rest of them put away. Well, thrown in the bottom of the wardrobe and stuffed into the chest of drawers, but off the floor at least. After a while she could even see the floor for the first time since she had moved in. She took her dirty plates and mugs to the kitchen and washed them up. She was pleasantly surprised to find things she had lost like hair slides and pens.

She began to feel pleased with herself and looked forward to showing it all to Annie when she came in. Except she couldn't, because of the mural. She had almost forgotten about it, she had got so used to living with it. Every day she had been doing some more. She found a pencil now and drew her father sitting on top of a chest. Her mother was there too but when she was young, that shy girl with the hare lip. And there was Annie, dressed in the tightest of dresses and the highest of heels, looking at paperwork with her reading glasses between her teeth. Violet decided that she would say sorry too. She wasn't sure exactly for what, but at least it would clear the air. Even if she got shouted at she wouldn't mind. She missed Annie, she needed to tell her that, she missed her, even the arguing.

When she'd finished she looked around the room with satisfaction, everything in a place where she could find it. That could only be a good thing, it had been such a pain to always be rummaging around. She even wanted to find clean sheets, but made the rudimentary mistake of stripping her bed first and then couldn't find any. Violet climbed up on to the bed and started to bounce. The ceiling was so high that she couldn't, even with her hands raised, reach it. This pleased her. The bed was unlikely to break, it had been bought by Annie and was of durable construction, as was the mattress. Always the best for Annie, always the best. I miss Annie, she thought, does Annie miss me? She thought of her dad, so small in his hospital bed, and his speech about beautiful things. She felt both proud of herself for going and sad to have met him only when he was so ill. She got down from the bed and found another pencil and started to write a list. She included some of the things on the walls in it.

Annie. Too many artists to name except Francis Bacon because he's too scary. Hydrangeas but only the blue ones. My mother's hands. Herons landing. Gymnasts. Old ladies with the marks of rollers still in their hair. The shadows that leaves make on tarmac when the sun is directly overhead. The moors in winter. Birch trees. Short-haired dachshunds. Chocolate cupcakes with chocolate icing. Thick snow. Geishas. Puppet theatres.

By the time she had stopped writing half an hour had passed. She read the list out loud to herself. She went and made herself a cup of tea. She read the list again. There was something wrong with it, she couldn't think what it was, but it was a good list anyway. Maybe she could draw a picture for each one, put them all together in one pocket-sized notebook, and that way she could carry them around with her and look at them when she felt rubbish. She liked this idea. Her father had been right, beauty was important. I shall go out and buy Annie flowers, she thought. Annie likes roses. I'll buy her yellow roses. And when she comes home I'll give them to her. Her phone rang and for once Violet could find it and answered it right away. It was Sam.

'Do you want to come round?' Sam said.

This is Grace's extremely bad hangover

It was a sign of her burgeoning maturity, Grace thought, that Eustacia's house was now the only place in which she ever woke up on the bathroom floor. And Eustacia's floor had the advantage of always being clean enough to eat off. In fact, if you had to choose a loo to throw up in and a bathroom floor to sleep on, you couldn't do better in the whole of England. It would have been pleasant to lie down there if it wasn't tiled with tiny tiles and therefore cold and uncomfortable. Can you get piles from lying on your side? Or does your bum have to be in contact with the cold surface? Is getting piles from sitting on cold surfaces a myth? She decided to pull herself together and using the loo as a prop she crawled up on to it, she weed, she flushed. Ow. Very loud the flushing. She went to pull her knickers on but the knickers around her ankles were pale pink with a pink bow in the centre front. They were not Grace's. She did not have any pale pink knickers. She had never owned anything pink in her life, much less anything with a bow on. Where did they come from? Had she stolen them? Had she found them? What if she had been kidnapped and her knickers had been exchanged for others by her kidnappers? But where did the kidnapper get them from? His wife? That was sexist, a kidnapper could perfectly well be a woman. Was she or he wearing hers now? Ugh. Grace hoped they weren't the ones which were slightly stained because she hadn't been doing any washing lately. Were the ones she was now wearing clean? Could you catch things from somebody else's knickers? She leant over to smell them but then she fell off the loo on to her head. On to the tiles. Ow. Which were cold. She was however at least now nearer the knickers. She smelt them. They smelt of washing powder. Ecover. So, she concluded, they were likely to be Eustacia's. But why was she wearing Eustacia's knickers? Then the door opened and closed. Then she looked up. Her timing was out. Maybe she was not her at all, she was in fact Eustacia and that was why she was wearing these knickers. Because after all this was Eustacia's bathroom. She would check. She crawled towards the sink. The door opened again with a cold swish of air. This time it didn't close though. She looked up and round. It was Eustacia.

'Smile, you're on candid camera.' She was laughing. For Grace, it had always been and would always be a lovely thing to see her sister laugh.

'What are you laughing at?' Grace asked. She thought she might have sounded grumpy.

'You, my love,' Eustacia said, laughing so hard she had to wipe the tears out of her eyes.

'Why?' Grace asked.

'Because at nine o'clock in the morning, it's funny to see one's thirty-two-year-old sister crawling across the bathroom floor with her bare bum in the air.' She was laughing still.

'These aren't my knickers, you know. I was kidnapped,' Grace said, kneeling up and pulling the knickers on properly.

'You gave Jeremy a shock,' said Eustacia.

'What?'

'That was him that opened the door just now.'

'Shit! And what did he say?'

'"Your sister is lying semi-naked on our bathroom floor." I asked if there was any vomit and was she still breathing, and he had to leave the room.' She started giggling again in a teen-age way.

'Stop laughing at me. Anyway, that's not true,' Grace said.

'Which bit? The bathroom floor bit or the nakedness?'

'They're not my knickers.'

'They're mine,' said Eustacia.

'I knew it! They smelled like your knickers! Why am I wearing your knickers?'

'You wet yours.'

'I what?'

'You wet yours. You were laughing so hard you weed yourself. We were playing two person Pictionary.'

'How much did I have to drink?'

'Too much. Don't worry. The rest of your clothes are in the washing machine. You were sick on them and then you refused to put anything else on apart from the knickers and you refused to get off the floor and so I left you in here. Now would you like to come and have breakfast. That way Jeremy can get in for his shower.'

She reached down a hand to pull Grace up. Grace took the hand and then stood and looked in the mirror over the sink. The marks of the tiles were imprinted on one cheek so that she looked as if she had been lying on mesh. Eustacia, as usual, looked not at all the worse for wear.

'Do you think he was shocked?' Grace asked.

'By the fact that at your advanced age of life you were exposing yourself on our bathroom floor?'

'Are you going to make me a proper breakfast?'

'Not if you harangue me.'

'With eggs and bacon. I want eggs and bacon.'

'Do you remember who is coming to lunch today?' Eustacia took the opportunity to clean the taps with a piece of loo paper.

'The queen?' Grace asked, wondering what she could do to ameliorate her appearance. She put in the plug and started to fill the sink with cold water.

'No,' said Eustacia.

'Is it worse than the queen or better?'

'Difficult question. There is more than one.'

'Manchester United?'

'Not all of them are male.'

'I give up.' Grace splashed herself so violently with cold water that Eustacia drew back.

'Your sisters,' she said.

'Oh my God!' Grace turned to her, face dripping.

'My thoughts exactly. I only remembered when I woke up.'

'Have you got any food?'

Eustacia passed her a towel. It was of course a clean and fluffy towel and smelt of Ecover, most unlike all her towels which were rat grey and threadbare. Grace rubbed at her face.

'Unlike you I go shopping.'

'Shopping, what's that? I only ever eat cat food.'

'I'm glad, you know.'

'About what?'

'That you've split up with Sam.'

'So am I.'

'Really?'

'It wasn't, I mean she wasn't, doing me any good, was she?'

'You weren't yourself. And, well, that one time I saw her . . . she left a very poor impression.'

'I think that's the most negative thing I've ever heard you say about anybody.'

'I felt like she was taking you away from us and you seemed to have been so unhappy recently, I think you've made the right decision.'

'I don't know if it was so much a decision as a cataclysm. And I think I'm going to be sick.'

'Whatever it was that stopped you seeing her and I don't expect you to explain all of it, I'm pleased.'

'I am going to be sick.'

'Well, come and be sick in the downstairs loo then so that Jeremy can go in the shower without encountering vomit.'

This is Annie getting her own back

Annie went and touched up her make-up in the loo in the café. The mirror was spotted black and there was a strong smell of drains. Not as bad as it might have been, her face, she'd been expecting worse to be honest. She took a pencil to her eyebrows and then she straightened up her collar. She found some bright red lipstick in her bag and put it on. For the first time in a while she felt like herself.

She walked into the advertising agency and asked to see him. The receptionist said he was busy, as though he was the most important man in the building. Annie didn't like the look of her, too thin, her hair brittle, and Annie felt the temptation to pull it. She wasn't in a waiting mood and so she bypassed the girl and walked into the office. The girl shrieked after her but Annie cast her a glare so evil that it would have stapled most people's feet to the floor and she shrank back into her desk. The office was one of those open-plan places of low cubicles staffed by hip young things in casual clothes as though pretending this wasn't a real workplace but a fun place to hang out. Annie saw Laurence at the far end of the room, talking to a young girl with her hair in a ponytail with his body inclined closely towards hers.

'Laurence,' she said loudly enough to be heard by everyone. 'I've come for the money you owe me.'

He did at least have the sense to look both shocked and embarrassed.

'Let's hope,' she said, 'that none of these young ones in here have loaned you anything either. Let's hope so. You like to take pretty girls for a ride, don't you?'

Not surprisingly all eyes were on her.

'He owes me twenty thou, sorry, twenty thousand, so you know. And just so you know too, I'm a lawyer and I'll be getting that money back and then some. Won't I, Laurence?'

'I don't think you have much of a choice,' said Annie. She had parked her car outside Laurence's building. They had had a drive there of stony silence.

'But Annie darling . . .' said Laurence. She had an urge to punch him and get it all over with.

'Annie darling nothing. You'll get me my money, or I'll see you in court.'

'You don't have any proof,' he said.

'Could be yes or could be no. But I can sure as hell ruin your reputation if I feel like it. I suggest you sort things out.'

'I don't have that much cash, you know that.'

He stared straight ahead out of the window and so did she, a smile on her face that he couldn't see. Lying? She was good at telling lies from truth. Or used to be.

'I'll take it in tuppences if I have to. And your flat?'

'Mortgaged to the hilt.'

'I'll take your shirts then.'

'You're not serious!'

He looked at her then, as though his shirts were more important to him than his other worldly goods.

'Try me.'

This is Violet and her decision

Violet walked past the park to get to Sam's and thought how she would always associate Sam with here, the trees, the lake, the ducks. The world did make you love all of it, she thought – tarmac and rain and nasturtiums and the smell of warm grass and music coming out of car stereos and traffic lights.

When she got to Sam's she rang the buzzer and waited. She watched Sam approaching through the shadowed glass that gave on to the hall. It would make an interesting picture that, the light and shade. Sam opened the door and stepped forward and hugged her.

'Violet,' she said, 'nice to see you. Come on up. You said you'd been away?'

'Yeah,' said Violet, as they went up the stairs, 'I've been to France to see my dad.'

'I didn't know your dad lived in France. I thought your family lived in Cheshire.'

'This was my biological dad. My real dad. Heh, you stuck up my picture.'

On the wall in the living room was a drawing Violet had done of the inside of Sam's kitchen, with all the bottles and jars on the shelves in minute detail.

'I like it a lot.'

'Good. I'm glad you've got it. I made a list.'

She held out the list she'd made to Sam. In the end she'd needed two pieces of paper.

'That's my list of things that are beautiful.'

'That's nice,' said Sam, who glanced at the pages quickly and then handed them back to her. 'Do you want a cup of tea?'

'No,' said Violet, 'I'd like you to look at the list please,' and gave it back to Sam.

'Sorry, Violet, I don't get it. Paula Rego? Who is she?'

'Never mind. I noticed something, about the list, and I wanted you to see it. Could you please look again?'

This is Annie and Laurence's last hurrah

He unlocked the door of his flat and she pushed past him, went to his bedroom and started to go through the cupboards and the drawers. She dared him to stop her but of course he didn't. He'd better not bloody try to restrain her. She'd have him on the floor in seconds. She supposed that he knew that. She was becoming increasingly happy in a way she hadn't felt for a long time.

'Annie, please don't!' he said, but made no attempt to stop her.

She started to throw things on to the floor and in the process heard glass smash. She reached down carefully and picked up some boxer shorts that she hoped were clean. Underneath was a large gilt picture frame with cracked glass in it. Two cute blond kids with gap teeth and a woman with that pinched horse face of the posh and dieted and with expensive-looking blond hair. Dyed, thought Annie, but dyed properly. That was what had been missing from the middle of the mantelpiece then, she thought suddenly. I knew I was right about that gap. She left it on the floor.

'Who's this then?' she asked. She could see he had about

given up. She didn't feel surprise though, only amusement. 'What are their names?'

'Maisie. Oliver. And that's Claudia,' he said, pointing at the woman in the photo.

'Where do they live?'

'Harrogate.'

'Handy,' said Annie.

'Annie, I . . .'

'And that house, the lovely one you surely have there, is that mortgaged to the hilt too?'

'Actually, it belongs to . . .'

'Right, of course it does. She's the money. Figures. Well, I'm glad you married it. Sensible you. She looks like she could do with some food, though. And so what happened to my twenty thousand, Larry? Was it gambling after all?'

He looked at the floor. She could see a slight bald spot developing on the top of his head. Funny, she'd never noticed it before.

'No, not that,' she said. 'Drink. No, not that either.' She waited for his answer but none came. 'Hmm,' she said. 'You're a quiet one.'

She resumed her throwing of objects only now she threw them at him. He stood and let them hit him. Jesus, she thought, he's not going to bloody cry like he did that time. There was definitely a moist look to his eyes. She threw a box of cigars at his groin but he defended himself in time.

'Go on then,' she said, 'I give up.'

The floor was strewn with ties and socks and yes, there was the giant packet of condoms. I knew it was somewhere, Annie thought with satisfaction.

'I didn't want her to think less of me,' he said at last.

'I presume you're referring to that woman in the photo.'

'Yes. She's such a force of nature.'

'You mean she has your balls in a vice?' asked Annie. She sat

246

down on the edge of the bed and folded her arms. Laurence remained standing, hands over his groin, like a footballer in the wall waiting for a free kick.

'No, no . . . I want her . . . I want her to be proud of me. She thinks I'm doing well at work, you see. She thinks it was a bonus.'

'You gave my money, my hard-earned money, to your wife to make yourself look better?'

'It's not as if you'd miss it, Annie,' he said.

'I beg your pardon?'

'You must be raking it in. What's a few thou to you?'

'It's my "few thou", that's the point. It's not yours to give to your horse-faced wife!'

'You're making way too big a deal out of this. It's hardly anything. And you gave it freely, I didn't coerce you, did I?'

Annie looked at the floor and took a deep breath.

'Oh right,' said Laurence, 'I should have taken your background into account.'

'What's that supposed to mean?'

Annie looked up.

'I didn't factor in that to someone like you this amount of money is a bigger deal than I thought. Must be a mindset kind of thing.'

'To someone like me?'

'To someone who was brought up the way you were. I mean, I can see your father has done well for himself but it's not hard to work out where your family comes from. Your mother has plastic plants in the conservatory for God's sake! She uses "serviettes". "Would you like a serviette, Laurence?" And they have a horrible kitchen, horrible. I mean who matches their toaster to their kettle to their oven gloves? The effort it took me not to laugh.'

'What are you saying about my family?'

'There's nothing wrong with being nouveau riche, Annie, nothing at all. You shouldn't be ashamed of where you come from. Horny-handed sons of toil and all that. But you might want to stop using the word "lounge". It does you no favours.'

Annie had options. She was aware she had options. But she decided, as she so often had in the past, to take the shortest route. She kneed him in the bollocks and then he did cry.

'Laurence,' said Annie, as he lay on the floor, 'I'm not going to cut up your shirts, which I think is very kind of me. I am also not going to ring your wife, which I think is even kinder. Neither am I going to take you to court as you well know. I'm going to take exactly what I want, which is what I should have done months ago. Now where are your keys? Are they in the "lounge"?'

This is how Grace's family eat

Grace sat looking at her family. Their table manners were largely atrocious. The twins were shovelling in Yorkshire pudding like there was no tomorrow, perhaps aware that Tess would soon notice and reinstate the macrobiotic policy. Augusta was pushing her food around her plate and eating next to nothing, only stopping now and then to glug glasses of Diet Coke as if she was in a desert and had suddenly reached an oasis. Bella always talked with her mouth full and she and Tess were discussing, for some reason, sheep parasites. Only Eustacia ate neatly, dividing her plate into food groups and putting them delicately into her mouth. Jeremy had had to go to bed because he had felt a cold coming on, having got completely soaked trying to get Twister out of Tess's car in the rain after the twins had gone into a sulk.

'I've got something to say,' said Eustacia.

'Like what?' said Bella, stuffing her food into one corner of her cheek.

'It might seem foolish to you, Bella,' said Eustacia. 'To all of you.'

'What is it?' said Tess.

'Are you getting Botox like Mummy does?' said Augusta.

'No, Jeremy and I have rented out the house.'

'Are you going on a round the world trip?' said Linden.

'Can we come?' said Rowan.

'What? Why?' said Bella.

'Oh no, you haven't,' said Grace, 'please tell me you haven't!'

'Yes,' said Eustacia, 'I have. There was nothing else for it. At least for a while, until, you know, well, you know.'

'You are completely and utterly insane,' said Grace.

'What the fuck is going on?' said Bella.

'I'm moving back to Ravel Corner. With Jeremy obviously. Next week.'

Nobody said anything for a while, not even the twins.

'Anyone else want to comment?' said Bella. 'Because I agree with Grace, you've gone completely round the twist. Why would you want to do that?'

'Who else is going to look after them?' said Eustacia firmly.

Tess was considering her carefully.

'I think,' she said, 'that is a very noble and brave decision and I wholly condone it. After all, Eustacia's job, unlike ours, is portable. And Jeremy is going to retire early. It seems sensible to me.'

'Thank you,' said Eustacia. 'Bella, I understand your objection, I do, but we've made up our minds. And I had suggested that Grace and, well, that Grace come with me if she wants to.'

'And she said no? Well done, Grace, at least someone in this family is sane,' said Bella. 'Apart from any of the other million objections, what on earth would you expect Grace to do with her time up there?'

'I've thought about that,' said Eustacia. 'If she wanted to, she could work online or even over the phone. I've researched it.'

'I am here,' said Grace. 'I am sat right here in front of you.'

'And then Grace, perhaps you could, if you wanted to . . . we would help you.'

'This is an interesting conversation, for once,' said Rowan.

'It's not bad,' said Linden.

'I could what?' said Grace.

'I know you think I don't know, but I do.'

'Know what?' said Rowan and Bella simultaneously.

'You won't have to do it on your own.'

This is Annie and this is Violet

Annie, having reverse parked the Jag carefully on the kerb outside, opened the door of her flat with a sigh. It had been a long day, and she badly needed a gin and tonic. She hoped she had some lemons. Violet was standing in the living room with her hands behind her back.

'I'm sorry, Annie,' she said, 'please forgive me,' and she held out a bunch of yellow roses. 'I know they're your favourites.'

Annie went up to Violet and hugged her hard, which surprised Violet so much that she nearly toppled over and dropped the flowers. Annie was not the instigator of hugs, she was the reluctant huggee. Those were the rules.

'Thank you,' said Annie, taking the flowers. 'I'm so glad you're back. Are you back? Because I've been a right cow and I've been worried you'll leave and move in with that bitch.'

'Oh that,' said Violet, 'that's over.'

'Because you're so much better than that woman,' said Annie. 'You could do so much better, you know you could. It doesn't matter who you want to sleep with or what you are but couldn't you pick someone decent? Did you say "over"?'

'Completely over.'

'Thank God,' said Annie. 'Did she break up with you? Because I can go round there and give her a piece of my mind if you want.'

Violet laughed.

'No, I broke up with her.'

'Well, I never,' said Annie.

'She wasn't on my list, you see. Lichen was on there. Ryoichi Kurokawa installations were on there. But not her. At first, I thought I'd made a mistake and so I read it again and again and she wasn't on it. And the more I thought about it the more I realized something. That she's a nice enough person, although I know you don't think that obviously, but she's just been a distraction so that I don't have to think about everything else that's actually wrong with my life.'

'Well, I could have told you that much ages ago! What did you say to her?'

'I said, "I don't want to go out with you any more, Sam, because you're not on my list."'

'What bloody list? And you're not upset?'

'I went to see my dad. He's dying. It put things in perspective.'

'You what? Where?'

'In France.'

'You went to France by yourself?'

'Are you proud of me?'

'I certainly am. I took Laurence's Jag.'

'Brilliant! Any particular reason why?'

'It's a long story. You saw your dad!'

'It's a long story.'

'I've been going to therapy. I don't want to have children. Well, not right now.'

'Stop one-upping me! I've decided to go to the doctor, I think I'm depressed.'

'Do you want to see a video of my twenty-year-old mother online singing Patsy Cline?'

'I've got three half-brothers in France!'

'I kneed Laurence in the bollocks!'

'And you've won!' Violet hugged Annie again. 'I've got something I really need to show you in my room.'

This is Grace

Grace drove into her street and parked. As she got out of her car she saw Dolores walking her pugnacious Yorkshire terrier, the one that thought it was a bull terrier and attacked dogs many times its size. It growled at Grace.

'Grace,' she said. 'Where have you been, my girl?'

'To see my family.'

'Good. Good. The family is important. That girl Sam was outside your house just now. She asked if I had seen you and I said no, I never see you, and it is a terrible pity. It is a terrible pity, come to my home. Come now. I have chorizo. I thought that you had broken up with her?'

'Sam? When?'

'Just now.'

But Grace was already running away.

'Chorizo!' Dolores shouted after her.

As Grace turned the corner she saw Sam's back. She was moving in that way that people in Leeds do when they are head down into the wind going up a hill.

'Sam!' she called. Sam turned around. She smiled and came back towards Grace.

'Grace, I was looking for you. But you didn't answer your door.'

They stood two feet away from each other. What is the protocol? thought Grace. Shake hands? Kiss on the cheek? Spit?

'I've been away,' said Grace. 'What are you doing here?'

'I wondered if you wanted to go out for a drink.'

'What?'

'We can go wherever you like.'

'But you said . . .'

'What did I say?'

'That you never go back on yourself.'

'It's only a drink, Grace.'

'But why?'

'I missed you.'

Grace looked at Sam. She was smiling her beautiful smile and there was a moment when the sun came out overhead and illuminated her and she turned her face up to it and yet Grace thought, no. No. I will not. If she had been a child, she would have stamped her foot. Sam looked cold, her jacket was too thin for the day, and Grace thought no, I'm not going to offer you my coat. Or lay my head down in that puddle at your feet. I'm not going to invite you in for a cup of tea that may or may not lead to something further. I am going to give you nothing.

'No,' said Grace.

'No for today? Because I could make tomorrow after work.'

'No. I don't want to go for a drink. Thank you.'

'OK,' said Sam, still smiling, looking like she didn't believe a word that Grace was saying. 'Are you sure?'

'Yes,' said Grace.

'Come out for a drink,' said Sam. 'We can go to that pub you like.'

'No,' said Grace.

'Why not?'

'Because you are a horrible person and I want nothing more to do with you.'

She turned her back on Sam and went back down the street

quickly and it felt like her heart was missing, like it had been scooped out of her chest with an ice-cream scoop and dumped on the ground. She forced herself not to turn around. She opened the front door of her house and went inside. As she looked up the stairs she imagined, as she always did when she came into the house now, Sam sitting halfway up them, book in hand, and the way she would look up and smile when Grace stood at the bottom. The days and days that she herself had sat on the very same step and cried so much that she had left a wet patch on the wallpaper where she had leant against it. She bolted the door and walked up the stairs and sat on what she thought of as 'Sam's step'. Next to her she could still see the watermark.

What was that thing called, Grace thought, where you think about what you wanted to say before and are annoyed that you didn't say it? Well, I said it. And instead of feeling guilty about this, she felt better. She had told the truth. She didn't want to be with someone like Sam. No, she wanted a nice girlfriend who didn't cheat on her and leave her an emotional wreck. She wanted to be able to sleep properly at night and get on with her life. I can be different, she thought, if I want to. I stood up to Sam just now, I don't have to be such a walkover in the future. I don't have to be stepped on by someone who doesn't care about me. She thought about all the clients she had had who spent years bemoaning the one who got away even though the one who got away had been a monster. I don't want to be like them, she thought. It was naïve to put all my expectations on one person, to want commitment so badly from someone who very obviously didn't want the same thing. I was stupid. So what do I want? She pattered her fingers on her knees. She wondered if Sam would come and knock on the door and what she would do if she did. She knew what she would do – not let her in. Sam was the big bad wolf and she had behaved like an easily led to destruction Red Riding Hood. But not any more. She, she realized, wasn't even that interested in thinking about what Sam might be doing now. What she was interested in, ever since Eustacia had said something this lunchtime, was how it was that Eustacia knew the one thing she had never told anybody? The one thing she wanted more than anything, more even than she had wanted to fall in love. She had secretly hoped that Sam would be a part of it but she had picked the most unsuitable person she could find. Perhaps she had done it on purpose to sabotage herself. Because she thought it was impossible. But what if it could be easy? A family was anything that you wanted it to be, she should be the first to acknowledge that. She was thirty-two, it wasn't that old. She had some money. And she could rent out her house like Eustacia had done and that would give her more. What if I could? she thought and then, what's to stop me? Let Sam go off on her own messed-up path trailing destroyed women in her wake, Grace decided then and there, I will go the way I want to go, and I will start right now. She went downstairs and into the back room and found her laptop and switched it on. And then she went on to one of the websites that she never told anybody she looked at, the ones where you could buy exactly what you lacked from a fairytale prince of your very own.

This is Violet and this is Annie

'Well,' said Annie, 'far be it from me to comment.'

'Is that all you're going to say?'

'I told you that you could do what you liked with your room.'

'No, you told me, quite forcefully and on many occasions, to keep it in my room.'

'And you've done that.'

'I have, yes. You're being very calm, Annie. Look, I've even got some on the carpet.'

Annie shrugged.

'I don't care. I like it, what you've done. I always thought you could be an artist. If you concentrated enough.'

'Did you?'

'Yes. I'm sorry I never told you that you're any good before. I should have.'

'Because I had this idea, I know it's probably daft, probably really daft.'

'What?'

'What if I applied to art college? My dad has given me some money. And I could get a loan too. I mean, I have no idea if they'd take me and I'd have to get a portfolio together.'

'Well, you're not chipping down parts of the wall to take them to an interview, I can tell you that much now. I think it's a great idea. Do it.'

'Just like that?'

'Exactly like that.'

'What's happened to you? Have you been taken over by aliens? You don't like it if I leave toothpaste on the sink, let alone this mess.'

'Well, I've messed up too, haven't I? I thought you were going to move out and I didn't seem to be able to stop it. And I had a towering row with my mum about kids and I lent Laurence twenty grand, if you can believe that, and then there's something else.'

'Wow! So what else? Is it a bad thing?'

'No, a good one.'

'Go on then.'

'I got headhunted. It's an amazing job. I get to travel all over the place.'

'Sounds good.'

'It'd be based in Dubai.'

'That would be really cool.'

'Did you not hear me? I said "Dubai".'

'And I said "really cool" like I was about eight and not twenty-eight, but never mind. Have you taken the job then?'

'I told them no.'

'Why?'

'I thought because of my mum. Because of what she expects of me. But I'm past that now, I reckon. And then there was Laurence but it turns out he was a complete waste of my time. Not to mention my money. To be honest it was mostly because of you. Because I'm worried about you. About you being depressed. I can't leave you here on your own, can I?'

'Because I can't look after myself?'

'Basically yes.'

'Say what you mean.'

'Yes.'

'Annie,' said Violet. 'I'm going to be fine. Would you sell the flat if you went?'

'No, I wouldn't do that, it's a good investment.'

'Then maybe I could stay here and if you wanted to you could rent out the other room to cover the mortgage. And I'd pay my way properly.'

'That doesn't matter.'

'It does. I'll work part-time in the shop as well as maybe going to college. And I'll go to the doctor, I promise I will.'

'It's too much pressure on you.'

Violet went and held Annie's arms.

'I'm a big girl. I can look after myself.'

'No, you're not. You're tiny.'

'I'll wear heels. I know you think I can't do it, but I can. I can, for once in my life, learn to look after myself. I don't want to be a princess trapped in a castle any more.'

'Often I have no idea what you're on about.'

'Do you want to go?'

'Yes. Yes, I do.'

'Then let's go and see if Manfred has an undiscovered bottle of champagne and toast your new job.'

'Are you sure? Absolutely sure?'

'Yes,' said Violet. 'Annie, I love you and I want you to be happy and if that's what will make you happy then I want you to go.'

Annie looked at her with great concentration and said, 'I love you too, Violet. Champagne it is then.'

'Champagne it is.'

This is Gabriel Marshall Eppington

Gabriel could hear Aunt Eustacia hoovering and this sound was battling with Great Aunt Beatrice's favourite music which was something called opera and the banging Uncle Jeremy was making up on the roof. He enjoyed the mix-up of noises and started to try and make up a little song to go along with them. Out of the window he could see Great Aunt Beatrice and Cyril in deckchairs on the lawn, both fast asleep. They had their heads back and their mouths open. He hoped no flies would fly in.

'Gabe,' said his mother, 'you've got to finish your reading.'

Gabriel liked learning to read, it was his favourite thing to do apart from recreating Ancient Roman battles with Cyril; they used plastic dinosaurs for the Romans and farm animals for the subjugated peoples. That and riding his pony, Fred; Beatrice was teaching him to do rising trot.

'K is for kangaroo,' he said. 'If we made a very strong apron could you put me in the pocket?'

'I'll see what I can do,' she said.

Gabriel put his hand up to touch his mother's earrings where they were swinging in the breeze. She carefully detached his hand and kissed the top of his head.

'Can I have earrings when I'm older?'

'If you want to,' she said, 'but I must warn you that getting it done does hurt a lot. They have to put a needle through your ear.'

'I don't want them then,' he said.

'You are my very best decision,' she said.

'I know, you've told me that,' he said, although he wasn't really sure what it meant. 'L is for llama.'

'And love,' his mother whispered in his ear so that it tickled, 'and love.'

Acknowledgements

Thank you to Penguin for giving me such a wonderful opportunity and for saying that I was a writer from the beginning.

Thank you to Siena Parker for making the road to publication such an enjoyable experience.

Thank you to my fellow writers from WriteNow 2016/2017. I wish you all the success you deserve.

Thank you to Katy Loftus for mentoring me and teaching me how to plan.

Thank you to my editor Isabel Wall, whose calm and inspiring presence has been so key to me completing this. Her love for the book has made all the difference.

Thank you to my agent Anna Power at Johnson & Alcock for her good sense. If I ever have to go to war, I'm taking her.

Thank you to Gel for helping me to get my confidence back.

Thank you to Frances for reading and for getting me down from mountains.

Thank you to Rachel for many years of shotguns and nighties.

Thank you to my family and especially my parents for their loyalty and bravery. I owe you everything.

Thank you to my siblings who are the best people I know.

Thank you to my nieces and my nephew and my godchildren. Do what you want to do with your lives and be who you want to be and don't let anyone tell you any different.

Thank you to Paul for taking me back and for being my home.

This book has no dedication but I would also like to thank

Sarah who always believed that I could. We all miss you, sweetheart.

Thank you to all these good people for never giving up on me. Because of you I never gave up either. I believe this to be the key to life. That and Lindt bunnies.

We love stories.

Fact or fiction, long or short, exploring distant lands, imagined worlds or your own back yard – anything can be a story, and every place has stories waiting to be told. And we want to find them.

Do you have a story to tell? Want help cutting through the jargon, answers to your burning questions or advice from top authors, agents and editors across the industry?

Find out more about how to get published at:
www.penguin.co.uk/publishmybook